DANGEROUS DISGUISE

She was no longer Mary Eugenia Victoire Marshall, Duchess of Runceford, Marchioness of Lyndale, Countess of Fare, the belle of the London season and the catch of the Marriage Mart.

She was humbly-born governess Mary Marshall, found in tatters on the highway and taken to the home of the Earl of Leighford, where she was now adored by his young nephew, Robin, befriended by his kindly housekeeper, Mrs. Heaven, and increasingly noticed by the earl himself.

The first step had been accomplished. So far so good. But the most difficult part of her impersonation still lay ahead. Being in the earl's employ was most pleasant—but what would happen when she found herself in his arms . . . ?

NORMA LEE CLARK was born in Joplin, Missouri, but considers herself a New Yorker, having lived in Manhattan longer than in her native state. In addition to writing Regencies, she is also the private secretary to Woody Allen.

Norma Lee Clark
The Daring Duchess

A SIGNET BOOK

NEW AMERICAN LIBRARY

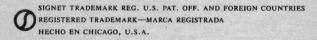

SIGNET, SIGNET CLASSIC, MENTOR, ONYX, PLUME, MERIDIAN and
NAL BOOKS are published by NAL PENGUIN INC., 1633 Broadway, New
York, New York 10019

First Printing, August, 1988

1 2 3 4 5 6 7 8 9

PRINTED IN THE UNITED STATES OF AMERICA

1

"Fetch the screen for her grace's chair," commanded Lady Hyde as she entered the drawing room, her magnificent bosom going before her with all the grandeur of the prow of a ship breasting the waves.

"It is really unnecessary, Aunt," murmured her niece, "the night is quite close."

"Nonsense. There is always a draft there. Well, why do you stand there gaping?" barked Lady Hyde, rounding on the hapless footman who had hesitated at her grace's demur, not sure whose orders he had best obey. At Lady Hyde's question, however, he gave a slight jump and scuttled across the room to fetch the screen, which he set up around the back of her grace's chair before the fire.

Her Grace Mary Eugenia Victoire Marshall, Duchess of Runceford and Marchioness of Lyndale, Countess of Fare, Baroness Marshall of Malloway, and various other titles and dignities, sank into the chair assigned to her and began to apply her fan. "You know I am never bothered by drafts, Aunt. I am quite revoltingly healthy."

"I am happy to be able to agree with you. And we need not seek far to find the reason. Loath as I am to puff up my own consequence, I think I may take full credit for having brought about such a gratifying state of affairs by my preventive measures, one of which is to take very good care to see that you do not sit in drafts."

Unable to refute this, Mary remained silent. No doubt, she thought, her aunt had some claim to the truth on her side, for there could be no denying that Lady Hyde had done everything in her power to ensure that

1

her niece was wrapped in cotton wool since the age of three, when she had taken over her care. The first three years had been in the hands of fate with only her mother and her nanny to care for her. The nanny was still part of the household, though now, of course, with no child in her charge, but the former Duchess of Runceford had died when her daughter, Lady Mary, was but three years old. Lady Hyde, a childless widow, had then descended upon Mallows, the family seat of the Marshall family where she herself had grown up, to console her grieving brother, the duke, and had remained to take control of his household and his daughter.

The poor Duke of Runceford, vowing never again to marry, and having but the one child, a daughter, was granted permission by his king for the title to be re-maindered to her and to the heirs male of her body, and had then departed this life not eighteen months after his beloved wife. The world ascribed his death to a broken heart, but his sister, the Countess of Hyde, maintained stoutly that it was no such thing, but the result of a putrid throat contracted by sitting about in wet stockings after a day's shooting in the rain.

However it came about, the Duke of Runceford had died, leaving his daughter a duchess in her own right and under the guardianship of Lady Hyde and his old friend Lord Fitzedward. Lady Hyde allowed no interference in the raising of the little duchess, however, and Lord Fitzedward, a retiring bachelor, showed little inclination to do so. He was a captain in the army and seemed for the most part to be in foreign countries. Mary had seen him only twice, the last time when she was twelve, and he had been very careful to offer no suggestions. He did, however, send her delightful presents from time to time.

Mary had wondered often since she had reached the age of reason, as she was doing at this moment, what it would be like to be plain Miss Mary So-and-so. Hedged about as she was by a household of people all dedicated to her care, she had little idea what such a life could be like. Indeed, she had no idea at all, for the nearest she had ever come to a plain Miss Anybody, was Eliza Foote, a distant cousin of Lady Hyde's, who had resided at Mallows since Mary could remember, as a sort of lady-in-waiting to Lady Hyde. Miss Foote was middle-aged and self-effacing, being too happy at having any home at all to resent Lady Hyde's bullying. She was the daughter of Lady Hyde's second cousin, who had married far beneath herself when she had taken the Reverend Jonas Foote. She had been carried off to a life of penury by the Reverend Foote, who had subsequently died penniless, leaving his wife and eight children to manage as best they could. Lady Hyde had offered Eliza a place as her companion and she had been with her for twenty years, the last fourteen at Mallows.

Despite their long acquaintance, however, Miss Foote had never called Mary anything but "your grace," but then neither had anyone else in the household with the exception of old Nanny, who was tolerantly allowed to refer to her former charge as Lady Mary, and of course Lady Hyde who called her Mary. There had been a time shortly after her father's death when Mary had thought "your grace" was her name and had referred to herself by that appellation, telling her aunt firmly one day that "Your grace will not eat that nasty porridge." Lady Hyde had not been amused by this quaint mistake and, after berating the nursery maids for giggling, had set Mary straight in no time at all, . . . and she had made sure that she finished every bite of her porridge.

There was one other "miss" in Mary's life, though they had never met. This was Maud Bryce, a distant relative. She also was an orphan, though her circumstances were far different from Mary's or from those of poor Miss Foote, for she had been left in comfortable circumstances by her parents. True, she could not afford to keep a carriage and did not go to London for the Season, but she lived in her own house with an income sufficient to keep it up and provide her with some of the smaller luxuries, such as a cook and a maid. Miss Bryce wrote to Mary faithfully on every birthday to extend her felicitations and occasionally included some snippets of her life that intrigued Mary no end: she had attended the Hon. Mrs. Herbert's strawberry party, she had stood up to dance twice with a Mr. Hodgson at the Daggleston Assembly, her rendition on the pianoforte of a Mozart sonata had been much applauded at Sir William and Lady Jameson's evening party.

Lady Hyde snorted contemptuously at all this, calling it a gaggle of nonsense about footling nobodies, and why Maud Bryce should presume that her grace of Runceford would have the least interest in it she, Lady Hyde, could not for a moment imagine. Mary was interested, however, and always replied warmly to Miss Bryce's letters, though since Lady Hyde not only read all Mary's correspondence, but dictated her replies, she was always forced to rewrite her letter to Miss Bryce in what Lady Hyde termed a more "seemly" way, thus eliminating most of the warmth. Lady Hyde said that in her opinion Maud Bryce was much too pushing and should not be encouraged.

"The next thing we know we shall have her on the doorstep claiming her connection, and she is not a real relative in any sense of the word. She is . . . Let me see now, yes, I have it. She is the daughter of the brother of your mother's sister's husband. There, now! I am surprised she has the presumption to write to you at all."

"Oh, I am sure she meant no real harm, Lady Hyde," twittered Miss Foote, conciliatingly. "Perhaps she is only lonely."

"She does not sound lonely with all the social activity she indulges herself in. I for one cannot approve of a young girl in her circumstances putting herself forward in such a way. Clearly she has had no one to guide her in the proper way to conduct herself."

"I am sure you are right as always, dear Lady Hyde. How fortunate you are, your grace, to have had your dear aunt to show you the way," breathed Miss Foote, unwilling to disagree with anyone, least of all Lady Hyde.

"There is no need for you to point that out, Miss Foote. Naturally her grace is well aware of her good fortune."

Mary retreated into her own thoughts as she always did when her aunt began dictating how she was to feel, for Lady Hyde's was a formidable personality and Mary had only recently emerged from childhood into her seventeenth year and had always been, for the most part, a biddable, good-natured girl. She was happy to be shed of governesses, dancing masters, French instructors, and the schoolroom and was looking forward to her first Season in London as a grown-up young lady, and to a certain amount of freedom and adventure. Not that Lady Hyde and Miss Foote, as well as her steward, her butler, her chef, several of her footmen, her abigail, and her chaplain would not all be accompanying her to London, but surely they could not all accompany her when she went out, and there would be many parties, sometimes several in one day! Oh, she was very much looking forward to London.

Months ago a Madame Thiery had been summoned from Paris to make Mary's gowns for this grand come-out and an entire room on the second floor was slowly filling with Madame's efforts. The court-presentation gown, being the most important, was completed and Mary went at least once a day to gaze upon its splendor. She had dreamed in the beginning of her consultations with Madame Thiery of something very sophisticated in red velvet with black lace. Madame had trodden firmly upon this dream, having very strong ideas of her own upon what was appropriate for a *jeune fille* making her first appearance before her sovereign. She had been equally as firm with Lady Hyde's suggestion of celestial blue.

"White," she had stated unequivocably, "the petticoat of spangled tissue with a deep van-dyked flounce embroidered with leaves and roses, the robe and train of white velvet lined with the palest shell-pink silk. She will wear her mother's tiara and white ostrich feathers with it."

Having spoken her mind on the subject, she allowed all debate on the subject to be carried on without her participation and proceeded to make the dress she had described.

As a sop to Lady Hyde there was a nearly completed ball gown of celestial-blue gauze, a rose-pink silk—"rose, *ma petite,* but on no account scarlet for a young girl. *C'est impossible*"—a lemon sarcenet, and a sea-foam-green muslin, as well as walking dresses, day dresses, dinner dresses, and carriage dresses. Mary's favorite after the court gown was her new riding costume. It was of a dark lavender-broadcloth with a high, rolled collar and a deep cape *à la pelerine.* There was a broad belt with a steel clasp and a high ruff of double-plaited muslin that sloped to a point at the bosom. With it she was to wear a dashing little hat of amber-colored velvet with a band of the same velvet formed into leaves, high boots of lavender-blossom kid tied with amber-colored bows, and York tan gloves. Mary considered it the most sophisticated costume she had ever owned, and it seemed to her to add at least five years to her age.

She spent hours dreaming of herself riding in the park in this costume, attended by a handsome young gentleman who flirted with her outrageously. This dream always ended with her doubts of being able to attract any young gentlemen, much less handsome ones, for she had no illusions of being a great beauty who would set London on its ears. Her hesitant queries to Lady Hyde regarding her looks were met with quelling lectures on "Beauty is as beauty does" and "Well-enough-looking for all normal purposes." Lady Hyde did not believe in young girls being too much complimented upon their looks, saying that it gave them airs and made them vain.

There was certainly nothing wrong with Mary's looks, for though she might not be a great beauty, she was freshly attractive. She was perhaps slightly taller than average, slender-boned, and graceful. Her hair was brown, and her eyes, her best feature, were long and well-set, and of a vivid green. Apart from that, her features were undistinguished, creating neither a profile to sigh for nor one to animate disgust.

Though she might have had little confidence in her looks, she had great confidence in Madame Thiery and felt that, when arrayed in her magnificent creations, no one would notice faults in her face or figure, depending, of course, on whether she could contrive not to trip or drop her fan or blush scarlet the first time anyone looked at her. Oh, if only Aunt would have allowed some parties here this past year or so to help her learn to keep her countenance in company.

Lady Hyde, however, had said there were too few families nearby to make such a thing worth wasting time upon.

"There are only the Fortmains, and they have only those three dowdy daughters, all on the shelf these five years, and the Robeson-Smythes, and their eldest boy is betrothed to a girl I cannot approve of and the youngest is but twelve."

"There are the Herveys and the Carescotes . . ." began Mary in protest.

"What! You would suggest receiving at Mallows Lady Hervey, whose father was an ironmonger? And Sir Merwyn Carescote is nothing but a jumped-up little baronet of two years' standing. He does something in the City, I have heard," she added in tones suggesting that the "something" was too discreditable to mention.

"But there are young people in both families and it would be so pleasant to—"

"You must be all about in your head, my girl, to even think of such a thing. People like that need only to get a foot in the door to presume they have an open invitation to come just whenever they choose. The next thing you know we should be having them paying morning visits and sending invitations and boasting of the acquaintance to all their friends. Not to speak of their callow sons nosing about for the chance to snatch up your fortune and make their own sons Duke of Runceford!"

Mary could not help smiling as she remembered this

speech and at how quickly her aunt had jumped from the suggestion of an evening party to marriage. She knew it was hopeless to pursue the matter. She would just have to remain content with the limited joys of Lady Hyde's friends, who were considered suitable guests. All elderly and settled and safe . . . and terribly, terribly dull. If only she were a boy, she thought, she would not be so fettered. Boys, even seventeen-year-old boys, were sent to Oxford and went on tours of the Continent and were allowed to go up to London at will, not to speak of being able to attend parties whenever they liked without having to apply to anyone for permission.

She had little doubt other seventeen-year-old girls were not so plagued with restrictions as herself. She would be willing to wager any amount that the Hervey and Carescote daughters, probably even the Fortmain spinsters, led a very merry life with parties and balls every night of the week. Why, even Maud Bryce went to assemblies and strawberry parties. Mary wondered what a strawberry party could be? It sounded delightful.

"Mary!"

"What . . . Oh, I beg your pardon, Aunt, I was dreaming, I think," said Mary bemusedly, turning away from the fire to face Lady Hyde.

"I should think you must have been. I have spoken to you three times and here is Mr. Goodenow made his bow to you with no acknowledgment at all."

"I am sorry, Mr. Goodenow, that was most remiss of me. Has dinner been announced?"

Lady Hyde frowned reprovingly at her, for it was one of Mary's jokes that the chaplain, Mr. Goodenow, knew instinctively when dinner was to be announced and timed his arrival in the drawing room to the exact half-moment before Salcombe, the butler, appeared at the drawing-room door. "Yes, it has, and if you are now ready, I believe you have kept us all waiting long enough. Salcombe, fetch her grace's shawl."

Salcombe signaled to a waiting footman who hurried

away even while Mary, taking Mr. Goodenow's arm, protested that she was quite warm enough.

"Now you may be so, but the dining room is always chilly," declared Lady Hyde authoritatively. "Please put your shoulders back, child. Lady Connaught commented upon your posture only last week when she dined here."

"I do not care a whit for Lady Connaught's opinion," retorted Mary, stung into rebelliousness.

"That is a very rude remark. Lady Connaught is a very old friend of this family and meant only to be obliging, for she would not want to hear from the queen after your presentation that your posture needed improving. You know that she is a lady-in-waiting and that the queen confides everything to her, and she will be certain to let me hear of it."

"Then it seems the queen is unfortunate in whom she places her confidences."

"It distresses me to find you in this pert and irreverent mood," said Lady Hyde icily. "I hope you are not sickening for something."

Mary bit back any response to this, for if her aunt even suspected she were "sickening for something," all hopes of leaving for London in a week would fly out the window. Gone would be the delightful prospect of shopping for all the furbelows to accompany Madame Thiery's gowns, not to speak of wearing them at her presentation at court and at all the balls and parties.

Instead, she would be put to bed and smothered with feather quilts and hot bricks and treated to disgusting paps and gruels. The doctor would be summoned, perhaps even a specialist from London, and there would be no hope of even leaving her room for a week.

No, she must not jeopardize London for the dubious pleasure of asserting herself. Surely after her come-out her aunt would realize she was no longer a child. If not, it was only four years until she became of age according to her father's will. That seemed aeons away to her now, but she must contrive to endure it. And, after all, London was only a week away!

2

The London *ton* was in a veritable ferment of excitement at the news that this Season was to see the come-out of a duchess in her own right! Never in living memory had there been such a phenomenon. Curiosity was rife as to her looks and her fortune. She was variously described as a regular antidote and a ravishing beauty and her fortune to be anything from a mere two hundred pounds a year to riches beyond the wildest dreams of avarice. That she was seeking a husband was of course understood. For what other reason did girls make come-outs and have Seasons in London? This caused much fevered speculation upon who was eligible to consider himself possible as a suitor for such a girl.

Young ladies due to make their own come-outs this Season were gnashing their teeth at the unfairness of such unprecedented competition, and dressmakers were working around the clock in a frenzy of activity preparing gowns demanded for the extra balls and entertainments planned for the young Duchess of Runceford.

Competition was high among the hostesses to entertain her and invitations for a month to six weeks in advance were already flying about, causing not a little enmity when dates clashed. Clever hostesses had sent their invitations down to Mallows in order to ensure the duchess's presence at their parties, while others were content to send them to Carlton Terrace to await the arrival of Lady Hyde and her niece, and much hand-wringing and bitterness resulted when those not so far-sighted found the duchess already promised for a certain date. It was felt by all that no party could be considered a success if her grace the Duchess of Runceford were not be to present.

One date was sacrosanct—the night of Lady Hyde's ball for her niece. Cards for this had been sent out three weeks before their arrival in town and had caused much heartburning among the unfortunates who had failed to receive one, and not a little flaunting on the parts of those who had. Lady Hyde's list had been concocted with the help of Martha, Lady Furness, wife of that prominent Parliamentarian and present Cabinet member, Lord Alexander Furness. Lady Martha was an old bosom bow of Lady Hyde's and, being much in society, knew exactly whom it was important to include and whom important to exclude.

The steward of the household had been sent by Lady Hyde to London some weeks ago with instructions regarding refurbishing Marshall House and hiring extra servants, most especially a French chef, since, except for Lady Hyde's once-a-year visits for shopping, Marshall House was kept closed and under dust covers. There was a great deal to be done to ready it for occupation and for the entertainment of guests. Madame Thierry had also been dispatched—the glorious presentation gown and the other finished costumes packed into enormous baskets—and she was now installed in the third-floor sewing room bullying a bevy of young seamstresses over the construction of even more confections for the duchess.

Mary, released from hours of tiresome fittings, could settle to nothing in those last days before departure and spent most of her day on horseback, galloping wildly about to use up her healthy energy. She would return late in the afternoon, cheeks glowing and eyes sparkling, her spirits high but her restlessness unabated, to face a long quiet evening with her aunt and Miss Foote.

At last, however, the day of departure arrived. The trip itself was uneventful, spent mostly by Mary in gazing out at the passing scenery, trying to imagine all the coming events. Would she manage not to wobble when she curtsied to the queen? Would anyone ask her to stand up with them at the balls or would she be forced, shamefully, to sit beside her aunt all evening? Or, worse, be lead out onto the floor only by the antiquated gentlemen friends of Lady Hyde! Was she destined to meet the man in the days ahead whom fate had singled out as her husband? Her heartbeat accelerated at this thought, but she very sensibly quieted herself by deciding it was very unlikely in her very first Season, and after all, there was plenty of time for all that. Now, first, there was pure pleasure to be anticipated and her first taste of freedom.

The few days in town before Mary's presentation at court were given over to the acquiring of gloves, sandals, silk stockings, fans, ribands, and bonnets. Then the great day was upon them. Mary was bathed and powdered and perfumed, then set down before her dressing table and put into the hands of a famous hairdresser, Mrs. Mimms, hired for the length of their stay in London. Lady Hyde, fully dressed and already attended to by Mrs. Mimms, came to oversee the proceedings. She was magnificent in purple satin and a towering turban with diamond spray and plume, and was prepared to be very dampening if the hairdresser showed any signs of ambition in regard to Mary. The woman knew her business too well for that, however, and the waving brown hair was brushed until it shone and then pulled back simply from her face into a waterfall of curls down the back of her head.

Then Mary stepped into the hoops, still *de rigueur* for a court presentation, and the shimmering white gown was lifted over her head and carefully draped over the hoops, before the pink-lined robe with its train was put on. The Runceford pearls, retrieved from the bank vault for the occasion, were fastened, heavy and resplendent, about her throat in three strands of large perfectly matched glory; and the Runceford diamond tiara was carefully set upon her head and the curling white ostrich plumes attached. The long white gloves were smoothed over her elbows, and she was handed her fan and turned to the mirror. For a long moment she stared in disbelief at herself. Was it possible that glimmering figure was herself? Then she gurgled with laughter.

"What on earth are you so amused about?" demanded Lady Hyde, somewhat indignantly as she herself had been moved to tears by the youthful beauty of her niece.

"I was thinking of ugly ducklings turned into swans." Mary laughed. "Thank you, Madame Thiery and Watts and Mrs. Mimms and dear, dear darling Aunt for all your labors. I hope I shall not disgrace you all by falling on my face before her majesty."

There was much tongue-clucking and murmured disclaimers and she was wafted out of the room and down to the waiting carriage through a throng of servants waiting in the hall to catch a glimpse of her. The gasps of admiration and oohs and ahs so gratified Mary that when she reached the door, she turned with a little wave and a blinding smile, thus enslaving them all to her. They were agreed that their duchess was just like a fairy princess and surely there could be none fairer in the whole city of London, if indeed in the entire world.

Mary was assisted into the Runceford state carriage, the ducal arms emblazoned upon the doors, and because of her hoops and train, she had the seat all to herself while Lady Hyde rode facing her with her back to the driver. Mary felt her whole body trembling with nerves and excitement and tried to scold herself into a calmer frame of mind. She was ordinarily of a serene temperament, becoming even quieter in upsetting situations, but this occasion defeated her. To be at the beginning of her adventure, to be actually on her way to meet her queen at this very moment and actually wearing the delicious white gown she had gone to gaze upon every day back at Mallows! These realizations succeeded in overcoming her usual self-possession.

They followed a long line of carriages, much slowed

down by the ladies' maneuvering of their hoops out of the carriage doors, but finally arrived at the door themselves and disembarked. They were met inside by Lord Furness, who was to escort the ladies. He was a tall, portly, dignified gentleman, very much alive to the importance of his task, having heard little else for the past fortnight but gossip about this little duchess in her own right. With her upon his arm he was guaranteed to be the cynosure of all eyes tonight, and he intended to make as much political capital of it all as possible. He was also not a little gratified to discover that his charge was as pretty as she could stare, for he liked pretty girls very much, and a plain girl would have not have bestowed quite so much glory upon himself.

He escorted the ladies up a very grand staircase and through a series of very grand reception rooms into the queen's drawing room. The rooms were all thronged with gorgeously gowned ladies and elegant-looking gentlemen in black or in uniform or in the pastel satin coats and knee breeches of the last century on the more die-hard elderly gentlemen.

At first the rooms seemed to swim with color and the glitter of jewels reflecting the flames of thousands of candles, and Mary saw nothing clearly, but as she steadied herself and looked about, she found every head turned toward her, and as they passed, there was a continuous wave of deep curtsies and bows as though a wind blew through a wheat field. It took her some moments to realize with a shock that they were curtsying to her, as taking precedence over every other woman there! That is, until they came into the drawing room itself, which was filled with a great many ladies of equal rank or higher, including a number of duchesses, three royal princesses, and the queen herself. The crowds parted before her and there sat the queen, smiling graciously upon her as she was led forward and introduced by the master of ceremonies, who called out all her titles and dignities. She swept to the ground in a deep curtsy and was helped to arise by that gentleman's firm hand. He had much experience in these matters and knew young girls were nervous at such times and needed a strong support.

The queen held out her hand and Mary moved forward to take it with a shy smile. "Well, my dear, it is a pleasure to me to meet the only subject I have with just your title, indeed, such a title as no queen has known for many hundreds of years."

"Your royal highness is very gracious," murmured Mary.

"A very pretty behaved child, Lady Hyde. I congratulate you," said the queen, turning to Lady Hyde, who curtsied and murmured her gratification. Then Mary was led around to make her obeisance to the three royal princesses, who spoke to her as graciously as had their mother. After that she was introduced to a great many people whose names she could not remember, and engaged in a great deal of conversation that she could only hope did not reveal her to be a complete want-wit.

Then a gentleman approached who introduced himself as Colonel MacMahon, private secretary to his royal highness, the Prince Regent, who craved to have the honor of having the Duchess of Runceford presented to him.

Mary could not know how rarely Prinny attended his mother's drawing rooms and that he was here today solely with the object of meeting her, for his curiosity had been much piqued by all the gossip about this young duchess. She was led up to him, and she again swept a deep curtsey, not at all wobbly this time, and he reached out his own hand to raise her. "Well, well, Duchess, so very young and so very pretty," he said, still retaining her hand, indeed, now it was captive within both his own. He turned to bow to Lady Hyde and nod familiarly to Lord Furness. "And this is my friend, Mr. Brummell. No doubt you have heard of him. He is nearly as renowned as you are yourself."

Mary curtsied again without replying, for she had

never heard of Mr. Brummell and was embarrassed by the prince's remark about herself. She plucked up her spirits, however, after a moment and made some comments of her own, and soon they were all chatting comfortably together though she could never afterward remember what was said between them. Lady Hyde did not join in this conversation, being too much displeased by the prince's continuing to hold Mary's hand, but even she dared not reprove him. She contented herself with swelling up her formidable bosom to even more formidable proportions and staring fixedly at the joined hands, hoping the prince would feel her displeasure and desist.

Later, on the way home in the carriage she waxed indignant about the liberty taken. "But, Aunt, he is only an old man. Why, his stays creaked when he moved," protested Mary. "It was just the same as when Lord Dachett does it at home."

Now, Lord Dachett was a particular whist-playing crony of Lady Hyde's who dined frequently at Mallows and Lady Hyde was not pleased to hear he indulged himself in holding Mary's hand.

"Who is Mr. Brummell?" Mary asked after a moment.

"Quite nobody, really, though he is very close to the Prince Regent and is received everywhere. He is called Beau Brummell and is considered a great dandy. It is said that he bathes every day." Lady Hyde's voice expressed her astonishment at such a fact, for though ladies, of course, bathed frequently, gentlemen were not known to be so nice. She herself knew a certain old viscount who was only bathed when he was too drunk to resist those who were determined to clean him up.

"I liked him very much," Mary declared, "better than the Prince Regent actually. Did he receive a card for the ball?"

"Yes, and no doubt he will come—and perhaps bring the Prince Regent with him."

In the five days intervening before Lady Hyde's ball

to present her niece to society she had, in consultation
with Lady Furness, arranged a series of dinner parties
with the object of introducing Mary to some suitable
young people so that on the night itself she would not
feel herself to be surrounded by total strangers. In this
way Mary met the Hatchworth twins, the real beauties
of the Season, two adorable creatures with guinea-gold
curls, blue eyes, and dimples; Lady Charlotte Gray,
daughter of the Earl of Huxton, and her younger sister,
Lady Amanda; and several other young ladies and some
young gentlemen, all wealthy, of impeccable blood-
lines, and either titled or due to inherit titles. These
young people were of course accompanied by their parents or near relatives.

Of the young men there were three who were clearly
Lady Hyde's favorites, for she was loud in their praises
to Mary. They were Lord St. Hillaire, the Hon. Mr.
Basil Forbes, and Lord Kynvet. Lord St. Hillaire was
the heir of the Marquess of Ardman, whose ancestors
stretched back in an unbroken line to a knight in the
train of William the Conqueror. Mr. Forbes was the heir
of Viscount Holcomb and an immense fortune. Lord
Kynvet had already inherited his title as Earl of Kynvet
as well as the family tendency to a stoutness foretoken-
ing later obesity.

Mary found them all rather dull despite Lady Hyde's
praises, but she was too grateful for her aunt's thoughtfulness to say so. She liked all the young ladies very
well and realized how much easier her coming ordeal
would be with these familiar faces about her.

On the night, the young ladies did not fail her. They
swarmed about her, greeting her as old friends with
kisses on the cheek and with loud exclamations of pleasure over the house, the decorations, the music, and
Mary's gown, which was indeed one of Madame Thiery's
finest efforts. It was of sheerest white tissue over sea-
green satin and seemed to hang straight and slim as a
column from the high waist when Mary stool still, but

when she moved the artfully cut column floated behind her entrancingly.

The ball was a triumph, certainly the first great "squeeze" of the Season, for everyone invited was there, and the staircase, reception rooms, and ballroom swarmed with guests. All Mary's fears of being forced to sit with her aunt for lack of partners proved groundless, for she had more requests to stand up than dances to give them. Unfortunately, she was engaged, through the manipulations of Lady Hyde, to open the ball with Lord Kynvet.

He bowed as deeply as his girth permitted before taking her hand to lead her out. "Duchess, you must allow me to say how greatly honored I feel."

"Oh?" she replied, knowing she sounded simpleminded, but, really, how was one to respond to such a remark?

"To lead you out for your first dance," he replied solemnly.

"It is very kind of you to say so, sir."

"No, no. Privilege, I assure you. Not an everyday thing for me, you see."

"You do no often attend balls, my lord?"

"Oh, forever. I mean to say, a great many. But one does not often have the pleasure of standing up with a beautiful duchess."

His other conversation was equally as pompous and she found it very laborious. But it would soon be over and there were hours of joy before her. She adored dancing and never tired, but she hoped her other partners would not feel obliged to make conversation if they were no better at it than Lord Kynvet. As it turned out, there were not a few who were and who were not backward in flirting either, and though it nonplussed her at first, she quickly got the hang of it and quite enjoyed it.

Just before it was time to go down to supper there was a great stir in the crowd, which denoted the presence of royalty, and the Prince Regent entered with his entourage, which included Mr. Brummell. Mary immediately requested her partner to lead her off the floor and made her way to the prince, who stood in conversation with Lady Hyde. He again took Mary's hand and held it while he complimented her upon her looks and her gown. He remained only a half-hour and then left, claiming a pressing engagement. Everyone was very impressed with the great honor he had shown the duchess, not least Lady Hyde, despite the handholding.

Mary tumbled into bed at half-past four in the morning, the music still singing in her ears, her feet still itching to move. She was not in the least tired, she told herself. It was her last conscious thought before she fell abruptly into sleep.

In the weeks that followed there were many balls, as well as dinner parties, musical parties, breakfast parties, visits to exhibitions and museums, and morning calls. Sometimes there were two or three of these in one day, necessitating the services of Mrs. Mimms and changes of costume. There were also rides in the park, when she was resplendent in her new lavender-blossom habit, suitably followed at a discreet distance by a groom in her livery.

The first of these rides was with Mr. Forbes, and he was openly admiring. "I must say, Duchess, that habit is slap up to the echo."

"I beg your pardon, Mr. Forbes?"

"Your riding dress. All the crack, I assure you."

"Oh?"

"Yes, monstrously becoming."

At last she understood that he was complimenting her, and thanked him. She was proud of her riding habit and it was kind of him to notice it, but unfortunately Mr. Forbes followed each of his remarks with a most disturbing high-pitched laugh. A giggle really, she thought, that at first startled her, but became increasingly irritating until it began to scrape upon her nerves. Apart from this, his conversation was almost exclusively concerned with comments upon the smartness or otherwise of the costumes, horseflesh, and various equipages they encountered on their ride. He seemed to have no other interests nor any idea of how to conduct a gay and witty conversation such as she had imagined back at Mallows when she pictured herself riding in the park. Of course, she felt little inclination to flirt with Mr. Forbes, but at least it would have been more interesting than this.

However, she met many friends and acquaintances as they rode so she was not confined exclusively to Mr. Forbes' conversation and giggles, and in time she rode with other young men who were more interesting and more inclined to flirt, though none who touched her heart any more than did Mr. Forbes.

By this time there were not a few young men who decided that it would be foolhardy to miss such a great opportunity of bettering their fortunes and came to Carlton Terrace to make their proposals. Some of these thought they were truly in love with the pretty young duchess; some were forced to marry money to carry on their lives of idleness, having been trained for nothing else and not only unable to earn their bread, but unwilling. Others were mere adventurers. All first encountered Lady Hyde, who learned their business very quickly and as quickly dismissed them. There were only three allowed to make their offers to Mary, and they were, of course, Lady Hyde's three favorites.

The first of these was Lord Kynvet, who spoke pompously of the propriety of such an alliance of two great houses, of matching fortunes, of his friends' approval of such an alliance and also of Lady Hyde's approval, but nothing of love, not even of affection. Mary rejected his proposal so decidely that he was out of the drawing room ten minutes after entering it.

Then came Mr. Forbes, who lasted longer only because he approached the business so circuitously it took Mary some time to discover his purpose. He was, however, dismissed just as cursorily when she did discover it.

When cautiously questioned by her aunt, Mary replied indignantly that she could not understand by what right they thought they might approach her on such a subject since she had never given them the least encouragement to do so.

"But, my dear, I suppose when a gentleman finds he has fallen in love he has the right at least to let you know it. How else can marriages be made?"

"Love!" cried Mary scornfully. "Nothing was said of love by either of them. They were no more in love with me than I with them."

"It so often happens that love comes after—" began Lady Hyde.

"Not for me. I shall never marry where I do not first love."

Then came Lord St. Hillaire, and it was more painful to Mary, for while she felt nothing at all for Lord Kynvet or Mr. Forbes and was convinced they felt nothing for her, Lord St. Hillaire was a different matter. Not that she loved him in the least, but she liked him well and had become aware that he had fallen in love with her. This sad state of affairs made her refusal all the more difficult. Lord St. Hillaire was a shy, blushing young man with a peculiarity about his face that had taken her some time to define. She had finally realized that his face was unnaturally wide and that his features were grouped closely in the center. It was not unpleasant, only strange. It reminded her of a cartoon drawing of the sun as a jolly deity. She thought of this characteristic being passed on to his children, or their children if she accepted him . . . Oh, heavens, no!

After a great deal of circumlocution Lord St. Hillaire managed to blurt out his profession of love and his proposal in so choked a voice she feared he was strangling. She thoughtfully poured him a glass of wine, which he gulped down gratefully. When the color had somewhat receded from his face, she spoke.

"I am certainly honored and flattered by your proposal, my lord, but I must decline it. I have no wish to marry for some years yet."

"But—but—I do love you most f-f-fearfully," he said heartbrokenly.

"I am sorry, Lord St. Hillaire, but I cannot return your feelings. Perhaps I am too young to love as yet," she said gently, genuinely touched by his sincerity.

"I have been too p-p-precipitate. I should have allowed you more time to become better acquainted with me. You do not positively dislike me, I hope?"

"Oh, not in the least. I have enjoyed our times together and hope that we may always be friends."

"You will not forbid me to hope? Please say that I may t-t-try again."

He looked at her so pitiously that she could not bear to deny him, though she knew very well she could never love this man as a woman should love the man she married. She graciously bowed her head and, rising, held out her hand to him in dismissal. It made her miserable to see anyone so unhappy. She had never dreamed of having it in her power to hurt another human being. She had thought of London as being all pleasure, never thinking that unhappiness might figure in it as well. Well, if nothing else, she thought, to console herself, I have learned a great deal about how to conduct myself during this visit.

However, the business managed to cast a pall over her that she could not shake off. She begged her aunt not to allow any other young men to approach her on the subject of marriage. Even flirting lost its flavor when she realized it might be seen as encouragement, and she had as yet met no young man she wanted to encourage. They had now been in London six weeks and it was gradually borne in upon her that she was no longer enjoying the endless rounds of parties, the endless changing of costume. It seemed to her that she always met the same people and that they always said the same things. Her spirit began to crave the country now as fiercely as before it had craved London. She knew that she might again become restless and bored there, but she had hopes that now that she was definitely "out," she would be allowed more freedom at home.

She expressed her feeling to Lady Hyde, who had begun to long for the peace of Mallows herself. She was too many years out of practice to enjoy the hectic gaieties of a London Season any longer, and too many years old to take the long, grueling hours of chaperonage required for a "toast." She missed the quiet days and the small dinner parties and games of whist with her country friends.

So it was agreed between them that they would set out for Mallows in four days. Regrets were sent out for previously accepted invitations and the servants ordered to begin packing. The servants who had accompanied them to town were sent ahead with the boxes, as well as Mr. Goodenow and Miss Foote in the smaller carriage.

As London drew farther and farther behind them Mary began to relax, happy to see hedgerows and fields once again, to have no pressing engagements to rush about to and from, not to have her hair dressed several times a day and be forever changing her gown. She had loved the beautiful gowns, and the theaters and spectacles and the dancing, but she had found the people of London less than enchanting. They seemed unreal to her somehow. Where are the "real" people? she wondered. Are there such people? Maybe I am looking for something that doesn't exist. I'm not sure I even know what I mean by "real." Perhaps these are the real people I have been meeting and it is myself who is out of step. Perhaps their empty chatter and endless gossiping is the only real world for a duchess, and in another Season or two I will find myself marching to their steps contentedly and accepting the proposal of a man I do not love because it will be a suitable "alliance."

Would she ever receive another proposal at all? she suddenly wondered in panic. Had she been foolish to refuse Lord St. Hillaire? He was very nice and she had liked him. Lady Hyde insisted that love came later, after marriage. Perhaps she was right. What if she never had another offer from a man she liked? Was she doomed to a life on the shelf with no son to become Duke of Runceford all because of some dream that had no basis in reality? Oh, why had her mother had to die before bearing a son? Why had her father not done his duty by marrying again and producing a son instead of laying his burden upon his daughter's shoulders? Was it possible to love someone so desperately you could not go on living without them, as they said of her father? Perhaps he had truly died of a putrid throat as her aunt claimed, and she was basing her dreams on something that had never existed.

Mary tried to imagine a love like her father's for her mother, but could not make it personal to herself, having no memory of being loved to guide her. Though she knew her parents must have loved her, she could not remember them. Nanny had loved her, of course, but she was a stern Scotswoman, not ever given to cuddling and kissing, any more than had been Lady Hyde. Her parents' deep love for each other seemed like something read in a romantic novel, yet it had imbued her entire life and she had built her dreams of what she wanted upon it.

She tried to imagine being head over ears in love. She closed her eyes and tried to conjure up an imaginary lover who would create such feelings in herself, but the faces of the various young men she had met in London intruded themselves and she turned away in disgust. She could not love any of those, even Lord St. Hillaire. They were all too—too shallow and too young. She tried again and a shadowy image began to form itself—an older, strong-featured face. With a jolt she realized she was picturing the face of her father as he appeared in the portrait over the dining-room mantel.

I suppose it is only natural, she thought in amusement, that he should become my beau ideal, being the only man I have been at all familiar with for all these years, even though only through a portrait, and one I associate with real love. He had been thirty years old when the picture had been painted, which seemed an immense age to her. No wonder those callow London youths had appeared to disadvantage.

Would she ever be likely to meet someone like her father? Certainly not at Mallows, for as her aunt had so succinctly pointed out, all the young men who could possibly be considered of a marriageable age were impossible socially. Lady Hyde would never allow her such a marriage as might be found in the local families, even if Mary were to fall in love with one of her neighbors.

But there was the winter season in London to come and perhaps then she would meet someone to capture her heart. She was of an optimistic nature. If today did not come up to expectations, tomorrow might be wonderful! In the meantime there was dear Mallows, where she could ride as much as she chose, ramble through the woods, swim in the pond below the orchards—though this last was strictly forbidden. Still she did manage it on days when her aunt went out to visit her friends and allowed Mary to stay at home, a rare event. Though she was never supposed to be alone on any occasion, she had grown quite adept at slipping the leash when out of her aunt's sight, and her maid and the grooms were sympathetic on those occasions and never reported her to Lady Hyde.

Mary slipped easily back into her old ways and for three weeks enjoyed herself thoroughly. Then, inevitably, she began to long for companionship. She decided that she should invite a friend to stay with her and counted over in her mind some of the young ladies she had met in London. She decided at last upon the Hatchworth twins, who were chatterboxes but gay and good-natured with it, and with her aunt's permission she wrote inviting them to Mallows for a long visit. Alas, they wrote back a cheerful letter saying how despondent it made them not to be able to come to her instantly, but they were promised here, there, and the other place for months to come. Mary realized that she should have thought of these things long ago, as apparently they had, and secured some guests while still in London. The fact was, she decided dolefully, she had no real friend, no bosom bow. She began to feel very sorry for herself.

Then a new thought occurred to her. At breakfast one morning she confessed her failure to obtain a guest for company. "But I think it will answer better for me to go away for a visit, Aunt."

"Go away? Good lord, child, we have not been back three weeks. However, if you are feeling restless I could write Lady Fitzwilliam and Lady Deburgh. I am sure they would be only too delighted to have us and—"

"No, no, Aunt. That is not at all what I have in mind. I would like to go and visit Maud Bryce."

"What? What is all this nonsense? Maud Bryce! Why, she could not possibly entertain someone in your position."

"But that is just the thing. I do not care to be entertained in that way. I had enough of that in London and I have it here. I should like to go quite incognito as plain Miss Marshall."

"And I am to go as plain Mrs. Hyde, I suppose," snapped Lady Hyde.

"Of course not. I—you see, Aunt—well, the truth is I should like to go alone."

"Out of the question," returned Lady Hyde with finality. "Miss Foote, I see you have finished your breakfast. Perhaps you could go up to my sitting room and commence sorting out those embroidery silks I brought from London."

Miss Foote, whose presence until now had been ignored as usual, had been listening with rapt attention to this odd notion of her grace's. Now there was nothing for it but to fold her napkin and slip away as she was bid. Lady Hyde sipped her chocolate in silence for a few moments to compose her mind.

"Now, my dear child," she said at last in a tone of sweet reasonableness, "what is all this foolishness? Surely you must see that I could not allow you to go off alone in such a harum-scarum way. I should not be doing my duty as aunt or guardian to allow a seventeen-year-old girl to go off unattended."

"Nearly eighteen now, and I could take Watts," conceded Mary, not sure if plain Miss Marshall would travel with her own abigail, but willing to acknowledge that propriety demanded that she have a traveling companion.

"Miss Marshall may travel with only her maid. The Duchess of Runceford cannot. It would not be commensurate with your dignity."

"But I do not want to go as the Duchess of Runceford! Do you not see, Aunt? I want to be away from all of that for a time. A month—a fortnight even. It isn't that I want to forget my duty to my father. I could never do it even if I did want to. I will marry, and it will be a man you will approve of, and God willing, the marriage will produce an heir to carry on the name. But that is for the rest of my life! Is a fortnight so much to ask for now, just to lay the burden aside for a brief time and learn how it is to live without hundreds of servants and retainers and all the bowing and scraping and 'your grace' this and 'her grace that.' "

"Oh, my dear," began Lady Hyde, interrupting this passionate outburst, torn between love and duty. Really, Mary could be most persuasive when she wanted something, however biddable a girl she was most of the time. "I am sorry, but I fear what you ask is impossible."

"Oh, please do not say so, dear Aunt," cried Mary, rushing eagerly into the wedge created by her aunt's sympathetic response. "I would take the small carriage and Watts, and there would be Storrs to drive. He could put up at a local inn and bring you reports every day if you like so you would not worry. No one would know. I would write Maud Bryce and swear her to secrecy. I shall just be her relative, Miss Marshall, come for a visit. I promise you I will not flirt or fall in love with anyone unsuitable. You know you can trust me when I give you my word. Oh, do think upon it, Aunt. Do no refuse me out of hand."

"Mary, my dear, I cannot—"

"Please, Aunt, only say that you will consider the matter. Otherwise I do not know what I . . . Oh, lord, sometimes I feel as though I want to ride out someday and just keep going until I find someplace where they have never heard of the Duchess of Runceford."

Lady Hyde felt as though every hair on her head rose separately and quivered, as a chill of fear spread throughout her body all the way to the tips of her fingers and toes. "Mary! Please, do not say such things! You could not do such a thing to me, surely?"

"Of course I would not. Forgive me, Aunt, I did not mean it, truly I did not," said Mary, contrite when she saw Lady Hyde's white face and fear-filled eyes.

"Thank you, child," said Lady Hyde humbly. "I will go upstairs to my room now for a bit. I think I must lie down. I will—I will think over what you have proposed and let you have my answer tomorrow."

A day of fretting brought Lady Hyde to the conclusion that some concession must be made, and a sleepless night of pondering the scheme Mary had proposed brought a grudging admission that it would not be such a terrible thing to allow her to go. She appeared at the breakfast table the next morning pale and hollow-eyed. Mary looked at her apprehensively, not with any real hope.

"Mary, I have decided that you may go upon this visit."

Mary rose with a whoop of joy and astonishment and rushed around the table to embrace her aunt enthusiastically, while Miss Foote looked on in bewilderment. Was it possible Lady Hyde was going to allow her grace to go off in such way? It seemed that she was because she immediately began laying down strictures.

"You must take a footman also, Mary, for protection on the roads. George, I think. He is the oldest and most reliable. It can only be for a fortnight, mind, and you must—"

"Anything! Anything you say, dearest darling Aunt. Oh, best of all aunts in the world! I shall obey your least command!" Then she danced away to the door. "I must go at once to write Maud Bryce to propose myself." She disappeared through the door, but an instant later popped her head back in to say, "What if she cannot have me? Would not that be the outside of anything after all this?" Again she disappeared.

"No fear," said Lady Hyde hollowly.

4

Miss Maud Bryce came down for breakfast and looked approvingly about her neatly furnished dining room. The maid entered at once with her dish of buttered eggs and the toast rack, placing them before her mistress, bobbing a curtsy, and then pouring out a cup of chocolate from the silver pot as she had been trained. Miss Bryce nodded, approving and dismissing at once, and the maid withdrew.

The mail lay beside Miss Bryce's plate, but she only glanced at it, approvingly again, for she liked receiving letters. It gave her a feeling of importance. To make sure she received them, she kept up a prodigious correspondence with everyone she had ever met, however briefly. She never opened her letters until she had finished her breakfast, however, since she did not consider it ladylike to read while she ate, and also because she was somewhat greedy about her food.

Opposite her, on the wall over the sideboard, was a large, gilt-framed mirror in which she studied herself as she ate, practicing daintiness in every movement of fork and mouth in anticipation of dining out, deploring as she always did the fact that the necessary chewing required was not of any great attractiveness to the human face. She was gratified, however, to note that the strong sunlight streaming through the windows upon her face did not reveal any lines as yet. She was five-and-twenty and each time she acknowledged that fact it was with a clutch of panic in her heart occasioned by her still-unmarried state. She had set her cap at every eligible man to come her way in the past eight years with no success. Her failure to find a husband was a matter of true bewilderment to her. She was gently bred, of good family, with her house and six hundred pounds a year to offer, and not, in her own opinion, so ill-featured or ill-formed as to be considered an antidote.

She was in truth a well-enough-looking young woman, with brown eyes and hair and a fine complexion. She lacked inches and was somewhat plumpish, it is true, although she could not be called fat. However, her brown eyes were neither limpid nor sparkling, but had a depthless flatness and smallness of size that made them an insignificant feature. She was not aware of this, of course, and flashed them flirtatiously over her fan in a well-rehearsed style at all the gentlemen. She was always well and tastefully dressed and, except for discreet flirting, behaved with great propriety.

In a way she was right to be bewildered by her lack of a husband, for she had much to offer. She was, however, too proud to take someone beneath her in the social scale, a humble curate or lawyer's clerk, who would have had her gladly, and gentlemen who would enhance her social status seemed oblivious to her attractions.

Still watching her movements in the glass, she wiped her lips and fingers, moved her plate to one side, and took up her letters. She read the first rapidly and put it aside to reach for the next of thick, creamy, expensive-looking paper. Curiously she turned it over and there in the red seal was the Runceford crest. Her heart leapt with excitement, for she had never received a letter from the duchess except in response to her own birthday greetings. To think it had been there all this time while she ate her eggs unknowingly! Reverently she broke the seal and began to read. She pushed back her chair and rose to her feet excitedly, then sat down and read the letter through once more slowly.

A smile of pure bliss spread over her face. Her grace was proposing herself for a visit. Cousin Maud, she addressed her and signed herself Cousin Mary. Only wait until Lady Jameson heard of this and Mrs.—but, no, quite incognito she says, as plain Mary Marshall. Of course it must be just as her grace—as Cousin Mary wanted.

Maud rose again and hurried away to her small sitting room to pen an answer at once assuring Cousin Mary of how happily she would welcome her as plain Miss Marshall for a fortnight, or for as long as she could be spared by her friends. The letter finished and set aside for posting, Maud began to plan for her grace's entertainment. At least two dinner parties, small ones, of course, for her dining room could not seat more than ten, but they would be very elegant with at least four removes. Those not invited to the dinners could be asked to drop in for morning calls. Of course her grace—Cousin Mary, she corrected herself, she really must remember—would come in her own carriage so they could go out for drives into the countryside on fine days.

Then Maud went off to consult with Cook about the dinner parties, in the process nearly biting the tongue out of her mouth to prevent herself from actually naming her guest by title. Maud was so filled with her budget of news it seemed she must burst if she could not share it. It was then necessary to decide where Cousin Mary would sleep, as well as arrange accommodations for her maid. It took only moments to decide that there was only one bedroom commensurate with her grace's dignity and that was Miss Bryce's own. This room had been her parents' room, the room where Maud had been born, and, as such, was larger and more grandly furnished than the others. Maud and her maid, Hetty, began immediately to empty the cupboards and drawers and carry Maud's clothing into a smaller bedroom across the hall. At the back of the hall was a sewing room that they made ready for her grace's abigail, who would certainly consider herself too grand to share a bed with Hetty. There was a full day's work involved in accomplishing all this, which fortunately left Maud with

no time to go out to the shops, for otherwise it is doubt-
ful she could have kept her secret through the day.

There were, however, four more days before the great
event. During the next morning Maud managed to inform most of her friends that she was to be honored
with a visit from her "Cousin Mary." She slightly em-
phasized "cousin," hoping, perhaps consciously, that
some would be wise enough to make the connection
without having to break her word. No one seemed to
do so, despite all these years of talking about her con-
nections with the Marshall family, who had been dukes
of Runceford for hundreds of years. Everyone smiled
and remarked how pleasant it would be for her and they
would look forward to meeting any relative of hers.

Maud had barely returned home, feeling somewhat
frustrated, when Lady Jameson was announced. Maud
was much flustered, wishing she had had time to go up
and smooth her hair at least, for Lady Jameson was
eminently important to Maud's plans, being the aunt of
Mr. Hodgson, a young man who figured largely in her
hopes for the future. He was Sir William Jameson's heir,
and if all went as Maud planned, she herself would one
day be called Lady Jameson.

The present Lady Jameson was well aware of these
aspirations and was determined to squelch them, for to
her mind dear Cecil could do very much better for himself than Miss Bryce and her six hundred pounds a year.
She had not ever previously called upon Miss Bryce,
though as a gentlewoman of the county she had invited
her to dinner from time to time, especially as there were
very few young women of suitable breeding available to
be invited to entertain dear Cecil. This morning, however, word had reached her through her servants that
Miss Bryce was expecting a visit from a relative, and
being insatiably curious as to the affairs of all her neighbors, Lady Jameson had condescended to pay a morning
call to learn what she could. She had heard often—as
who in the county had not—of Miss Bryce's illustrious

relative, the Duchess of Runceford, but never of a Cousin Mary.

After a brief preliminary exchange of courtesies, Lady Jameson came bluntly to the point. "I have heard you are to have a visitor, Miss Bryce."

"That is so, Lady Jameson, my Cousin Mary," replied Maud demurely.

"I do not believe I have ever heard you mention such a relative before. What is her full name?"

"Mary Marshall, my lady."

"Marshall? Then she is a connection of the Runceford Marshalls, I take it?"

"Oh, yes indeed, Lady Jameson," replied Miss Bryce with a smile and a significantly raised eyebrow, which Lady Jameson missed entirely.

"Some cadet branch, I assume, for there was only the duke and his sister, Lady Hyde, and she is childless. Not a close connection, I take it?"

"Oh, on the contrary, Lady Jameson, a very close connection, indeed," cried Maud, her eyes widened to a bright stare straight into those of Lady Jameson. If it had not been so unladylike she would have winked to convey her message. Poor Lady Jameson was so obtuse!

"Close? But how—I mean to say—"

Maud smiled enigmatically and again raised her eyebrow, willing her visitor to grasp her meaning.

Lady Jameson stared at her blankly for a long moment, then almost perceptibly one could see the wheels beginning to turn. "Mary . . . Marshall," she said slowly. "But surely you do not mean . . . Is it—?"

Maud raised her hands in mock dismay. "Oh, you must not take me up so quickly. I meant nothing at all, I assure you. Only that plain Mary Marshall has proposed herself for a visit and I will be delighted to receive my cousin." She could barely suppress a grin of pure pleasure, for nothing would so surely impress Lady Jameson in her favor as the news that the Duchess of Runceford was so close to Miss Bryce that she would propose herself for a visit.

"Ah! I see—plain Miss Marshall. Quite incognito, is that it?"

"Now, you must not ask me such questions, my dear Lady Jameson, for I vow I would not be able to answer them," said Maud, but at the same time giving Lady Jameson a little reassuring pat on the hand to make sure Lady Jameson did not mistake her. "I hope you and Sir William will come to dine one evening to meet her. And Mr. Hodgson, of course. I shall be sending out cards in the next few days."

"Naturally, I shall look forward to meeting your, ah, relative, Miss Bryce," pronounced Lady Jameson majestically.

She took her leave then and Maud was left to contemplate her guilt in having betrayed her word to Mary. However, in only a few moments she was able to console herself with the knowledge that she had not actually said anything in so many words, and she could not help it if Lady Jameson chose to interpret those words she had said in her own way.

Lady Jameson had no qualms at all about telling the whole story to Sir William and Mr. Hodgson that evening at dinner. "But you must remember to address her as Miss Marshall when you meet her, for she does not want her title used. We shall have to entertain her here, of course. I hope you will not think of going back to London soon, Cecil." Lady Jameson was already entertaining ideas concerning her nephew and the Duchess of Runceford. After all, they were both young and unmarried, and young people had a way of falling in love.

"No fear, Aunt. I would not dream of passing up an opportunity of paying my *devoirs* to her. Heard all about her in London. All the crack this last Season, you know. A regular toast, I heard."

Cecil could not resist passing on this *on-dit* to his friend Captain Beaumont as they were out riding together. This gentleman, of course, passed it along to his mother, and in no time at all it was generally known through the village and the surrounding countryside that

Maud Bryce was to be visited by the Duchess of Runce-ford. Every woman with the least pretension to gentility decided she must entertain the visitor, and by the day of Mary's arrival, four invitations had already arrived and been accepted by Maud.

As Mary's carriage rolled down the high street of the village of Sturrett, she found it somewhat odd that there were so many people strolling up and down and that all the shop doors were filled with staring people. What a very dull place it must be whose inhabitants find so much entertainment in a passing carriage, she thought, forcing herself to look straight ahead. Watts, sitting opposite her with her back to Storrs, the coachman, and George, the footman, looked from side to side and distinctly saw a woman begin to drop a curtsy, before being nudged by another lady. Oh, oh, here's trouble before we start, thought Watts. Someone has let the cat out o' the bag for sure. And no bad thing, so far as Watts was concerned, for she didn't hold with all this incognito nonsense. Duchesses should be called by their proper titles and be treated accordingly. What was the point of being ladies' maid to a duchess if they went about in a plain, poky carriage like this with only two horses and no attendants to announce her mistress's glory. As for this visiting Miss Bryce, it was beyond anything foolish. How was she, Watts, to be treated in a house with only two servants? Why, at Mallows, Miss Nancy Watts was third in the hierarchy of servants, with only the housekeeper and the butler above her, and great respect was paid to her by everyone.

They drew up before a modest little house, and before George had let down the steps and opened the carriage door, Miss Bryce came flying out her front door followed by a maid. As Mary stepped down, Miss Bryce threw her arms about her.

"Welcome, welcome indeed, dear Cousin Mary," Maud cried happily.

Mary drew back, attempting to straighten her bonnet, which Miss Bryce's enthusiastic embrace had knocked awry. "Thank you so much. How kind of you," she murmured.

"But do come inside at once. You must be weary from your journey. Hetty," ordered Maud, "help bring in the cases and show Miss Marshall's maid upstairs."

Mary was ushered inside and looked about approvingly. The hall was small but well-proportioned and the drawing room furnished in excellent taste.

"I hope you will take a glass of wine. You must be parched," said Maud, hurrying to a side table where a tray was set with a decanter and glasses.

"No, I thank you, Cousin Maud. I am not in the habit of taking much wine except with my dinner." After some few moments of stilted conversation regarding the hazards of the road, Mary said she would like to step up to her room to lay aside her bonnet and freshen herself after all the dust of the journey.

"Of course, of course. Dear me, how very remiss of me not to have thought. Do come along at once."

Mary found Watts awaiting her, with a clean gown unpacked and spread upon the bed and hot water in the basin. Watts helped her out of traveling costume, waited with the towel while Mary washed, then took down her hair, brushed her curls until they shone, and rearranged them. She then helped Mary into the fresh gown of white figured muslin and handed her a clean handkerchief before holding open the door.

When Mary reappeared, somewhat shyly, in the drawing-room door it was to find her cousin sitting with three other ladies. "Oh, here you are, dear Cousin Mary. Please allow me to introduce my guests to you. This is Mrs. Herbert and Miss Speers and Miss Olivia Speers."

All the ladies had risen to their feet and seemed to quiver expectantly as they eyed her with avidity. Mary dropped a curtsy and murmured how pleased she was to make their acquaintance and they each curtsied back. They remained standing until Mary had seated herself in the chair Cousin Maud led her to. She thought they were all uncommonly formal here in Sturrett. The ladies stayed only twenty minutes, and before leaving, Mrs. Herbert avowed how she looked forward to seeing her for dinner three evenings hence, and the Miss Speers that they hoped she and dear Miss Bryce would be coming to a small musical evening on the next night.

"What a very social life you do lead here, Cousin Maud. Was that the Mrs. Herbert of the strawberry parties?"

"Why, yes, fancy you remembering that. She has a lovely little place about two miles from here and—" Before she could continue, Hetty was at the door to announce two more ladies, and after they had gone, three further callers were shown in. Mary was quite astonished. She had met more people in two hours than she had met in all her years at Mallows. Was it possible that this sort of thing went on everywhere but in her own home?

"Now, dear Cousin Mary," said Maud as she returned from showing out the last visitors, "we must go up at once to change for we are to dine with the Entwhistles."

"Dine out?"

"Unless you would prefer not. Perhaps you are too weary?"

"Oh, no, not in the least. I shall enjoy it very much."

No wonder Cousin Maud's letters were always so full of these things, thought Mary as Watts again helped her into another gown and rearranged her hair. They seem to entertain one another continuously. She was to become even more amazed as the days went by, for every day brought callers and every evening a party until on Friday Cousin Maud's own dinner party brought about Mary's first evening at home. It was to be very small, Maud assured her, consisting of only Sir William and Lady Jameson, their nephew Mr. Hodgson, and Captain Beaumont, none of whom, surprisingly, Mary had as yet met. She was glad of this because she would now have to start repeating herself on evening gowns. Not having dreamed of so much dining out in so small a place, she had brought only a few for her fortnight's stay.

Lady Jameson, when she was introduced, curtsied to the floor and Sir William bowed profoundly over her hand. Mr. Hodgson made an elaborate leg and pressed his lips to her fingers much longer than was necessary. Captain Beaumont, a dashing-looking gentleman, murmured, "Honored, your gr—Miss Marshall," and everyone froze. Mary, being unsure of what she had heard, only greeted him graciously. Everyone suddenly began talking at once and Mr. Hodgson led the captain aside and murmured in his ear.

Mary thought it odd in the extreme when her Cousin Maud called out to Sir William to lead Mary in before Lady Jameson. Surely Lady Jameson took precedence over plain Miss Marshall. She stared at Maud in astonishment.

"Oh, you must not mind how we go on here in Sturrett, Miss Marshall," declared Lady Jameson, gallantly coming to Maud's rescue. "We always insist on the honored guest leading us in."

Maud laughed a little wildly, her face flushing up at the realization of how nearly she had come to giving the game away out of carelessness, when she had been so much on her guard all this week and made sure everyone else was also.

The talk became general over the meal and there were no further incidents. The ladies retired to the drawing room at the end of dinner, leaving the gentlemen to their port. When at last they were all reunited over the tea tray, it was easily to be seen that the gentlemen had not stinted themselves, for they were all very jolly, declining tea and continuing to laugh immoderately over one another's remarks while the ladies had theirs.

At one point Sir William, who was seated beside Mary upon the sofa, leaned toward her and patted her hand. "Pleasant evening for us all, my dear. Don't know when I've enjoyed myself more." He leaned closer and breathed boozily, "Always makes a party go when there's a pretty gel." Lady Jameson frowned at him warningly and he straightened himself up, muttering, "S'truth, by the Lord Harry. Not often you find a pretty gel with a ti—"

"Dear Miss Bryce," said Lady Jameson loudly, "I think we must be leaving now. Perhaps you wouldn't mind asking for our carriage to be brought around."

In the hallway as they made their farewells, Sir William possessed himself of Mary's hand and held it while he said good night. Then he patted her cheek and told her she was a pretty child "with no airs or consequences about you at all, as many a one in your position would flaunt for all she was worth. Believe me, m'dear, I—"

"Miss Marshall, it has been such a pleasure," said Lady Jameson, stepping firmly between them. "You dine with us next week, I believe. I shall very much look forward to seeing you again."

It seemed to Maud that Mr. Hodgson had pressed her hand quite meaningfully as he bade her good night, and had smiled most intimately into her eyes. She was well-pleased with the evening despite all the little heart-stopping moments. She took Mary's arm as they ascended the stairs to their rooms and chattered happily. She found Mary somewhat silent and unresponsive and assumed she was tired. She kissed Mary's cheek, bid her to sleep well, and tripped happily across the hall to her own room.

Mary stared broodingly into the glass as Watts brushed her hair with long soothing strokes, but she did not see herself. She was thinking of Sir William's last remark. No matter how she looked upon it, she could only take one meaning from it. Then her mind went back over each puzzling event of the evening, each one only confirming her growing suspicions.

"Your grace is tired tonight. I vow this Sturrett is nearly as bad as London, and we have not brought nearly enough gowns. You shall stay in your bed tomorrow with a tray and see no one all day.''

"No, Watts, I am not in the least tired, but—"

"Yes, your grace?"

"I tell you what it is, Watts. Those Jamesons and Captain Beaumont know who I am.''

"Lord love you, your grace, and so does everyone else here.'' Watts laughed merrily.

"What? Why do you say that?'' demanded Mary in dismay.

"Why, didn't Cook and that Hetty admit as much to me the first day we came? They heard it from the Jamesons' servants. I questioned them about it later and found everyone around here knows.'' Watts related all this with some satisfaction, for her own status had risen accordingly.

"But you should have told me, Watts.''

"Why, I supposed you knew, your grace. What with all these women calling, people staring when you go out and everything.''

"But—but this is dreadful!''

"Now, your grace mustn't get into a taking over it. No doubt Miss Bryce confided in a friend she thought she could trust, but these things have a way of getting around. She meant no harm, I'm sure. It's all a play, like, and no one will let on to you, since they know you don't want it.''

"I must go away at once. I cannot look these people in the face with their knowing and my knowing they know. How could I have been so stupid? It is horrid— horrid! Pack the cases at once and send Storrs word to bring the carriage around at seven. And you are to say nothing of this discovery to the servants here, Watts.''

"Now, your grace, you needn't—"

"Do as I ask you, Watts,'' said Mary in a voice that brooked no argument. "I must speak to Miss Bryce now.'' She swept out of the room, leaving Watts staring after her in dismay, for she was not at all eager to leave, having begun a flirtation with a footman from the Jamesons'.

Mary rapped at Maud's door and, when she was bid to enter, did so, closing the door behind her. Maud was already in her bed, though her candle was still lit.

"Miss Bryce, I find it is necessary for me to leave in the morning."

"Leave? Oh, dear me, Cousin Mary. Has there been bad news? Is Lady Hyde—"

"Lady Hyde, so far as I know, is enjoying her usual good health, but I have had some unpleasant news from Watts. It seems I am discovered." She said it lightly, not allowing herself to express accusation, but the slow, dark flush that spread up Maud's face to the roots of her hair was as good as a confession.

"I assure you I have never—" Maud muttered, her eyes everywhere but meeting Mary's own.

"No, no, please do not say anything. It was all my own foolishness and will be a lesson to me for the future. We will say our good-byes in the morning, so I will wish you good night now. I have ordered my carriage for seven." She left the room before Maud could reply, and softly closed the door behind her.

Maud turned away to bury her face in her pillow and sob. It was all the fault of that stupid Sir William, who never knew how to carry his wine! After blaming everyone but herself for a fruitless quarter of an hour, she sat up and wiped her eyes. What was done, was done and could not be changed, but it was not all bleakness. After all, she had been here, and everyone knew now that the Duchess of Runceford cared enough for her relative to pay her a visit. Mary would put a good face on it before the servants, Maud was sure of that, so no one need know why she was leaving. It could be put about that her guardian had demanded her return. The good of the visit had been done and could not be taken away and Mr. Hodgson and Lady Jameson would remain impressed. With these thoughts she was at last able to fall asleep without too much trouble to her conscience.

5

Mary came down to breakfast dressed for travel and greeted Maud civilly. When Hetty was in the room to serve them, both ladies played out a little charade for her benefit, and when she was not present, they remained silent. Maud could think of nothing to say that could possibly ameliorate the situation and Mary was so out of charity with her "cousin" that she could hardly speak at all. She finished her breakfast and waited politely for Maud to finish before rising.

"You will, I know, make all the proper apologies to your neighbors who had so kindly planned parties for this next week and explain how sorry I am to be called away."

"Yes, of course, cous—your grace."

"Thank you very much for having me. I know you have gone to great pains to make everything here pleasant and comfortable and I have appreciated it." She held out her hand. "Good-bye, Miss Bryce."

Maud shook her hand and bobbed a curtsy and Mary went out into the hall, where Watts awaited with a cloak. She put it over Mary's shoulders as Mary pulled on her gloves. Hetty waited to open the door and curtsied her out. George helped them into the carriage, put up the steps, and closed the doors. He then mounted up beside Storrs and they rolled away from the house and out of Sturrett. There were very few people about to see them go as it was barely half-past seven. Mary had been determined to make the entire journey in one day.

She gazed silently out of the window, wondering how

43

she could have been so childish as to think all could have gone as she had planned. Of course, she had not known Maud Bryce when she had made her scheme. Now she realized that Maud was not the sort of girl to keep such a secret to herself. She also knew that Maud was not the sort of girl she could have made a friend of. Maud was a social climber and a snob of the worst sort, for one thing, but also she was too lacking in warmth and naturalness to attract someone of Mary's cheerfully good-natured openness. Just the same, it had been dreadfully sly of Maud to betray her confidence and then, knowing everyone in the village was aware of her identity, to allow her to play out the farce for a full week. It was so absolutely shaming for Mary. She could only hope she never came face to face with any of those people again.

Suddenly the carriage tipped violently, dumping Mary unceremoniously into Watts' lap. She pushed herself back onto her precariously leaning seat to meet George's anxious face peering in at her through the window.

"Are you all right, your grace?"

"Nothing worse than a crushed bonnet brim. What has happened?"

"A wheel cracked, your grace."

"Good Lord, and we've not been on the road for an hour. Well, what is to happen now?"

"Storrs will walk into the next village. He says it can't be more nor five mile to Bortonford."

"Oh, dear. Well, we shall just have to wait, I suppose. Thank heaven it is not cold. Help us out, George, and we will sit on that bank. The seats are too tilted to be comfortable."

In all, the delay took three hours. When they were at last able to set forth again, Mary decided they would have to stop at Bortonford for refreshments, as it was now midday and her servants had had nothing to eat for at least six hours. By the time they had reached Bortonford and eaten, another hour had passed. Mary thought it was now impossible to reach home on the one day and, after consulting with Storrs, decided they would put up for the night at Scathin, which was reputed to have a fine coaching inn. Storrs thought they could easily reach it by six o'clock.

They set forth again and the slow, jolting hours passed. Mary put her weary head back against the squabs and dozed fitfully. She was wakened by a shocking clap of thunder. She straightened herself painfully, rubbing her aching neck, and peered out into a day suddenly dark as night with heavy clouds. The rain began very suddeny, a heavy, obscuring downpour that forced Storrs to slow his pace. The warm summer day was gone, and Mary and Watts huddled shivering in their cloaks. Mary took out her little pocket watch and found it was a quarter-past five. Well, another forty-five minutes and they would be in Scathin. She was very much looking forward to a fire and hot food and a bed.

Then the carriage stopped completely and George was there in the driving rain peering in at her. It was so dark she could barely see his face. "The bridge is out up ahead, your grace. There's a sign posted. We'll have to make a detour to get to Scathin. Storr's can't be sure how long it will take as he's not at all familiar with the road we are to take."

"Well, go on, then. We cannot just sit here."

The carriage turned into a side road that was little more than a country lane, with the hedges brushing at the windows as they passed. It was an exceedingly rough road and Mary and Watts rattled about like two peas in a box. Mary peered out anxiously but could see nothing but hedges for a time. Then they were passing a field and she looked hopefully for lights, thinking that if they found any sort of habitation, they could stop and get inside until the rain had let up somewhat, but there were no signs of life to be seen. Then, abruptly they entered some woods and the rain seemed to slacken in its force as the trees took the full brunt. Mary leaned back with a sigh.

"This has certainly been an ill-omened journey, has it not, Watts? I begin to wonder if it will ever finish."

"There now, your grace, you are overtired, but the worst is over now and we'll soon be warm and comfortable at the inn."

With these words several things happened simultaneously. There was a loud, barked order, the carriage halted abruptly with a great deal of protest from the horses, followed almost immediately by a gunshot and a yell of pain. Mary and Watts stared at each other with wide-eyed horror for a second or two before Mary reached for the door handle.

"No, your grace, don't you—"

"Someone is hurt. I must see—"

Then the door was wrenched open and a very unattractive face was thrust inside. Black eyes, sharp and glittering, took them in and a red mouth set within a great deal of black facial hair parted over execrable teeth in a wide grin. "Females, by God!" he shouted, and reached out to clamp upon Mary's wrist. "Come out of that, wench, and let's 'ave a look at cher," he said, and yanked Mary so suddenly out of the door she would have fallen in the dirt had his grip not been so firm.

Watts screamed, "Let go of her, you wretch. How dare you?"

"I dares plenty, lass. Now, then, you, missy, gi us yer purse."

"I am not carrying money, if that is what you are looking for. My maid has a few pounds for our needs on the road. I heard a shot. Was someone hurt?"

"Well, yon coachman thought to be brave and got hisself winged," confessed the man with a grin.

Mary attempted to release her arm to go to Storrs, but when the man only gripped it harder, she called out, "Storrs, are you hurt badly?"

"Aw, never mind the old gent. He won't stick his spoon in the wall yet. Now, let's have yer geegaws, missy, and I'll take the money you're carrying also."

"You are welcome to what I have. Watts, hand out

my dressing case.'' Mary was grateful for her decision to bring no jewels of any great worth on her visit to Sturrett.

The case was handed out and there in the dark and rain the man opened it up. He pawed through the contents while Mary looked about. Storrs was holding his shoulder, but was still upright on his seat, and George was peering down at her with frightened eyes. To one side sat two men on horses holding the reins of a third horse.

''What cher got there, Pike?''

Pike threw down a handful of brooches and chains in disgust. ''You playing games with ole Pike, now, be'ant cher, missy? Where's the real stuff at?''

''I assure you there is nothing more.''

''Be damned to that for a lie and you in yer fine rig and yer servants. Who be ye now?''

''You mind your language, villain. This is the—'' began Watts furiously.

''I am Miss Marshall. I am governess to the children of Sir Paget, ah, Peckham. This is his carriage and these are his servants,'' Mary said loudly and firmly for the servants' benefit, for it would never do to allow these men to know her true identity.

''Gi over, Pike. Take the doins and lets git out o' this,'' called out one of the men.

Pike stood scratching his beard for a long moment. ''Naw, there's bound to be plenty o' blunt in this business somewheres. This Sir Whatsis, now.''

Mary spoke quickly. ''Yes, he is a very wealthy man. We will go and get some money for you. I myself will bring it back to you at this spot in—''

Pike roared with laughter. ''Oh, ye do be clever as a cageful of monkeys, missy. You'll go bring it, eh?'' He went off into another gale of laughter as he jerked his head at the man holding his horse. The man brought the horse alongside Pike, who, without loosing his hold on Mary, got himself into the saddle. ''Get the case, Jem. We mights well have it. Now, missy''—and with a sud-

den heave, he pulled Mary onto the saddle before him—
"you'll just come along o' us and this here lot will go
pick up the money from old Sir Whatsis, see? An 'un-
nert pounds, we'll say, and when they comes back, we'll
let cher go, all fair and square."

"George," called Mary, "help Storrs down and into
the carriage. You will have to drive. Watts, find something to bind Storrs' shoulder. Take careful note of the
road, George, so you can find your way back." Mary
spoke as calmly as possible, though her heart was
bumping so hard it was painful and the hand that had
bruised her wrist was now about her waist in so tight a
grasp she felt the breath was being squeezed out of her.

Abruptly Pike swung his horse around and galloped
off into the trees, followed by his men and the shrieks
of Watts. Once these had faded away Mary curled up
her free hand into a fist and swung it around with all
her force straight into Pike's eye. She had refrained from
any action while her servants were in sight or hearing,
for she knew that despite everything they would have
attempted to come to her aid, and these men were
armed. At least one of them was, the one who had shot
Storrs. Now she had no compunction about fighting for
herself and landed her blow as neatly as a boxer.

Pike let out a roar of pain and loosened his hold on
her to put his hand to his eye and she leapt to the ground
to land, after a stumbling run, in an ignominious heap.
She scrambled up and began to run, but it was too late.
All three men jumped down and had her before she had
gone three yards, tearing off her cloak in the process.

"Yer would, would yer, little she-devil," growled
Pike, boxing her ear so that her head rang.

"Handy wi her fives, ain't she, Pike?" said one of
the men with a cackle.

"Shut yer trap, Jem, or I'll draw yer cork for yer,"
snarled Pike, wrenching Mary's hands behind her back.
"Fetch the rope, Maggs."

Pike proceeded to tie Mary's wrists so viciously tight

that she cried out. He then hauled himself back into the saddle. "Throw 'er across in front o' me," he ordered.

"Bring my cloak first, if you please. It is very cold," Mary ordered in her most imperious voice.

Maggs snatched it up and put it about her shoulders before Pike could speak.

She completed her trip hanging head down across Pike's saddle. Fortunately it was not a long journey, for nothing she could have imagined could have been so excruiatingly uncomfortable. In less than ten minutes they had reached their destination; a dismal-looking hovel, as far as she could make out when they pulled her off and set her on her feet.

Pike pushed her ahead of him through the door into a dirt-floored room. "Git them lamps lit and a fire going," he ordered. Mary, shivering in her damp clothes nearly blessed him for this, but in a moment learned her mistake. He pushed her over to a low door and through it into blackness and left her. Presently the lanterns bloomed and some of the light penetrated to her. She was in a tiny room, little more than a closet added to the main room. It was also dirt-floored and the rain had seeped through the cracks in the board walls to turn the dirt to mud around the edges. In the center was a pile of rags that she assumed was someone's bed. Even in the near darkness it looked so unsavory she pulled her skirts away fastidiously to keep from touching it.

She could see the fire burning up now and longed to join the men huddled about it, but was too proud to ask them for anything. They had set a pot of something over the fire and presently a faint aroma of a stew of some sort reminded her that she was hungry. The men talked about their recent adventure and the division of the spoils.

"Tol yer wi' that bridge out we needn't to go all t'way t'main road. They's bound to come this away. T'aint no other way ter go," Pike gloated. "Pour out t'grog, there, Jem. 'Twas thirsty work."

Mary huddled miserably against the inner wall beside

the door, willing some warmth from the fire to reach her. Her shoulders had begun to ache intolerably from her arms being stretched back, and she began to wrench and jerk her wrists in an attempt to loosen the rope, but only succeeded in rubbing her wrists raw.

"The rain's stopped, Pike. Let's go out again. Mayhap another carriage be coming along there tonight."

Pike declined this suggestion and an argument ensued. At last Jem and Maggs opted for trying their hands once more since the night was so young and left. Pike poured himself another drink and sat scratching his beard.

It was intensely quiet, with only the crackle of the fire and rain dripping from the trees breaking the silence, and Mary, for some reason, became more frightened than she had been so far. She hardly dared breath for fear of reminding Pike of her presence. She tried to reason herself out of her fear by telling herself that he would not dare kill her, after all, for the imaginary Sir Paget would not hand over good money for a dead body. She set herself to trying to count how many hours it would take the servants to reach home. If they didn't stop at Scathin, which was, say, an hour from here, they could reach Mallows in two or three hours. But of course they probably would have to stop at Scathin for Storrs to be attended to and to bate the horses. Another hour. It could not be more than six o'clock now, and in five hours it would be eleven o'clock. Then an hour at Mallows for Lady Hyde's hysteria and to put in a fresh pair of horses and at least four to return. With the best luck in the world they could not get here with the money before four or five in the morning! Her spirits sagged, for she now knew all the things that could go wrong and delay them for even longer. Would Aunt have a hundred pounds in the house? Lord, what a thing to think of? she chided herself. Will I feel better if I stand here thinking of all that could go wrong? It is not so very long, and anything can be endured if one sets one's mind to the job.

She saw the light in the room brightening, and stiffened. It was Pike approaching the door with the lantern. He held it high and looked about quickly. "So, there yer be, missy. Not quite so high and mighty now, be ye?"

"And you are not so handsome," she retorted unwisely as the lantern light revealed an eye already nearly swollen shut and turning black. She earned another head-ringing box on the ears that knocked her to her knees. At least it's not on the same side, she thought dazedly.

He jerked her to her feet. "Too clever by half's what you are," he snarled. "Too much eddicachun's yer problem. I'm agin eddicatin' females. They's only good for one thing that I knows of." With that he reached out, put his hand to the neck of her dress, and with a jerk ripped the fine merino cloth all the way to her waist, exposing her chemise and half of her proud, small, high-set breasts. She screamed and turned away, but he swung her around again and flung her onto the heap of rags on the floor. As he attempted to fling himself upon her, his nose came into violent contact with her raised knee and spurted blood copiously. He stood up, cursing, and pulled a filthy rag from his pocket to stanch the flow.

"Now listen to me, Pike," Mary began quickly, taking advantage of the moment, "I am only a poor girl trying to earn her living, just as you are. I am the sole support of my poor widowed mother and four little brothers and sisters. I was educated so that I could support them and also to find a husband above my station in life to help me take care of them. Would your mother approve of what you are thinking of doing to a poor girl like me, who's only trying to earn bread to feed her family? Do you think any man will marry me if you— if you—and I doubt if even Sir Paget will pay if he knows, for he is in love with me and he will be vengeful if he thinks harm has come to me, and I will tell him, you may be sure. And they will be bound to come back armed. Sir Paget will no doubt come with them and he is a crack shot, I assure you. You had best be satisfied with your hundred pounds, which you'll not get if you—if you—''

''Arrgh!'' roared Pike nasally from behind his blood-soaked rag, ''shut yer trap. Yer makin' me head ache with all yer yammering.'' He turned and lumbered out of the room and back to his place by the fire.

Mary scrambled away from the makeshift bed and huddled on the floor by the wall again, all her pulses racing and her breath coming in gasps of relief. She didn't know for sure what had been so nearly her fate, but she knew it was something vile. Even the memory of the brief contact of his hand at the neck of her dress, touching her throat, sent shudders through her. It is only a reprieve, she thought wildly, he will brood on it and come back.

It was quiet, though, for a considerable time, with only the clink of the bottle against his cup to signify that Pike was drinking. Presently even this stopped, and snores began. He was asleep!

After a time Jem and Maggs returned, cursing their lack of luck in not finding another hapless traveler to hold up. They settled down with the bottle between them and presently their jokes and snickers about the state of Pike's face died away and their snores joined his in loud chorus.

Now, she knew, if ever there was to be one, was her chance. There was no point in any further attempts to loosen her wrists, though she could not prevent trying a few twists, which set her raw wrists to throbbing and stinging. She shivered uncontrollably now with cold and excitement and longed for her cloak, but it lay where it had fallen when Pike had thrown her down and she could think of no way to pick it up, much less get it over her shoulders.

She began edging her way through the mud along the board walls, pushing against each one experimentally to find if one were loose. She did find one at last that

gave to the pressure of her shoulder and was, fortunately, in a corner away from the door. As she continued to press, it squeaked against the nails and she
halted, holding her breath. There was no interruption
of the drunken snores, so she continued to press, stop-
ping when the squeaks became too loud and then continuing until it had given way enough to enable her to
squeeze through. She stood there in the utter darkness
for a moment. The rain had stopped, thank goodness.

She heard the soft snort of a horse and her heart leapt
in hope. But, no, that was impossible. There was no
way to get onto the back of a horse with her hands tied
behind her. She would have to go on foot. She set off
at once into the trees, leaving in the opposite direction
of the front door and the path they had used when they
had brought her here. Until she judged she was well
away from the house, she tried to step softly, but then
she began to run, blundering along, nearly blind in the
pitch black. She ran, branches clawing at her hair and
face and tearing at her gown, fallen branches, rocks,
and unexpected dips in the ground sending her sprawl-
ing again and again, and occasionally a full-tilt encounter with a tree trunk leaving her reeling about in a daze.
It seemed hours before she stumbled out of the edge of
woods and fell flat onto her face in a ditch half-filled at
the bottom with icy water. She lay there, winded and
gasping, until she had recovered her breath and then
knelt up to peer out. There was a well-made road before
her. She sank back onto her haunches. I will wait here
until daylight and then, when a carriage comes along, I
will get out into the road and make them stop and take
me up, she decided. She leaned her shoulder wearily
against the muddy side of the ditch, and despite the fact
that she was sitting in cold water, her head sank forward
and she slept.

6

The night hours crept by interminably for poor Mary as she sat cramped against the side of the ditch, the ache in her shoulders near agony by now. She thought it was not possible for a night to go on for so long. So much had happened to her it seemed days since that fateful abduction, but it had all happened in much less time than she imagined. In fact, it was not long after ten o'clock on the same night when she had reached the ditch, though she had been sure most of the night must have passed when she had escaped from the hut.

However, at long last the blackness became gray, and when she had roused herself from her last fitful doze she was able to assure herself that the night was truly over. Now, besides her pain, her raging thirst and hunger, she was more fearful than ever that Pike and his men might find her, for surely they would not be long in waking from their drunken sleep and discovering her escape. No doubt they knew every inch of this woods and might even now be quartering it for her. She instinctively hunched down lower in the ditch.

At that moment, however, she heard horses and wheels upon the road. Thank God, a carriage at last! She struggled to her feet. The carriage came in sight, plodding along, the coachman nearly asleep. From the open window protruded a pair of boots and a raucous song filled the quiet of the morning. There could be no mistaking this for anything but a drunken gentleman returning from a night of carousal. She ducked out of sight. Rescue was desirable, even necessary, but she could not bring herself to be rescued by a person in such a condition. It might be jumping from the frying pan into the fire.

After another hour she began to wonder if she had been quite wise. Pike and his men could not be much longer in finding her, for it was definitely daylight now, with the just rising sun laying heavy bars of tree shadows across the road. She was faint with hunger and sheer fatigue, and was finally reduced to bending down and lapping up some of the muddy water in which she sat to moisten her throat.

Another hour, or so it seemed, had gone by before she again heard the sound of an approaching carriage. It came from a different direction than the first and was rolling along at a fair clip. She scrambled out of the ditch and into the road. She would take this one no matter who was inside it. Anything would be better than Pike!

The coachman saw her and called out something to his passenger. The carriage came alongside her and halted. She stared into the dark, scowling face of a man who was looking distinctly annoyed at being stopped. Over his shoulder could be seen the wide-eyed face of a very small boy.

The man saw an apparition such as he had never beheld. A woman, her hair in wild tufts starting out from her head Medusa-like, her face raked by scratches that had bled tracks through the mud that covered it, her gown torn into strips and hanging open revealingly over her bare bosom, the whole caked with mud.

''Please, sir,'' she begged, turning half around, ''please untie my wrists.''

For a second he stared disbelievingly, then he opened the door and jumped down. Taking a folding knife from his pocket, he cut her bonds. She screamed as she tried to bring her hands around and then her kees sagged. He caught her before she fell.

''Proudie, come down—quickly, man!'' The coachman climbed down. "Take my cloak off and help me wrap her in it."

When this had been accomplished, she was lifted into the carriage and propped into the corner. The man managed to get a few drops of brandy from his flask down her throat. In a moment she opened her eyes and essayed a groggy smile. "I'm all right now, truly. It was only—"

"How many hours have your wrists been bound in that position?" he asked curtly.

"Since about six o'clock last night."

"Good God—fifteen hours! Proudie, whip them up, if you please. I am Charles Leigh and this is my nephew, Robin Leigh."

"How do you do, sir. I am . . . Mary Marshall. I was returning to my, ah, place of employment last night when we were set upon by footpads. When they found no money or jewels enough to please them, they took me for ransom. My—the coachman was shot. Not seriously, I hope, and they were sent on to collect money from my—employer—for my release."

"But then you managed to escape, I take it?"

"Yes. They began to drink and then slept and I got away. That was hours ago."

"No need to talk anymore now. Just try to rest quietly and we will be at Hachett's Hall soon." He turned away to stare out the window and she sighed gratefully and leaned her head back against the squabs. The pain in her shoulders was beginning to ease, but now the feeling was returning to her hands and that was almost as bad. Still, she was safe now and soon there would be warmth and food. All the spirit that had kept her resolute for so many hours fell away and the tears she had refused to allow herself before came oozing from beneath her closed eyelids to run in runnels through the dirt and blood on her face.

She felt a tiny hand creep into her own and looked down to find the little boy nestling close to her and looking up at her with great sympathy. She managed to

smile reassuringly at him and then closed her eyes again,
comforted by his warm little hand and body as he leaned
confidingly against her.

After a time the carriage turned sharply off the road
onto gravel and Mary opened her eyes. The little hand
in hers squeezed convulsively so that she had to bite her
lips to keep from crying out. Not for anything, however, would she loose that little hand, for she had begun
to realize that he was not only comforting her, but also
himself. She wondered why he should need comforting,
poor little mite. He could not be more than four years
old.

The carriage halted before an imposing but sadly ne-
glected mansion, and the front door opened immediately. A pleasant-faced, comfortable-looking woman in
spotless white apron over her black dress came bustling
out.

"Well, my lord, and so you are back," she cried as
Charles Leigh descended. "And the little lad?"

"Good morning, Mrs. Heaven. Yes, we are back."
Robin was lifted out by his uncle and swept up into
Mrs. Heaven's arms.

"There now, isn't he a love?" she said delightedly.
Then her eyes nearly started from her head as the other
passenger was helped out and stood before her, looking,
to her eyes, like a bedraggled witch. Robin wriggled
out of Mrs. Heaven's arms and ran back to take Mary's
hand, nearly hiding himself in the folds of the cloak.

"This is Miss Marshall, Mrs. Heaven. She has suffered a great deal at the hands of some villainous footpads. Do you take her along and, er, make her
comfortable. A bath, I believe will be necessary, and
another gown. Now, Robin—"

"No. Stay with her," Robin muttered from the folds
of the cloak.

"Oh, very well, very well, as you like. Take them
both along, Mrs. Heaven. You will know what to do, I
am sure. I will be in for dinner at three as usual." He

hurried away, as though glad to wash his hands of these problems.

Mary loosed her hand from Robin to put her hand about his shoulders and press him close, for she could feel his little body trembling. They followed along behind Mrs. Heaven across a hall with a magnificent staircase, through a door at the back, down a long hall that led at last into a vast kitchen. There were huge fireplaces at either end, but only one had a fire burning in it and clearly all the business of the kitchen was done in that end of the room.

Mrs. Heaven called out to a young girl who stood stirring a pot hung over the fire. "Take that off for now, Betsy, and put a pot of water to heating. The big pot, mind. Now, ah, Miss . . . ?"

"I am Mary Marshall. Please call me Mary," she said, holding out her hand.

Mrs. Heaven rather reluctantly reached to take it—reluctantly because she could not quite forgive Robin's clear preference for this strange girl and also because she distrusted anyone who appeared in such a condition. However, she was a good-hearted woman and she would not refuse to shake hands on appearances alone, apart from the fact that the girl was obviously gently bred from the way she spoke. So she took Mary's hand, but as she did so, she saw the abraded, bloody wrist and cried out in horror.

"Merciful heavens! What has happened to you?"

"They tied my wrists together. I suppose I did that myself trying to loosen the ropes. It is not bad, truly."

Mrs. Heaven reached for her other hand and examined the wounds minutely. Then she looked up. "Those scratches on your face?"

"Oh, I did that to myself also. On branches and bushes when I ran away. It was so dark, you see."

"Betsy, fetch the hip bath into my sitting room and spread a sheet first to put it on. Well up to the fire, and fetch some towels. Sit you down here, Miss Marshall.

You'll take a cup of warm milk." She pressed Mary down on a stool at the fireside.

"I wish you will call me Mary, Mrs. Heaven."

"Mary, then, sit here till the water heats and Betsy and I make all ready, then you shall have a bath. We must wash your hair too, for it's all filled with mud."

Mary huddled before the fire with Robin in her lap; she sipped her milk until, after Betsy had struggled into the next room with the large pot of hot water, Mrs. Heaven called her. She set Robin on his feet and rose, but he wrapped his arms about her legs and clung.

"There now, Master Robin, sit you down there and let Miss—let Mary have her bath," said Mrs. Heaven.

"No," he replied firmly.

"Robin," said Mary, "you remember how I looked when I stopped the carriage in the road?" He nodded his head against her knees. "Then you know I am very dirty and must have a bath as your uncle ordered me to do. Now, you know a lady cannot entertain a gentleman in her bath, do you not?" Again she felt his hard little head nodding against her knees. "So if you will sit here, where its lovely and warm, Mrs. Heaven will give you—"

"Some cake," said Mrs. Heaven.

"Some cake to eat while you wait. I shan't be very long."

"I am also very firsty," he declared.

"Then you shall have some milk, Master Robin, Betsy, fetch them and stay with him while Mary has her bath."

This all being settled, Mrs. Heaven led Mary into the next room, her own sitting room, where a tub stood steaming before the fire. Mary hesitated and then removed the cloak.

"Dear Lord! Your gown," cried Mrs. Heaven, much shocked at the sight of the torn bodice and the wet muddied skirt hanging almost in strips. She said no more but pursed her lips together in grim anger that a poor young lady should be so treated by those filthy villains.

Her sympathies had been roused by the wounded wrists, but now she had completely lost her first antagonism and all her warm heart went out to Mary.

She helped her out of the gown—a fine one it had been, too, she noted—and then out of the undergarments, also of the highest quality and as daintly made as she had ever seen. She assisted Mary into the tub and Mary sank with a sigh of pure bliss into the water.

Mrs. Heaven stepped over to the door. "Betsy," she called out, "fetch Miss Marshall one of your gowns." She then returned to the tub and, when Mary had finished scrubbing herself, ordered her to put her head back and proceeded to wash her hair. She then helped her out and wrapped her in a towel she had warming by the fire, and wound another about her head. Then the wrists were spread with a soothing balm and bandaged and Mary resumed her undergarments and Betsy's gown, a dark-brown cotton. It was much too short for her, but otherwise not a bad fit. Betsy had cleaned Mary's smart kid half-boots and provided, unasked, a pair of her own thick knit stockings.

Mary went back to Robin and found him playing on the floor before the fire with a calico kitten. "Look, Mary, he came out of the wood box to play with me," he called out happily.

"Yes, darling, how lovely for you. Now I am all clean again I believe I should like a kiss."

"I don't have time now, Mary," he said, totally absorbed with the kitten's antics.

Mary and Mrs. Heaven exchanged smiles and Betsy giggled. Mrs. Heaven said, "Now sit down, Miss—"

"Mary," said Mary plaintively.

"—Mary, and let me comb out your wet hair." Mrs. Heaven patiently teased the snarls out of the long hair, and as the warmth of the fire dried it, it sprang into curls and waves that shone in the firelight.

"Thass purty hair, that is," said Betsy shyly.

"Thank you, Betsy." Here Mrs. Heaven handed Mary the few pins that had been left in her hair and she looked at them in bewilderment. At last she pulled her hair back and attempted to bundle it somehow into a knot. The few pins she had, however, were inadequate to hold so awkward a mass of hair and it all promptly tumbled down her back with a scattering of pins. Patiently she began to pick them up.

Mrs. Heaven, watching her, thought, I'd lay odds she's never done her own hair in her life. "Here, let me do that. It is hard when it is fresh-washed like that," she said kindly, and very deftly twisted the hair into a knot at the back and inserted the pins with a sure hand. "There, now. If you are tired, you can lay yourself down in there on my bed while Betsy and I get the dinner."

"Oh, no, Mrs. Heaven, though you are kind to think of it. Perhaps I could help you?"

"Not today," said Mrs. Heaven firmly. "If you won't lie down, just you sit there quietly. Such an adventure you have had," she continued as she bustled about the kitchen. "I declare the roads ain't safe for travel these days. Where had you been going?"

"I was returning to my place of employment from a visit. I am governess to the children of Sir Paget Peckham," replied Mary, not without a pang of guilt to be lying to someone so good and straightforward as Mrs. Heaven, but she was still determined not to reveal her true identity to anyone. If word got out that the Duchess of Runceford had been abducted, it would become the talk of the country. It might even get into the newspaper! She shuddered with horror at the thought of becoming the object of gossip and speculation.

A governess, thought Mrs. Heaven, with them underclothes fit for a queen! I never heard of a governess able to afford a chemise like that—worth as much by itself as every stitch I own put together. She began to question Mary about her adventure, and Mary told her the story, at least most of it. She did not feel able to speak of Pike's brutal attack. She told her about the black eye, however, and Mrs. Heaven began to laugh so heartily she had to stop work and sit down, while Betsy giggled helplessly, saying over and over, "She done landed him a facer," with great glee.

Robin liked the sound of this phrase and picked up the kitten to go dancing around the kitchen chanting it to himself in singsong. Presently there were sounds in the front hall. "There be master, Mrs. Heaven," said Betsy.

"All right, Betsy, I hear. Take up those potatoes into the covered dish. Master Robin, put down that kitten now and come wash your hands. Your uncle will be down for his dinner in five minutes."

"No. Don't want dinner," said Robin, dropping the kitten and running to Mary. He climbed into her lap and hid his face in her neck.

"Why, Robin, what is this? How can a great boy like you not be hungry for his dinner? Run along now with Mrs. Heaven and wash your hands. And after you've had your dinner I will be waiting right here for you."

"Oh, no, Miss—Mary. We all sit down together in this house," said Mrs. Heaven. "Master don't hold with separate meals, he says, when we're all working together. He says its a waste of good time."

Hearing this, Robin allowed his hands to be washed and they went into the dining room with Mrs. Heaven and sat down. Charles Leigh came in quickly and pulled out his chair. He stopped in shock when he saw Mary.

"Oh, it is you, Miss Marshall?"

Mary smiled demurely, sure that he had forgotten her existence since he had turned her over to Mrs. Heaven. But Mrs. Heaven knew that it was because he could not believe this pretty girl, despite the scratches, was the same creature he had brought home earlier. "Good afternoon, sir. Robin, say good afternoon to your uncle."

Robin looked down at his plate. He had not yet learned to like this uncle, who looked so grim and who had hardly spoken to him at all. Mary was embarrassed for Mr. Leigh. Robin seemed almost frightened of his uncle. She must contrive to find out from Mrs. Heaven

all about Robin and why he was here. Until this moment
she had been so grateful to be safe and clean she had
not even thought to be curious about the people with
whom she found herself.

Then Betsy came in with a roasted chicken and the
potatoes and, after placing them before Mr. Leigh,
seated herself beside Mrs. Heaven, rousing Mary to real
curiosity. What a strange household this was, to be sure.
The house seemed very grand. Perhaps Mr. Leigh was
the manager of the estate for an absent lord. She studied
his face covertly. It was burned brown by the sun, as
though he spent most of his life out of doors. His hair
was thick and dark, nearly black, and his eyes . . . What
color are they? she wondered. He looked up at that moment and caught her look. She lowered her eyes to her
plate. Blue, she thought. Not an unhandsome face, after
all, though her initial impression had been of hardness
and coldness, something about the eyes and the set of
his mouth that had struck her as unsympathetic. Then,
too, he had been so silent in the carriage after his brief
questions. No exclamations of outrage at her plight, or
even much concern beyond telling her she should not
talk anymore at the moment, which she had been grateful for at the time.

She ate her chicken and potatoes hungrily, and helped
Robin to eat his. Everything was very good. Though
Mr. Leigh had not spoken after his initial greeting, the
feeling around the table was not constrained. Mrs.
Heaven spoke to everyone—even Mr. Leigh—easily, and
even Betsy said a word now and then.

Slowly Mary was pervaded with a sense of content-
ment. She liked sitting here with all this household
about her. She liked the simplicity of the communal
meal. She liked especially Robin's dependency upon
her, a thing she had never experienced before.

At last Charles Leigh pushed aside his plate and
leaned back in his chair. ''You said you were returning
to your place of employment when you were taken by

the footpads, Miss Marshall. You will have to let them know that you are safe, of course."

Mary felt her jaw sag with dismay. Poor Aunt! She would be nearly mad with worry by this time, and in all these hours she had not given her a thought! But Mr. Leigh was staring at her and waiting for her reply. "Yes, yes, of course. I will write to him at once."

"Who is your employer?"

"Ah . . . Sir Paget Peckham. I am governess to his children. I will ask him to send the carriage for me as soon as possible."

"Yes. That will be best, for I cannot spare the horses to take you back, nor Proudie either, for that matter."

"Oh, of course not. I would not dream of—"

"You are welcome to stay here, of course, until he sends for you."

"You are very kind," she murmured.

"Mrs. Heaven, you will have to air a bed for Miss Marshall."

"Certainly."

"Mr. Leigh," said Mary, "I shall be very happy to earn my way by serving as Robin's governess while I remain."

"Very well. Thank you, Miss Marshall. Now, I must leave you. There is much work to be done before the day is over. Robin, you will do as Miss Marshall bids you." With that he rose and left the dining room.

What a peculiar man, Mary thought. So driven. "Does Mr. Leigh always work so hard, Mrs. Heaven?"

"My dear child, it is not Mr. Leigh," replied Mrs. Heaven somewhat scandalized. "It is Lord Leigh. He is the Earl of Leighford."

7

"**B**ut—but . . . Mrs. Heaven, I do not understand," cried Mary when she had recovered from her speechlessness. She was trailing along behind Betsy and Mrs. Heaven toward the kitchen carrying the bowl of potatoes. Robin, clinging with one hand to her skirt, carried his water glass in the other as his contribution to labor.

"Well, he is a very poor earl. His father gambled away the money, and his older brother mortgaged the rest to pay for his drinking and his mistresses. He died of the drink—or perhaps of the other, for all I know. At any rate, die he did, and Lord Charles Leigh came into nothing but the title and a load of debts."

"How does he live, then?"

"As you see. He works his acres as a common farmer, and none could work harder than he, I do declare. In the fields at daybreak, home for his dinner at three, and back again till sundown. He's determined to pay off the mortgages on this estate. The rest he sold to pay the debts. Oh, the fine grand manors all over the country the Leighs had, you wouldn't believe."

Mary sat down before the fire and Robin climbed into her lap and closed his eyes. Like all healthy young animals he had the ability to fall asleep instantly, and did so. "Mrs. Heaven," whispered Mary, "what of Robin?"

"Ah, the poor darling boy. My lord's younger brother and his wife were both taken with the diphtheria. There was no one else, so my lord went to fetch the boy here and was bringing him back when he found you. Doesn't seem to take much to his uncle, though, does he, poor lamb? My lord is something dour in his manner, though he means nothing by it. It's because he has so much trouble on his shoulders so young.''

"I suppose it is not easy to be lighthearted when one must work so hard,'' replied Mary with a great yawn.

"That's the truth of it, Miss—Mary. Now, that boy should be in bed, and no doubt you wouldn't mind it yourself.''

"Oh, I should like it of all things,'' breathed Mary tiredly.

"Here, let me take the child. We'll put him into his bed and then . . .'' But Robin woke at once when Mrs. Heaven lifted him from Mary's arms and began to cry. "Now, don't take on, Master Robin. You must go to your bed surely.'' She carried him up the back stairs, Mary following, Robin sobbing as though his heart would break and reaching out piteously for Mary over Mrs. Heaven's shoulder.

When they reached his room Mary took him and began to undress him, and his sobs abated. Once in his nightshirt, though, and placed in the center of the large bed, he began to cry so convulsively that Mary had to take him up again. He would not be soothed, crying that she must not go away and leave him, and at last Mary asked if she could not simply sleep here with him.

"Why, bless you, why not?'' said Mrs. Heaven with relief. "If you will not mind. I don't think you'll get much rest else. I'll just fetch you a bed gown.''

Presently the two orphans fell asleep wrapped in each other's arms and Mrs. Heaven closed the door upon them and went back to her kitchen, wondering what on earth they were to do with the boy when Mary went away.

The next morning Mary woke just at sunrise and stared in surprise for a few seconds at the tiny head nestled against her shoulder. Then she remembered everything and felt extraordinarily happy, happier than she could remember feeling for the past year at least since her childhood had ended. It was hard to believe that only a few weeks ago she had been in the midst of her first London Season, surrounded by the *ton*, being feted and courted and finding it all less exciting than her dreams of it had been. Her boredom had made her wonder where there were to be found "real people," and now she felt she had found them. For surely people who worked so hard and lived so simply, even though they were to be found listed in the peerage, must be as real as one could hope for. She looked down at Robin's round little face, flushed and dewy with sleep, his lashes looking impossibly long, and then leaned to kiss his warm cheek before slipping out of bed and over to the window. The morning was clear and shining, everything fresh and burgeoning into early summer. The perfect day for a good gallop, she thought, wishing her mare were here instead of at Mallows.

"Mary!"

She turned to find Robin sitting up. "Yes, darling, here I am. It is a beautiful morning, but very early. Shall we dress quite quietly and slip out to walk barefoot in the grass? It is lovely when the dew is still on it."

"Oh, yes," he breathed happily.

She went to the chair, where she found her clothes folded neatly, though she had no memory of having put them there the night before. Then she found her undergarments had been washed and ironed and she felt guilty and glad at the same time. She had never had the care of her own clothing before and had not thought last night, probably would not have thought even if she had not been so tired, that this morning she would have to face a crumpled gown and unfresh undergarments.

She dressed as quickly as possible, realizing as she struggled with the buttons that she also had never had to dress herself in her life. First there had been Nanny and then Watts, and she herself had only had to stand still. She fared better when she came to dress Robin, for she had had her dolls, after all, to dress and undress. There remained the problem of her hair, but as she knew it would be impossible to attempt to dress it herself, she left it hanging down her back. She would ask Mrs. Heaven to help her with it after breakfast.

Carrying their shoes and stockings in one hand and holding Robin with the other, she led him quietly down the back stairs, shushing him when he began to giggle with excitement and then giggling herself. When she opened the door into the kitchen, they both stopped guiltily, for there was Mrs. Heaven rolling out dough on the table and Betsy peeling potatoes at the sink.

"Well, well, here are the lie-abeds at last," cried Mrs. Heaven cheerfully.

"Oh, dear, Mrs. Heaven, are we so terribly late? The sun is barely up."

"We're going to walk barefoot in the wet grass," announced Robin importantly.

"Are you so? Well, go along, then," said Mrs. Heaven indulgently, "but only for a minute or so, mind. Then you're to come in to your breakfast."

They ran laughing out the back door, hand in hand. "Can't say as I ever heard of a governess like that," declared Mrs. Heaven. "Still, it's a good thing to see the child happy like. Slice some bread, Betsy, and give that porridge a stir."

While Robin spooned up his porridge with great appetite and Mary ate a large slab of bread and butter, Mrs. Heaven told her that my lord had said before he went out that Mary would find paper and pen on his desk in the dining room to write her letter, and if she left it, he would frank it for her. Mary, however, knew she could not allow that, for her letter would, of necessity, be addressed to Lady Hyde, not the imaginary Sir Paget Peckham.

"I should like to post it today, Mrs. Heaven. How far is the village?"

"About seven miles. You could never walk it. But I heard my lord tell Scraggs he'd have to go in this morning to pick up something he's ordered down from Lunnon. Scraggs could take it if you are quick like, for I

saw him going toward the stable a few minutes ago.
Betsy, run out and tell him to come up, there's a letter
to post.''

Mary rose at once and headed for the dining room,
but at the door she stopped short, then turned back to
ask as casually as possible, "Can Scraggs read, Mrs.
Heaven?''

"Scraggs read? Lord love you, where would Scraggs
be learning to read? What strange questions you do ask.''

Much relieved, Mary hurried away. She gnawed the
end of the pen for a moment anxiously. To write what
must be said needed thought and time, and she had
given it no thought until now, and now there was no
time. At last she wrote:

> Dearest Aunt,
> I escaped unharmed and then was rescued by very
> kind people. I am very well and very happy and you
> are not to worry about me, for I want to visit with
> these nice people for a little time. I will write again.
> With much affection from your loving niece, Mary

She knew her aunt would be much upset, especially
when she discovered there was no direction given in the
letter. Mary knew she was causing her aunt a great deal
of anxiety, but despite the guilt she felt, she was determined to stay for as long as she could as Mary Marshall, governess to Robin Leigh.

Back in the kitchen she handed over her letter to the
grinning Scraggs, who was waiting at the back door,
and returned to her cooling cup of chocolate. "I hope
you will not mind pinning up my hair for me, Mrs.
Heaven. I simply cannot seem to get the way of it. I
have brought the pins in my pocket.''

Mrs. Heaven obligingly twisted the hair into a knot
and pinned it up. "How you have gone on this time and
not learned to put up your own hair is strange like to
me,'' she said, probingly.

Mary improvised wildly, "Well, I have worn it down
until just recently, then I—I braided it, you see.''

Mrs. Heaven did not see, and thought it an unlikely explanation but held her tongue for the time being.

To change the subject Mary asked, "Does not Lord Leigh ever entertain or keep any kind of estate at all?"

"He says he has not time for fripperies now, and if he must work like a farmer, he will live like one. Mind you, he goes off for dinner to Squire Herries every so often, and then the squire and his missus and their daughter have been here to dinner a time or two, but none else. They do say . . . Well, never mind that, 'tis only gossip and I'll not repeat it."

"What are they like?"

"Who?"

"The Herries. Are they nice?"

"Well, the squire is a fine gentleman and a good farmer himself. All up on the newest ways and that. I can't say I care for his womenfolk much."

"Mary, can we go out and play now?" said Robin in tones of one whose patience is sorely tried.

"Oh, good heavens, darling, how quiet you've been. You certainly deserve to play. That is . . . Can I help you in some way, Mrs. Heaven?"

"No, child. You run along with Master Robin. That is your job. Who's to play with him when you leave I'm sure I'm blessed if I know."

Robin was very anxious to see the horses, but the stables were empty. Mary supposed the horses were all out pulling plows today, and of course Scraggs had one to take the cart to the village. In the home paddock behind the barn, however, there was one elderly mare who ambled over to the fence to stare at them with mild curiosity.

The cow barn was likewise empty, the cows having been taken out to pasture, so they wandered along to look at Mrs. Heaven's chickens and ducks. Robin had become strangely quiet and Mary twitted him. "I suppose the cat got it."

"Got what?" He looked up at her in surprise.

"Your tongue, little man." His hand flew to his

mouth and she laughed. "Not really, I was only teasing. But you are very quiet."

"Mary, are you going—going away?"

"Well, I cannot stay here forever, darling."

"Why not?"

"Because it is not my home. I must go to my own home one day or my friends will be worried about me."

He studied the ground in silence for some minutes. "My mama and papa went away," he said at last.

She knelt before him and pulled him into her arms. "I know they did, darling. They were very ill, you see. My mama and papa went away also when I was very small, but I know they did not want to leave me, any more than did yours."

"It wasn't because you were bad?"

"Oh, dearest Robin, no! Is that what you think? That they went away because you were bad?" His head hung lower. "Then you must never, never think such a terrible thing again about your dear mama and papa. They would never have left you willingly, any more than would mine have done. I promise you this is true, Robin, on my honor."

He leaned hard against her. "We are alike, aren't we, Mary?"

"Yes, darling. We are both orphans, but we have dear friends who love us and take care of us. I have an aunt and you have your uncle."

"Don't like him. Want you."

"That is only because you don't know him very well yet. He works so very hard, you see, and there's no time left for him to play with you. But he does love you and you will love him when you know him better. You have only been here one day. You must have patience with everything and it will come right. Now, let us go for a long ramble in those trees over there and see all the interesting places we can find. Perhaps we'll find a pond."

He went quite willingly and presently was chattering happily of all they saw, but Mary had the first real twinge of conscience about what she was doing for her own pleasure. She had not set out to attach Robin's affections—that had happened almost despite herself—but the results were the same. He was a little boy who had lost all he knew of safety and love and had turned to her at first because he was unhappy and she was crying and therefore must be unhappy also and he sympathized. Then she had become an anchor in a bewildering place with new people. Now, when she went away, as she must one day, he would feel again that he had been deserted. Was it fair for her to stay here a day longer, forging the bond between them ever stronger, only to leave him? On the other hand, he was so desperately alone and unhappy now and she was his only comfort. Was it not better to stay as long as possible to help him grow more confident and until he had learned to love his uncle and Mrs. Heaven and Betsy?

Since the last coincided so much with her own wishes, she thought it must be the best solution. In the meantime, she would do all she could to foster the relationship between Robin and Lord Leigh.

When they went back for dinner she decided she must put this policy into practice at once and turned to Lord Leigh. How formidable he looks, she thought, even while eating. The blue eyes stared intently at the space between the edge of his plate and the saltcellar, his brows drawn together into a frown. He always seemed so preoccupied, or at least he had done so on the three occasions upon which she had seen him. Still, he had been kind, if not demonstrative, in lending her his cloak and bringing her here, she told herself bracingly and clasped her slightly trembling hands tightly together.

"Lord Leigh."

Mrs. Heaven and Betsy, who had been speaking together, stopped and turned to her in surprise. Lord Leigh continued staring abstractedly into space.

"Lord Leigh," she said again.

He looked up at her blankly, his fork suspended halfway to his mouth. He put it down, wiped his mouth, and looked at her interrogatively.

"I was thinking it would be a treat for Robin to accompany you to the fields for a short time today to see the sort of work you do here."

He raised an eyebrow. "Tired of your job after only one morning at it, Miss Marshall?"

"Of course not," she protested, "I only—"

"I am glad to hear it. I am very weary of mine, I assure you, but despite that, I must give it every moment possible. I have no time to amuse children."

She felt the blood rush into her face at this snub and set her lips firmly to hold back the retort that rose to her lips, and resolutely continued with her dinner. However, when Lord Leigh rose, she pushed back her chair and followed him into the hall.

"Lord Leigh, I cannot allow you to think I was hoping to shirk my job. It was for Robin's sake that I spoke. He is very bewildered by all the changes in his life. He misses his parents dreadfully and you are his only relative and it would be helpful to him if you gave him some attention. He is only a baby, after all."

"I know that very well, Miss Marshall, and babies belong with women who understand their needs."

"Yes, I agree that most of the time that is true. But Robin lost a father also and you must naturally come to take that place in his life. Just a few words at the dinner table now and then would surely not take up too much of your valuable time," she finished, unable to prevent a touch of acid in her last words.

"Thank you for your concern, Miss Marshall. Now, if you will excuse me, my men will be waiting," he grated out through clamped teeth. With a bow he took up his hat and went out the door, barely restraining himself from slamming it. Damned interfering woman, he fumed silently, picked up half-dead in a ditch yesterday and today presuming to tell me where my duty lies. He was not the less angry because he knew she was right. He had hardly spoken two words to the boy yet and knew how unhappy and lonely the child must be. Oh, damn and blast!

Mary returned to the dining room, aware she had made him very angry and too angry herself to care. Cold, supercilious and heartless man, she said to herself indignantly. Three pairs of eyes met hers as she came in: Mrs. Heaven's interested, Betsy's round with awe, and Robin's fearful.

Mrs. Heaven hastily pushed back her chair. "Now, Betsy, stack those plates, and if you could take the platter, Mary, and Master Robin his glass, we'll get all cleared and washed up." Mary was grateful for her bustle, for she could not have spoken had she tried.

That afternoon Mary and Robin went on a tour of the house. "Nearly all the rooms are shut up and under dust covers now," said Mrs. Heaven. "My lord says it's foolish to try to keep it all clean when we don't use it. We open up the drawing room when the Herries come, of course, but for the rest, my lord sits in the dining room of nights. He had his desk moved in there to save having a fire in his study."

The house was very large and the rooms spacious and beautifully proportioned. It made Mary sad to see the silent rooms in their ghostly drapings. Her anger at Lord Leigh gradually melted as she realized all the sacrifices he had had to make to hold on to his ancestral home. He had not been raised to labor with his own hands in his own fields, to live so penuriously, scrimping on servants and space and fires, giving up the privileges that normally obtained to an earl. Of course, he was the second son and had not been raised to expect to inherit, but even second sons of earls did not expect to have to labor in the fields.

Of course he would have little time to give to his nephew. She began to realize how forward and impertinent she had been in speaking so to the man who had rescued her. Actually, it had been a foolish suggestion on her part, for of course he could not take Robin with him and keep an eye on him while he worked, and then, when Robin tired, interrupt his work to bring the child home again. Yes, it had been a stupid thing for her to propose. She became so engrossed in berating herself for her ill-thought-out suggestion that she quite forgot that her original intention had been a good one.

The next day at dinner she was still so oppressed in spirits she could not bring herself to raise her eyes from her plate and was therefore the more startled to hear Lord Leigh say, ''Well, Robin, are you getting to know the place?'' Robin flicked a wary glance at him and then hung his head bashfully. ''This is your father's own old home, you know, the place where he was born and lived until he married your mama. I wonder if you have found the pond yet where he used to swim?'' Robin did not answer. ''I'll wager you haven't. I shan't tell you where it is, but I will give you a clue. Beyond the paddock you will see a path.''

Robin, intrigued, peeked up at his uncle. Lord Leigh returned to his dinner and said no more.

Mary's flagging spirits suddenly soared. He might have been angry at her, but he had taken her meaning, after all.

After the meal Robin was ready to go find the path beyond the paddock at once, but Mrs. Heaven insisted upon a delay. ''You wait, too, Master Robin. You shall go presently, but for now you must possess yourself with patience. Come along, Mary, I've something to show you.'' She led the way up two flights of stairs to a room at the back of the house that was clearly used for storage. There, laid out on various pieces of discarded furniture banished from other parts of the house, was an array of feminine garments from the previous era. Panniered gowns of shimmering satins and brocades, fur-trimmed cloaks and large-brimmed hats with trailing feathers. Mary stared about, much puzzled. Robin immediately picked up one of the hats and put it on. It came down to cover his entire face.

Mary giggled. ''What on earth, Mrs. Heaven? Why are all these things lying about like this?''

''I pulled them out last night. I thought you might be able to wear some of them.''

"But—but—I cannot wear such clothes, Mrs. Heavens." She picked up a cherry-pink satin gown much trimmed at the low-cut neck and the elbow-length sleeves with creamy Mechlin lace, and held it up against herself.

"Well, I suppose not that. And of course, child, I didn't mean just as they are now. But the fabric is very good and one or two could be picked apart and made up into something more suitable."

"I fear I know little of dressmaking, Mrs. Heaven," said Mary regretfully, "though I thank you for your kind thought."

"Oh, as to that, I am very good with my needle. Just you pick out what you like and I'll make it up for you."

"You have too much to do as it is," Mary protested, "and this gown of Betsy's will do me well enough. It is another chemise and petticoat I need."

Mrs. Heaven smiled. "You will find those on the chair in your room when you go up."

Mary threw her arms about Mrs. Heaven and kissed her soundly on each check. "You are too good to me. But where did you find them?"

"Where I found all this. They were Lord Leigh's mother's things. I've never been able to bear throwing anything away. She was my own lady, you know. I was her maid when she was but a girl, and I came here with her when she was married, poor dear woman. But there, here is Master Robin being a dear, patient boy. You pick out something now and let's be done with it."

Mary sorted through the piles of gowns until she found two that were made of cotton—obviously house gowns for morning wear—and hovered between a lilac and a pale gray and pink print.

"We'll have them both," said Mrs. Heaven decisively, sweeping up the gowns. "Now, run away both of you."

Mary and Robin went away to the paddock to find the path that led to the pond.

8

The days passed quickly for Mary and Robin once they had found the pond. They spent part of every day there, returning wet and happy, and usually barefoot. Both had sunburned cheeks and Mary's dark-green eyes glowed like emeralds. She also had acquired a fine sprinkle of freckles across her nose. When Mrs. Heaven noticed them she found an old straw hat with a wide brim that she insisted Mary must wear when she went out. Though Robin would not be separated from her at night and they still shared the same bed, he no longer moped or cried or looked fearfully at his uncle. Some of this was due to Lord Leigh himself, who always made a point of exchanging a few words with his nephew at the dinner table now.

For all the household the high point of the day was this meal where they saw Lord Leigh. The two servants idolized him, and for Mary and Robin he had begun to exert a fascination, despite, or maybe because of, his taciturnity. He was so totally dedicated to his work he seemed like a saint, or at least a knight concentrating on the Holy Grail. One hesitated to interrupt his thoughts with mere everyday commonplaces.

It was a strange experience for Mary, used as she was to being the center of attention since she could remember anything, to find herself relegated to such a disregarded position. Strangely exhilarating also. She felt freed entirely from all bonds of Runceford responsibility. It was as though she had stepped out of an old skin and was newborn into another world. She rarely thought of Mallows or her aunt, and when she did, she quickly put aside her twinges of conscience, for she felt she must enjoy every moment of these days, since it was unlikely she would ever be free again.

Within a week Mrs. Heaven handed her the remade gown, the gray printed cotton. It was simply made, with a high neck ending in a small ruffle, short puffed sleeves, and long straight skirt below the high-waisted bodice. Its simplicity pleased Mary as well as the fact that it was in the style of the day.

"Oh, we're not so entirely out of touch with the world as you might think," said Mrs. Heaven when Mary exclaimed over it.

When she came in from the pond that day, Mary put on her new gown for dinner and Lord Leigh halted in midstride when he saw her, his eyes widening appreciatively. Betsy nudged Mrs. Heaven in the ribs and Mrs. Heaven turned a quelling glance upon her.

"Well, well, you are very fine today, Miss Marshall. Has your employer sent you your clothing?"

"Oh, no, sir."

"Really? Have you not heard from Sir Paget yet? How very odd."

"No—yes—I mean—Mrs. Heaven made this gown for me."

Lord Leigh sat down and began to eat his dinner, seemingly no longer interested in such a petty matter as gowns. From time to time, however, his eyes rested upon her, though she didn't notice it. It was Mary now who ate with a frown of concentration and an abstracted gaze into space. She was thinking furiously of what she must say about Sir Paget. She had not dared claim to have heard from him before Mrs. Heaven and Betsy, who would know she had not. She realized she had spun a web of lies around herself and she must either confess everything or keep spinning her web and bear the guilt. She opted for the latter, for to confess would mean to leave, and she could not bear to go away now, and besides, Robin was not strong enough to bear it yet.

Finally it came to her what she must do, and when Lord Leigh rose, she hastily pushed back her chair and followed him out of the room.

In the hallway he turned in surprise at the sound of her footsteps behind him. "Ah, am I to be scolded again, Miss Marshall?" he asked sardonically.

Mary flushed. "Oh, no. That was impertinent of me and I do beg your pardon. I have realized since that—that—"

"Please do not think of it, Miss Marshall. You were right in the matter. Was there something else?"

"It is about Sir Paget. I do not like to speak of my going away in front of Robin," Mary said, the color rising again into her cheeks at her barefaced lie, "but I have heard from Sir Paget. The children are down with—scarlet fever and he has advised me to remain here if it is possible until they are better. I—I hope—"

"Of course, Miss Marshall, you must stay as long as necessary." He smiled as he said this and with a little bow turned and went out the door.

Mary stood as though turned to stone. She realized she had never seen him smile before. How very different he looked when he smiled. She stood thinking of this difference until the clink of plates being stacked roused her and she hurried back to the dining room, avoiding Mrs. Heaven's eyes out of shame for the deceit she had just practiced upon her.

It was the day after this that Lord Leigh announced that Squire Herries and his family would be dining with him the next evening.

"You will want dinner at six o'clock, then, my lord?" asked Mrs. Heaven.

"Yes. I will take bread and cheese with me for midday. You will put Robin to bed early, Miss Marshall, and join us for dinner."

"Oh, no sir, I—I—"

"I can think of no reason why you should not agree to this simple request, Miss Marshall," he said coldly.

"Mrs. Herries and her daughter will be better entertained if another woman is present at the table."

"But I have no gown for such a dinner, my lord,"
protested Mary.

"What you have on will do perfectly well," he said
as he rose and made his exit.

Mary stared after him in dismay, then looked down
at her plain cotton print. How could she sit down to
dinner with the Herries women in such a gown?

"Never mind, child," said Mrs. Heaven, "I'll put
the finishing touches to the lilac tonight. I've made it
with a lower neck so it will be more suitable perhaps.
And I'll look out one of my lady's shawls to dress it
up."

"Don't want to go to bed early without Mary," said
Robin, his lower lip quivering ominously.

"Then you shan't," said Mrs. Heaven quickly. "You
shall stay in the kitchen with Betsy and me and help us
with the dinner."

Mary knew the moment she was introduced to the
Herries women that her presence was not going to make
the evening as entertaining to them as Lord Leigh had
hoped. Mrs. Herries was a small, thin, cross-looking
woman with two deep furrows between her brows and
sharp black eyes who glared her disapproval at finding
Mary there. Mary assumed she was displeased to be
asked to sit down at table with a servant and was se-
cretly amused. Mrs. Herries was just the sort of woman
who would be thrilled to be in the same room with the
Duchess of Runceford.

Her daughter was all pink and dimpled with bouncing
yellow curls and blue eyes, very like her father in looks.
Her manner, however, was very different, for he was a
kindly man. Miss Herries affected a wide-eyed stare of
disbelief at Mary's gown and then turned to raise an
eyebrow at her mother.

Both ladies were in full evening dress that somehow
looked ludicrous, but nevertheless managed to make

Mary feel somewhat rustic in her simple cotton gown. She curtsied at her introduction to Mrs. Herries, who only acknowledged it after a long, cold appraisal with a stiff nod of her head, and Miss Herries followed her mother's gracious example. The squire took her hand and made something of a fuss over her, telling her Lord Leigh had told him of her escape from the footpads and that she was a very brave girl.

They went in almost at once to dinner, which was served by Mrs. Heaven. The meal was a dreadful ordeal for Mary. Mrs. Herries looked outraged when Lord Leigh indicated that Mary should take the end of the table opposite him, and narrowed her eyes to dart glances at him and then back to Mary as though speculating upon her real position in the household. Miss Herries simply turned her shoulder to Mary and ignored her throughout the meal. Lord Leigh and the squire were already deep in agricultural problems and oblivious to all else, though when Miss Herries interrupted them with little quips and laughs, they paused politely to turn blankly courteous eyes upon her for a moment before they continued their discussion. Miss Herries was undaunted by this. No doubt she was accustomed to it, Mary thought wryly.

Mary was determined to do her duty and entertain the women as best she could, and her pride would not allow her to show she felt their snubs. She leaned toward Mrs. Herries with a gracious smile and said, "Do you have much society in this part of the country, madam?"

Mrs. Herries bridled, as though offended that she should dare speak at all. At last she snapped, "Enough, I believe."

Mary struggled on valiantly through the rest of the meal, receiving no help at all and only the most curt replies to her remarks. At last she looked up and met Lord Leigh's eyes and realized he was waiting for her to take the ladies to the drawing room. She felt a flash of resentment. Here he had sat, talking away to the

squire throughout the entire meal with scarcely a word
to the ladies, and now he wanted to be left alone for
more talk with the squire. She rose, however, and led
the way into the drawing room. Mrs. Herries stalked over
to the sofa before the fire, which was lit for the first time.
Mary had never seen the room with the dust covers off
and now discovered it was a lovely drawing room.

Miss Herries wandered over to the piano, but after
trying a few chords she realized it was badly out of tune
and sauntered away.

"Are you quite warm enough, Mrs. Herries?" asked
Mary seating herself opposite the woman.

"This room needs airing," replied Mrs. Herries.

"I believe Lord Leigh does keep it closed most of
the time, since it is so rarely used now," said Mary
politely.

A long silence ensued. At last Miss Herries came to
sit beside her mother. "How long have you been gov-
ernessing, Miss Marshall?" she asked carelessly.

"Why—almost a year," Mary replied, feeling her
color rise at the lie.

"Lord Leigh told my papa you worked for a Sir Paget
something, I believe."

"Yes, that is so, Sir Paget Peckham."

"How many children has he?"

"Ah—three. Three small girls."

"You seem very young for the work," said Mrs. Herries accusingly. "Is there a Lady Paget?"

"Oh, of course," said Mary hastily.

"Where did you say Sir Paget lives?"

"Why, in—in Wiltenden," said Mary, and then could
have bitten out her tongue for being so slow-witted as
to use the name of her own county.

"Wiltenden. I see," said Mrs. Herries, her eyes nar-
rowing again in a calculating way.

The gentlemen came in, to Mary's infinite relief, followed immediately by Mrs. Heaven with the tea tray.
When the tea was drunk, Squire Herries began making
his good-byes at once. "We keep early hours in the

country, you see, Miss Marshall." He took her hand. "It has been a pleasure, indeed. I hope we may meet again before you must return."

Mrs. and Miss Herries again acknowledged Mary's smile and curtsy with a distant nod, bid their host an effusive good night, and at last were gone, with Lord Leigh seeing them to their carriage.

Mary breathed a sigh of relief, then turned and picked up the tea tray. When she turned to the door with it, Lord Leigh was standing there. "Thank you, Miss Marshall," he said with his devasting smile. "I suppose Mrs. Herries raked you over pretty well, eh?"

"Nothing to bother me," she said with a proud lift of her chin.

"Detestable woman," he said feelingly. "I am sorry if she was rude to you."

"Oh, I took no notice of it, my lord. That probably was the rudest thing I could have done to her," she added with a mischievous smile.

He grinned in complicity. "No doubt it was a disappointment to her. Is that another new gown?"

"Yes. Mrs. Heaven's work. I hope it was—was all right?"

"Very becoming."

She knew she was blushing and cursed herself for such missishness. She turned away with the tray. "I— Mrs. Heaven will be waiting for this. Good night, Lord Leigh."

"Good night, Miss Marshall."

Mrs. Heaven was banging pots around with a great deal of energy, muttering angrily to herself, while Betsy, washing plates, watched her timorously. When Mary entered with the tea tray, Mrs. Heaven turned upon her.

"You shouldn't be carrying trays about," she said, snatching away the tray from Mary's hands.

"I hope I have not offended you, Mrs. Heaven."

"You . . . offend? Of course you would not offend me," cried Mrs. Heaven, banging the tray onto the table.

"But you are angry. What is the matter?"

"Ah, 'tis that Herries woman gets my blood boiling. Always with her nose in the air, pretending she's above us all, and her with no more idea of how to behave in company than that kitten!" She pointed dramatically to the rug before the fireplace, where Robin and the kitten lay curled together, miraculously still sleeping despite the banging of pots. "And she no more nor a curate's daughter, to be treating you so wickedly. You that's ten times more a lady, and well she knows it."

"Oh, well, I am but a governess, Mrs. Heaven," said Mary placatingly.

"That's as may be," replied Mrs. Heaven enigmatically.

"Her'll make a fierce mother-in-law to master," said Betsy with a giggle.

Mary, tiptoeing over to Robin, stopped short and turned to stare at her.

Mrs. Heaven said, "Hush your mouth, Betsy!"

"Thass what they do be all saying, Mrs. Heaven," protested Betsy.

"Do you tell me Miss Herries and Lord Leigh are betrothed?" demanded Mary disbelievingly.

"No, they are not! It's only that everyone knows she's set her cap for him and goes about the county dropping hints so folks have come to believe it's true. If wishes were horses, Miss Herries would ride for sure."

Betsy giggles appreciatively. "Oh, Mrs. Heaven, you do be sharp!"

"You get on with them dishes, young Betsy, and stop fooling about. The day that woman sets foot in this house as mistress is the day I pack my cases," she added grimly.

"Well, if it is any comfort to you, Mrs. Heaven, Lord Leigh shares your views of Mrs. Herries. I cannot say how he feels about the daughter, but surely he can look higher than that for a wife, however impoverished he is."

"That's the truth of it, Mary, for sure he can, and it's

to be hoped he will, however close he is to the squire. Of course, I don't suppose the squire would object to the match, but he would never push her onto him the way his wife does. She has no shame at all. To think of her dreaming that rag-mannered dairymaid daughter of hers could become a countess.''

Mary couldn't help laughing at Mrs. Heaven's eloquence, which sat Betsy giggling again.

Robin sat up blinking. ''Mary?''

''Yes, darling, here I am.'' She picked him up and he immediately put his head down on her shoulder and fell asleep again. ''I will take him to bed now, Mrs. Heaven. Oh, I should tell you that Lord Leigh was very complimentary about the gown, and I felt very grand. I do thank you for all your trouble for me.'' She kissed Mrs. Heaven's cheek and went to the back stairs. ''Good night to you both.''

They called out their good nights and continued with their work. Presently Mrs. Heaven said, ''And now you've seen how a real lady behaves, Betsy. That is my idea of what a countess must be. Sarah Herries indeed!'' She picked up a pot and banged it down to emphasize her point. ''And don't let me hear you repeating any of that stupid gossip again or I'll box your ear for you.''

9

Some days after this Mrs. Heaven told Mary that the old mare had been saddled up for her to ride. "My lord said he'd left her in the stable for you and you're to take Robin up before you."

"Hurray!" shouted Robin.

"But I have no habit, Mrs. Heaven," Mary protested.

"I found my lady's for you. It should fit a treat, for she was always slim as a girl till the day she died, bless her, and my lady's own saddle is on the horse."

The habit was not a bad fit, and though black, it had a high white stock to relieve its somberness. Mrs. Heaven and Betsy came out to the stables with Mary and Robin, and when Mary had mounted with the help of the mounting block, Mrs. Heaven lifted Robin up into her lap. Mary touched her heel to her mare's side and she ambled off slowly with Robin shouting and waving his hat with excitement.

Betsy's grin nearly split her face, but Mrs. Heaven, her hands folded under her apron, followed their progress with her head cocked to one side judiciously. At last she said, "She has a good seat." Betsy giggled. "Ignorant girl," scolded Mrs. Heaven, "that only means she sits a horse well. That's what they always said of my lady and Mary looks just as she did on a horse. Ridden all her life, I'd say."

Despite the mare's leisurely pace, Mary found it exhilarating to be in the saddle again. After they had ridden for three-quarters of an hour, they came upon some men clearing a ditch between the road and a field and

Mary pulled up to say good morning. The men stood up and greeted her, and among them was Lord Leigh. He removed his hat, wiped his forehead on his sleeve, and stepped up onto the road.

"Good morning, Miss Marshall. Good morning, Robin. She is not much of a goer, I'm afraid, but I thought you might enjoy a ride. Her name is Meg."

"Good morning, Lord Leigh," Mary replied, leaning forward to pat Meg's neck. "She's lovely. Thank you very much for your thoughtfulness. Robin and I are enjoying ourselves thoroughly. He should have his own pony in a year or so."

"Perhaps, if all goes well. I can see you have spent a lot of time on horseback, Miss Marshall."

"As much as possible. I love to ride," Mary was agreeing eagerly, then caught herself and stopped abruptly. "Though of course I have not been able—at least—well, as a governess, I mean." She felt herself coloring, though it was literally true that as a governess she had not ridden before this day. Why, then, does it feel like a lie? she wondered. She slanted a look at him to find him looking at her and for a long moment their eyes held before she dragged her own away, totally confused. Why does he look at me so? Does he sense my falseness? Her pulses were pounding for some reason, and if old Meg had been capable of it, she would have set her into a gallop at once to escape her discomfort in the situation.

"Can we go on now, Mary? I do not think Meg will care for standing about so long," said Robin politely.

Lord Leigh and Mary both laughed at this and Mary was able to make her escape gracefully. She raised her crop in a salute and he his hat, and they rode slowly away.

Lord Leigh stood staring after them until they had disappeared, then clapped his hat back onto his head and returned to his men, his mind filled with the image she had left burned upon him memory as she had sat upon old Meg looking down at him. He thought he had never seen a lovelier girl in his life. More beautiful girls, certainly, in his days as a young man about town in London, but none so freshly lovely as Mary Marshall.

His life in London, before the dreadful burden of his inheritance had fallen upon his shoulders, had been as blithe and carefree as any young man could wish for. Though his father had made him only a very small allowance, Charles Leigh as second son had inherited money from his mother that allowed him to do very much as he liked. He had liked what most young gentlemen of his station and means had liked: morning calls upon beautiful young ladies or rides with them in the park, grand dinners or a chop and a good claret shared with a friend at his club with a few rubbers of whist to follow, and, hopefully, a ball or an evening party to finish the night. And of course any number of light flirtations. Always light to avoid complications and because he had never met a girl who had inspired any strong emotion in him. Certainly nothing to compare to the feelings now coming to the forefront of his mind as he thought of Mary Marshall, feelings he was at a loss to account for. He had no business at all to be thinking of any woman at this stage in his life with so much still to do before Hatchett's End was safe.

For the past three years, since his brother's death, he had labored as the lowliest farmhand, with no time or energy for women, or even, except very rarely, thoughts of them. He had simply put his head down and slogged away at what must be done, his only break from routine his dinners with the squire. Of course, at these dinners he had come into contact with Mrs. Herries and her daughter, but he was hardly aware of them, certainly not as women attractive enough to divert his thoughts. Mrs. Herries he disliked and Sarah Herries he discounted. Her dimpled, blond prettiness held no charms for him, even apart from the petty inanities of her conversation.

He had no idea of the ambitions he had inspired in the female Herries breasts and would have been appalled had he known. Though he was as good as betrothed to Sarah Herries in the minds of his neighbors and their servants, he had no contact with the former and the latter would never have dared to allude to such a thing to his face.

Now, despite his whole-minded concentration on restoring Hatchett's End to a moneymaking estate, he found his thoughts more and more returning to this girl who had entered his life in so unusual a way, and he even looked forward eagerly to every encounter with her. The wretched, unappetizing creature he had rescued had surprised him that very first day, for despite the scratches on her face, the shining clarity of her complexion and the fineness of her bones that had emerged from the dirt had brought him up short. Each day since then he had become more aware of her, of the gleaming rich brown of her hair, of the slender appeal of her figure, which even the rough, ill-fitting dress she wore could not disguise, and most of all, the brilliance of her deep-green eyes.

He found himself beginning to wonder about her background. That she was gently bred he could not doubt, for such bones and air of breeding could not come from common stock. Perhaps, like his own, her father had died in debt, leaving his family to struggle for their bread, and the girl had been forced to become a governess to contribute to their support. She was very young for it, to be sure, but there was really no other avenue open for gently bred girls who must earn their livings.

He was even more convinced of his scenario when he saw her today, in his mother's old habit, looking to the manor born despite poor old Meg's inadequacies as a mount; the color in her cheeks was soft as roses, and her green eyes sparkled with happiness. He tried to avoid thinking of the moment when she had glanced sideways at him and their eyes had locked, but he finally surrendered to it and again felt himself sinking into those dark-green depths.

One of the men spoke to him and he shook the dream away impatiently. He had no time for daydreaming about a girl, any girl, but particularly one who would soon go out of his life as abruptly as she had entered it, never to be seen again. For he had no time to go chasing after her to Sir Paget . . . whoever. No, he had not time in his life now for such things as love and courtship, certainly not marriage. Not that he was in love, of course. Any man might react to a pair of shining eyes.

In the routine established since her first day, Mary spent the early evening in the kitchen with Mrs. Heaven and Betsy, with Robin, scrubbed and in his nightshirt, beginning to drowse in her lap over his bowl of bread and warm milk. The women had a light meal and then, when Robin finally succumbed to sleep, Mary would carry him up to bed and retire herself for the night. She never saw Lord Leigh after the midday meal, though she heard him come in and sometimes helped Mrs. Heaven prepare a tray for his supper. It was Mrs. Heaven, however, who served him.

One evening several days after he had first ordered Meg saddled up for Mary, Mrs. Heaven returned to the kitchen after taking in his tray to say, ''My lord's compliments and perhaps you would care to drink a cup of tea with him.''

Mary flashed her a startled look—almost one of fright, thought Mrs. Heaven—then she looked down at the sleeping Robin, heavy in her lap and said, ''I—I must take Robin to bed now.''

''Don't you be worrying yourself about him, bless his heart. I will take him up. He's so sound asleep he'll never know the difference.'' Without more ado she took Robin from Mary and carried him toward the back stairs. ''Betsy, get out another cup,'' she ordered before she disappeared.

Mary's heart felt like a frightened mouse skittering about in her breast as she slowly rose to her feet and shook out the skirt of Betsy's old gray dress, crumpled from Robin's weight. Her hair had come loose and fell down her back in its light waves. She had not bothered to ask Mrs. Heaven to pin in up again, thinking to be so soon in her bed. Now Mrs. Heaven was gone and she could not do it up herself and she felt untidy and ill-dressed to take tea with Lord Leigh, even had she wanted to do so, which she did not. She was sure he would ask her questions about her home and family and she hated the thought of even more lies that she would have to tell. There was something so straight and honest about his clear blue gaze that she felt sure he must see right through her to her deception. She had found it increasingly difficult to meet his eyes as her respect for him had grown. When she and Robin on Meg had met him and he had caught and held her eyes for what seemed an eternity, she had felt uneasily sure that he had found her out. Since then she had not only made sure not to ride anywhere near him, she had not been able to raise her eyes to him at the dinner table.

However, he had summoned her now and she must obey, for he was her employer and master of the house. Her knees trembled as she took up the teacup and walked slowly up the hall to the dining room. As she reached the dining-room door, however, some pride returned to her and she threw up her chin. He could not eat her, after all, and she would not allow herself to appear cringing and frightened before him. She had held her own with Pike, had she not?

When she entered, he rose at once from an armchair before the fire. She curtsied and he came forward to take the teacup from her and place it on the tray. "Thank you for joining me, Miss Marshall. I hope I have not kept you from your bed. Mrs. Heaven tells me you generally retire early."

"It is Robin, you see. He is still frightened to sleep alone."

"Yes, so Mrs. Heaven has told me. Please sit down, Miss Marshall. I have drawn up this chair for you. Perhaps you will pour for us."

The tray had been set on a low table beside Mary's

chair and she reached for the pot, willing her fingers
not to tremble.

"Tell me how you find my nephew, Miss Marshall.
It has been nearly three weeks now since you have had
charge of him."

"Oh, he is a marvelous child, Lord Leigh," she said,
forgetting her fears as she poured out and handed him
his cup, "so intelligent for his age, so loving and kind-
hearted."

"Yet still frightened?"

"Not as he was at first. Most of that was just because
he was not sure what had happened. People have a way
of not explaining such things as death to children, and
they fear what they don't understand. I remind him often of his mama and papa and now he has come to
accept that they are gone and speaks of them quite naturally. And of course he is becoming more accustomed
to this house and all of us. It is so good of you to take
the time to notice him more."

"It is due to you, I am ashamed to admit, for until
you spoke to me about it I had not fully realized my
responsibilities toward him." She blushed at this
oblique reference to that angry encounter and concen-
trated on her cup of tea. "Do you have any set method
for teaching young children?"

"No. I . . . Well, only to remember what I wanted,
as best I can, at that age. I was very much alone, like
Robin."

"Sir Paget's children are, I take it, very young girls?"

"Why should you think so?" she asked, suddenly up
in arms. Was he questioning her ability?

"Because no sensible parent would hire so lovely a
girl to be governess to a boy over ten years of age."

She blushed even more furiously at this, while silently cursing herself for doing so. She, with a Season
in London under her belt, so be put out of countenance
by a compliment!

"Do you still ride Meg?"

"Oh, indeed, every day, Lord Leigh. Robin does like it so. And of course, so do I."

"I thought to see you about," he said with a quizzical smile.

She dropped her eyes. Was he angry that she had not come near him to show him her pleasure? "Well, of course, we do not know the ways so well yet. We go where Meg takes us, more or less."

"I was thinking, Miss Marshall—of course, I do not know what Sir Paget, er, pays you—but I should be paying you also. I think no one who works for a living can quite go without his salary."

"Oh! Oh, no, no indeed, Lord Leigh," she cried hastily. "Sir Paget Peckham will continue my salary. I shall not lose anything. And after all your kindness I could not dream of accepting anything."

"Have you heard anything further from him?"

"No, no, I have not. But I am sure he will communicate with me when—when it is safe to return." She added this last in such forlorn tones that he felt his heart swell with happiness. She would not be glad to leave them!

"That will be a sad day—for all of us," he said meaningfully, with an intent look that she caught unintentionally and then was unable to look away from. She felt her heart constrict.

He watched the soft lips part in a gasp and could not help wishing that he might taste them with his own. He half-rose in his chair, his hands stretched out to her involuntarily.

She jumped up. "I must go to Robin now, Lord Leigh. He might wake and find me gone and be frightened. Thank you for—for the tea."

He rose and held out his hand. "Good night, Miss Marshall," he said softly. She was constrained to place her own hand in his, and at the warmth of the contact she felt an electric impulse shoot up her arm. She snatched her hand away, frightened by she knew not what.

"Good night, Lord Leigh," she gasped, and with a little curtsy hurried away.

He stood rooted, staring after the last flick of her skirt as the door closed behind her. Oh, Lord, he thought, now what am I to do? For he had recognized his own feelings at once. The touch of her hand had made it all clear.

He sat down again, stretched his long legs to the fire, and stared into the flames. The last thing he wanted was to be in love, for there could be no question of marriage for him for at least two years. It would take that long to reap any profit from the property. Would she be willing to wait? Was it even fair to declare himself under such conditions? On the other hand, it was not easy for him to contemplate the future Countess of Leigh slaving as a governess to Sir Paget's brats. Still, he could not ask her to leave her position and himself take on the support of her family when he barely had his head above water as yet. What a dreary prospect to offer a young, pretty girl. Yet pretty girls fell in love and were betrothed and often had to wait for the money to marry on.

Suddenly he sat up straight. Good God, he thought, what if she has already given her heart to someone else? Even if she had not, it did not mean she could ever love him. He had done little enough to attach her until tonight and she had seemed . . . frightened of him! This realization was such a blow that it quite literally dashed all his hopes for a few moments. But he at last recovered his spirits. She hardly knew him, after all, and their relationship until now had been so much employee and employer. The best way to mend this was to go on as he had tonight, showing interest and warmth until she had grown comfortable with him. And had she been in love with someone else, surely her first concern after writing Sir Paget would have been to communicate with her lover and he knew she had written no such letter or he would have heard of it. He felt sure her heart was still free, and since this was so, surely he could win it for himself. If she learned to love him, all their problems would somehow resolve themselves. On a surge of optimism he rose and took himself off to bed.

10

Mary, still awake beside the sleeping Robin, heard Lord Leigh taking the stairs two at a time on his way to bed and held her breath until she heard his bedroom door closing softly. She was not aware of doing so until she released it in a great sigh. How energetic he was at the end of such a long day filled with hard work, she thought wonderingly. She sighed again and turned restlessly on the bed. She thumped her pillow, pressed her head into it, and closed her eyes resolutely, but immediately those blue, blue eyes were gazing into her own, candid and quizzical, probing with their honesty, and she quailed before them.

Oh, why was she so enmeshed in these lies she feared to meet his gaze? Should she go to him tomorrow and confess? She began rehearsing the story in her mind. How she had at first been afraid to reveal her identity and then decided to continue in the lie for . . . for her own pleasure! No, no she could not tell him that. Yet she had no other reason. He would think her stupid and capricious for behaving so. He would be insulted that she had been afraid to reveal her identity to him for fear he would take advantage of her in some way. What a thing to have to confess to a man like Charles Leigh!

She got out of bed and went to sit by the window. The soft summer night was lit by the unearthly glow of the stars, and she stared and stared at them, willing some answer to come from them, but none came. Her mind toiled wearily among the unsavory facts and found no rest. At last she could only decide that she must avoid him as best she could as the only preventative for further lies, for she could not yet bring herself to return home.

Avoidance, however, was impossible, as she discovered on the next evening when he again invited her to join him for tea before bed. She was startled by this second invitation, though she realized at the same moment that she should have foreseen it and prepared an excuse. Now Mrs. Heaven had taken Robin from her and shooed her out of the kitchen before she could order her mind.

Again Lord Leigh rose to greet her as she entered, and led her to a chair opposite his own. Again he asked her to pour his tea. When this had been accomplished, he said, "Miss Marshall, I hope I do not frighten you for some reason?"

She had kept her eyes firmly on the tea tray, but now she raised her head abruptly, for she could not bear to admit fear of anything. "Of course not, Lord Leigh," she answered stoutly.

"I am glad to hear it, for I should be sorry if it were so. It is the last thing I would want." When she did not reply, he continued, "I presume Sir Paget will have informed your family of what has happened to you?"

She had a moment of speechless panic before she managed to say, "Oh, yes, of course."

"Good. How many of your family are still at home?"

"Well, only my aunt," she said, glad to be telling a truth.

"Oh? I had thought . . . Your parents are both . . .?"

"Yes. They both died when I was very young. My aunt raised me."

He felt a great relief. Only an aunt, who could without too much cost to the estate, be added to his own household. What dire circumstances the poor old soul must be in to be forced to send her niece out to work so young. What happiness it would be to work for both of them, to rescue this sweet girl from the bondage and reunite the poor lonely old aunt with her in his own

house. There was no need to wait two years. No need
at all. He could not set her up as a fine lady yet, but he
had a roof to offer her she could look upon as her own,
and any work she did would be in her own house. Surely,
provided he could win her love, she would be grateful
and happy to marry him.

For the next three nights she went in to him in the
evenings and endured as best she could his questions
about her life and her evasive answers. She felt his kindness and interest to be warm and genuine and could not
help wondering if he would still be her friend if—
when—he learned her true identity. Several times the
urge to tell him all was so sharp she could barely re-
strain herself from pouring out her whole story just for
the relief of being honest with him, but then the shame
of her own lies overcame her and she could not confess.

Then one morning he told them that he would be dining with the Herries that evening. She was relieved at
first, but then she experienced a feeling of being let
down. She retired early with Robin, but sleep came only
after what seemed hours as she imagined him across the
table from Miss Herries blond charms. If they were not
already betrothed, perhaps he was at this very moment
making his proposal in form. The thought pulled her
out of bed to the window again. He could not—surely
he could not! Oh, but he could, whispered the voice of
reason. She may look like a dairy maid to me, but men's
tastes differ in these matters and there must be something there if the whole neighborhood was convinced of
the betrothal.

Lord Leigh, however, happily immersed in agricultural talk with the squire, was as usual courteously at-
tentive when the women spoke, but grateful when the
squire reclaimed his attention.

At last Mrs. Herries raised her voice. "Lord Leigh,
I had a most interesting letter this week from my old
bosom bow living in Wiltenden."

"Wiltenden?" he repeated, trying to look interested.

''Yes. That is where Miss Marshall told us Sir Paget Peckham resides.''

Mrs. Herries ignored the warning glare directed upon her by her daughter. There had, in fact, been a raging debate between them over this matter, Miss Herries being of the opinion that such information as they had learned would only pique Lord Leigh's interest in the girl, and Miss Herries felt she could not carry much weight with such competition. He had never as yet shown the least sign of trying to attach her, but she had convinced herself that he would do so, given time, and once he had spoken she would know herself secure, for he would never go back on his word. Her mother, on the other hand, wanted the girl out of Lord Leigh's house, being well aware of the dangers of propinquity. Once the truth was revealed, the girl would have to go. Out of his sight would be bound to be out of his mind with Lord Leigh in his obsession with his estate. So she ignored her daughter and looked with avid eyes at Lord Leigh, who was looking rather blank.

''My friend is a Mrs. Robeson-Smythe, and when I wrote her our interesting tale about Miss Marshall—well, you will never guess what she wrote back to me.''

''No. I doubt I could, '' he said politely.

''Well, it seems there is no person named Sir Paget Peckham in Wiltenden or anywhere else in the county,'' she said with an air of triumph.

''Perhaps your friend is not acquainted with him,'' he suggested after a moment, feeling somewhat at sea.

''Her family have lived there for generations. It is not possible that she would not know him,'' declared Mrs. Herries decisively.

''Well, I feel sure there has been some misunderstanding somewhere. Perhaps you did not hear Miss Marshall perfectly.''

''I heard her very clearly, Lord Leigh, as Sarah can confirm. No, there can be no mistake in the matter.''

''Now, my dear,'' began the squire, ''clearly there has been—''

"No, Mr. Herries, there has not," his wife replied quellingly. "Mrs. Robeson-Smythe has, however, heard of a Mary Marshall. She very definitely is from Wiltenden."

"Ah," said Lord Leigh with relief. "It was only her own mistake, then. She only muddled things, no doubt."

"Yes, of course, that is how it was, my dear," said the squire placatingly.

Mrs. Herries visibly swelled as she produced her winning trump card. "Mary Marshall of Wiltenden is the Duchess of Runceford. She lives at Mallows with her aunt, Lady Hyde, but is now away on a visit. She is nearly eighteen years old. Mrs. Robeson-Smythe describes her as taller than average with brown hair. Now, what do you say to that? Can you still think there is a mistake?"

Charles felt such a rush of blood to his head that the room swan redly before his eyes for a moment. Then he pulled himself together. He would not give the woman the satisfaction of seeing she had disconcerted him. "No doubt there will be a reasonable explanation, Mrs. Herries. Now, Squire, what have you to say about putting alfalfa in that twenty acres to the north of Wombley Wood?"

They proceeded to a long discussion of the twenty acres at Wombley Wood and left Mrs. Herries frustrated and Miss Herries uneasy. Her mother had been wrong, she was convinced. Lord Leigh was bound to be intrigued by the prospect of a duchess within his household. A duchess! Good Lord, how could any girl hope to have a chance?

Once safely away from the Herries, Lord Leigh allowed his pent-up fury full rein. He had no doubt at all that he had heard the truth, and he felt defrauded, cheated, made a fool of! That he could be so naïve! He had actually contemplated marrying the girl to rescue her from, as he thought, a degrading situation.

He stalked grimly into the house, met by Mrs.

Heaven, who had, of course, waited up for him. "Send Miss Marshall down to me," he said harshly.

"Why, she will be asleep, my lord."

"Then wake her! Send her to me at once."

Mrs. Heaven did not dream of disobeying this stern command. With her heart pounding with fear she climbed the stairs hurriedly to Mary's room and entered.

Mary slept with Robin's head on her shoulder, her other arm over him protectively. Mrs. Heaven put a hand on her shoulder and shook it gently. Mary woke at once and gazed sleepily up at Mrs. Heaven.

"What—what is it?"

"You must come down, Mary. My lord wants you at once," Mrs. Heaven whispered urgently.

"What has happened? Is something wrong?"

"I don't know, my dear, but you must come quickly. He says you are to come down."

Mary eased her arm from beneath Robin's head and rolled over, putting back the covers. "My gown, Mrs. Heaven, the old one will do. Dear heaven, what can have happened?"

Her hair hanging loose, curling and waving down below her waist, her feet bare, she hurried down the stairs to the dining room. She pushed open the door without knocking and entered the room. Lord Leigh turned abruptly to face her, his brows drawn together in an intimidating frown and his blue eyes dark with anger.

He did not greet her, but spoke at once in a tight voice. "Sir Paget Peckham. He lives in Wiltenden, so you told Mrs. Herries."

"Yes—yes, I did," she faltered, more frightened of him than she had ever thought it possible.

"Yes, he does, or yes, so you told Mrs. Herries?"

"Yes, I told Mrs. Herries."

"And do you maintain this to be true?" He stared at her demandingly.

She could not tear her eyes away. She felt, in the glare

of his gaze, like a rabbit before a stoat. She could not have spoken had she known what to say.

"Well, Miss Marshall," he said, emphasizing the title sarcastically, "since you are governess to his children, surely you can tell me where he lives. You have written to him, I believe. Where did you direct your letter?" He waited, but she could only stare at him helplessly, pleadingly.

What on earth could she say to him? What did he know, and how did he know? Mrs. Herries, of course. That dreadful woman had made some remark, had planted some seed of doubt, but what could the woman possibly know? Should she brazen it out, trusting to his dislike of Mrs. Herries to carry her though? All these thoughts shot through her mind in less than seconds, and at the same time the sickness of shame at her deceit washed over everything. It was, it seemed, impossible to lie in the face of the blue blaze of righteous anger stabbing out at her from his eyes.

As though sensing the reason for her speechlessness he turned abruptly away to the fire. "Please answer me, Miss Marshall."

There was no help for her now; she was as incapable of lying to that broad-shouldered back as she was to his face. "I did not write to him," she whispered.

"There is, in fact, no Sir Paget Peckham living in Wiltenden, I take it?"

"No," she said starkly.

He turned to face her. Her head was up, her eyes met his unflinchingly, brazenly, it seemed to him, and he fed his anger on this thought. "So, it is all a farce, this playacting of governess? What shall I call you? Liar? Actress?"

"I am Mary Marshall," she said bravely, "that, at least, is truth."

"Ah! But not *all* the truth, is it? You are something more, I believe, than mere Miss Mary Marshall. What else are you?" he asked harshly. Her tongue clove to the roof of her mouth and she could not speak. All her pride deserted her in a moment in the face of his barely held in check anger, and her eyes fell. She could not face him. This seemed to enrage him further. "What? Too shy to confess *Miss* Marshall, now your little masquerade is discovered? What was it, some little game conceived by your idle London friends, bored with parties and gossip? A dare, perhaps? Who can carry it off successfully for the longest time? Or perhaps a little itch to imitate Marie Antoinette as the milkmaid to titillate the boredom of your life?"

"No—no—" she whispered in a stricken voice.

He was, however, in full stride now and could not have heard her no matter what protestation she made. He had been duped, he had been on the point of making a declaration to this girl, thinking to rescue her from a life of drudgery, even being inspired by his own sacrifice. Only to discover that all the while she had been laughing behind his back at his simpleminded acceptance of her story. She had made a fool of him!

"Well, your grace," he continued, "I am sorry to bring your little amusement to so abrupt an end, but I have no time for playacting. You may go back to your friends and tell them you were a great success. No doubt you will enliven dinner parties for a whole Season with tales of the gullible fool who was taken in by your dramatic abilities."

"Please, you must listen. You must not think—"

"Oh, I know very well what to think, your grace. Scraggs will be waiting in the morning to take your letter to your friends. I am sure they will send your carriage at once. At once, your grace!"

"But—but Robin . . . I cannot—"

"Please do not concern yourself any further with my family, your grace. I am quite capable of taking care of my own." He stalked to the door and opened it. "I will bid your grace good night." He stood waiting, holding the door, and there was nothing for her to do but go.

All dignity forgotten, she ran past him, her eyes beginning to brim with tears. She ran straight to the kitchen, where she knew she would find Mrs. Heaven, who never went to bed while her master was downstairs. She was sitting before the dying kitchen fire, a little frown disturbing her usually placid, round face. When Mary burst through the door, she looked up in alarm. Mary threw herself on the floor before Mrs. Heaven and buried her face in the old woman's lap and let loose all her misery and humiliation in heartbroken sobs.

Mrs. Heaven had been expecting trouble and was not so shocked as she might have been. She soothed her work-worn hands over and over the soft, tumbling brown curls and uttered soft words of comfort until the sobs abated and at last came to a stop. Mary sat up and silently accepted Mrs. Heaven's handkerchief.

In a few moments she turned her red swollen eyes up to Mrs. Heaven and whispered, "I am to leave at once, Mrs. Heaven."

"What has happened, dear heart?"

"He—he has found me out. He was very angry. Oh, Mrs. Heaven . . . " The tears welled up again at the memory and she turned away to hide her face in the damp handkerchief.

"Perhaps, if you think you can, you would care to tell me all about it. Only if you want to, you know."

So Mary told her: who she was and about her life filled with ceremony and her visit to Maud Bryce. Then of her capture by Pike and her escape and of how much she had liked life at Hatchett's End and had wanted so much to stay for a short time that she had told dreadful lies, and finally, some of the awful things Lord Leigh had accused her of. Then she began to weep again.

"It was that d-dreadful Mrs. Herries, I know, though how she found out I cannot imagine. Oh, why are there such c-cruel people in the world who take p-pleasure in being malicious and spoiling one's ha-happiness. I meant no harm and I n-never dreamed I could be hurting anyone."

"No doubt it was her, for he came in from there on

the boil, but your grace would have had to leave one day soon in any case and—''

''Oh, Mrs. Heaven, am I no longer to be Mary to you?'' wailed Mary.

''But, dear child,'' began Mrs. Heaven, scandalized, ''how could I do such a thing knowing—''

''Oh, please, please, Mrs. Heaven. Only for two days so Betsy and Robin and—and Scraggs need not know.'' She clasped Mrs. Heaven's hands and looked up into her face pleadingly, her green eyes swimming with tears. ''I must write my aunt first thing in the morning to send the carriage for me. Scraggs will take the letter. The carriage will be here the next day. Could you not manage it until then so that everything will be the same. I do not want everyone to know. They will think of me as—as he does, and despise me.''

Mrs. Heaven had to agree, for she could not have stood out against a request so piteously made. She made Mary a cup of tea and fussed over her and said she believed that Mary had meant no harm and that such little lies would be forgiven. At last she coaxed her up to bed and tucked her in.

Poor child, poor dear little girl, Mrs. Heaven clucked to herself. What a scolding he must have given her to put her into such a state. Mrs. Heaven remembered the icy voice in which he had ordered her to fetch Mary, the eyes spitting blue flames, and she did not blame the girl for becoming hysterical. She also had some inkling, which she was sure Mary had not, of just why he had been so very enraged, but she could only shake her head in sorrow, for she knew very well nothing would come of it now. Her heart ached, for she had had her own dreams for Mary and Lord Leigh. She was not in the least shocked to learn that Mary was the Duchess of Runceford. Hadn't she known all along, at least since she'd seen those undergarments, that the girl was something more than just a governess?

11

Mary slept only fitfully and each time she woke the memory of her dreadful scene with Lord Leigh flooded back, causing her to weep afresh. She dragged herself from bed before daylight, her head throbbing with pain, and went to sit at the window, laying her head on her arms on the windowsill. The cool predawn air laved her aching head and soothed her jumbled thoughts about those scathing accusations, Robin's reaction when he learned of her imminent departure, of the letter she must write, and what she must say to her aunt when she reached home.

Presently she heard Lord Leigh's door open and close and his footsteps going downstairs, heavy now, unlike his lighthearted leap up the stairs the other evening. Soon he would have finished his breakfast and be gone to the fields and she could go down and write her letter.

The light grew steadily brighter and soon a rosy glow announced the sun and she got up and began to drag on her clothing, wondering how she was going to be able to get through this day. Robin sat up sleepily and she forced herself to answer his bright chirpings cheerfully. She felt hollowed out and light-headed, as though her scalding tears had scoured out everything inside her and she was but a shell.

She left Robin in the kitchen and went to write her letter to Lady Hyde, begging her to send only a coach-man and Watts in the small, unmarked carriage as soon as possible. When she returned to the kitchen, a grinning Scraggs was waiting at the back door.

"My lord has told him to take one of the horses and deliver your letter by hand," said Mrs. Heaven, pursing up her mouth into a grim line.

Mary quietly gave Scraggs the directions for reaching Mallows.

Betsy kept casting furtive glances at Mrs. Heaven and at Mary's swollen eyes, but held her tongue. Robin chatted away obliviously. Mary decided she would tell him immediately after breakfast to give him the whole day to become accustomed to the fact that she must go. Scraggs would reach Mallows in something like five to six hours, and Lady Hyde would be sure to send the carriage in time to arrive first thing tomorrow morning.

"But why must you go?" demanded Robin when told.

"Because I have been away a very long time and my aunt needs me."

"I need you more," he said with comic seriousness, "because she is a grown-up and I am only a boy. I really think you had better stay here, Mary."

"It is not possible, my love."

He ignored this. "You must tell your aunt that you have a little boy to take care of and she will understand."

"Oh, darling," cried Mary, sweeping him up into a great hug, "I wish I needn't go, but I have no choice."

He wriggled free of this embarrassing display of emotion. "But I will have no one to play with me?"

Since this was unanswerable, Mary said quickly, "I will write to you every day. Every day, my darling, I promise you. Now, let us not waste the day. Shall we take some lunch and go to the pond?"

He agreed to this enthusiastically and seemed to forget her treachery. For him tomorrow was still too immeasurably in the future to have present reality. When they returned from the pond, she cleaned him up for dinner and sent him in with Mrs. Heaven and Betsy. Nothing could have persuaded her to sit down at the table with Lord Leigh, nor, she felt sure, would he expect her to do so.

Somehow the terrible day passed and tomorrow was upon her after another nearly sleepless night. Mary was up and dressed in the gray printed cotton before the sun when she heard quite clearly in the morning stillness the sound of the carriage wheels on the drive, and she knew it awaited her. Her room was at the back of the house and in a few moments she heard the back door open; she peeked out of her window to watch Lord Leigh stride stiffly across the cobbled yard and disappear toward the stables. I shall never see him again, she thought and felt her throat tighten with tears. She turned quickly away from her thoughts as she had vowed she would not cry this morning and make the parting miserable for everyone else.

Robin lay still sleeping, a faint dew on his brow, his round cheeks delicately pink, his rosy mouth a little open revealing his tiny pearls of teeth, and his lashes spread like fans from his closed lids. She longed to caress him, but if left alone, he would sleep for another hour. She was torn between the need to hold him in her arms and the need to spare them both the pain of parting. He would wake to Mrs. Heaven's presence and learn that tomorrow had come and his playfellow was gone. He might be mopish for a time, but children forget so quickly, she solaced herself. She had written a long letter for him which Mrs. Heaven would read to him when he woke up.

When she went down, Mrs. Heaven fussed over her with tea and toast, while a red-eyed Betsy sniffed as she washed up her master's breakfast dishes. Nothing was said of the waiting carriage or of Lord Leigh, Mrs. Heaven and Mary both pretending that nothing untoward had happened.

Mary took a last sip of her tea and rose to her feet. She took the letter from her pocket and handed it to Mrs. Heaven. "This is for Robin. You will go up to him as soon as I am gone so he won't wake and find himself alone?"

"Of course I will, my dear. You are not to worry yourself now."

"I shall write every day. Tell him that." She went to Betsy and embraced her. "Good-bye, dear Betsy, and thank you." Betsy let out a wail and threw her apron over her face as Mary left the room.

Mrs. Heaven came out to the carriage with her, and with Watts looking on with lively curiosity, the women embraced.

"Oh, dearest Mrs. Heaven," Mary murmured into the older woman's neck, "how good you have been to me. I shall miss you."

"And I shall miss you, dearest child. Don't say any more now or I shall begin howling like Betsy and disgrace us both. I will write how we go on, you may be sure."

Mary squeezed her tightly for another moment, then turned away blindly to the carriage. George was waiting to help her in and close the door. When he had climbed up beside Storrs, they at once rolled away down the drive. Mary leaned out the window to wave, but the figure of Mrs. Heaven and of Hatchetts End swam hazily through her tears. She sat back and gulped, trying desperately to control herself, but the sobs rose irrepressibly until at last she buried her face in her hands and gave way to her sorrow. Then Watts was beside her, pressing a clean handkerchief into her hands and laying a cloak tenderly about her shoulders.

Watts was burning with curiosity, of course. She longed to know what had happened to her mistress with the dreadful footpads, how she had managed to escape them, and more than all the rest, who were these people she had been staying with who caused her to weep so at parting. The house had looked very grand, but the old lady whom her grace had embraced so lovingly was not quality, of that Watts was sure. Then she would like to know what her grace was doing in that disgraceful gown. Watts was sure she had never thought she would see the day when her mistress would appear dressed so.

Her curiosity remained unsatisfied, however, for though presently Mary wiped her eyes and smiled wanly, she said only, "It is very hard to part from friends." After that she lapsed into silence that remained unbroken until they stopped to bate the horses. Then Mary roused herself, stepping out of the carriage, and went up to Storrs.

"Forgive me, Storrs, for not asking you at once about your injury."

"You was that cut up, your grace, as I could plainly see," said Storrs forgivingly.

"Yes, I was. But I am very glad to see you so well-recovered."

"Thank 'ee, your grace. T'were nothing so serious."

After this exchange she spoke pleasantly to George and resumed her seat in the carriage. The remainder of the trip was, for Mary, of an indescribable dreariness, which held no promise of ever ending.

They reached Mallows by late afternoon and clearly Lady Hyde had had someone on the lookout, for even as the carriage rolled to a stop she came running out of the door followed by Miss Foote and a swarm of servants who all bobbed and bowed and smiled to see her safely home again. George quickly let down the steps and Lady Hyde cried, "My child, my dearest child," as she held her tightly.

Mary was moved by all the genuine love and worry and relief it expressed. Lady Hyde led her straight up the stairs and she soon found herself in her own room being deftly stripped by Watts, who looked disdainfully upon the gray gown as she carried it away. Then, swathed in a wrapper, Mary sat down before a small, comforting fire and a light repast of chicken wings and a glass of wine.

She waited for the hovering Lady Hyde to begin scolding and complaining of Mary's treatment of her, but poor Lady Hyde was a broken woman. The appalling news brought her by Watts and Storrs of Mary's abduction had so overcome her that she had been ill for

several days. She had, however, sent George and another man off at once with the money demanded, but
they had returned at last only to report their failure even
to find the stretch of woods, much less the footpads.
Lady Hyde had fainted dead away at this news and had
been unconscious for over an hour. The doctor had been
summoned and had ordered bed and absolute quiet for
several days, during which Mary's brief note arrived
and had helped her to recovery. At least the child was
safe and unharmed. Still, as the weeks passed with no
further word, she had become more and more morose.
Her total helplessness to remedy the situation was so
fretting that she finally came to the conclusion that if
only Mary were restored to her, she would never say
another harsh word to her. She knew she would be
haunted for the rest of her days of guardianship by the
fear that Mary would run away again. She had not truly
"run away," of course, this time, but when the opportunity presented itself to be completely out of her aunt's
control, she had not hesitated to take it.

Now she could only sit opposite Mary and feast her
eyes upon her. The dear child looked healthy enough,
but her eyes were unhappy. Was she so sad to be in her
own home? At last Lady Hyde said hesitatingly, "Was
your ordeal very dreadful, my dear?"

Mary looked up blankly. "My ordeal?"

"With those dreadful footpads."

"Oh—oh, that," Mary said with relief. For a horrible
moment she had thought her aunt was referring to her
scene with Lord Leigh. That was the only ordeal in her
mind. The other she had forgotten even more quickly
than the wounds on her wrists had healed. She told her
aunt of all that had occurred with Pike and his men,
except for the few moments in which Pike had attacked
her and she had bloodied his nose. Somehow, that scene
was more frightening now than it had been at the time
and she had never been able to tell anyone of it, not
even Mrs. Heaven.

Lady Hyde was predictably aghast at her story and

had many questions. Inevitably they arrived at the point of her rescue and Mary sensed that her aunt was even more eager to hear of this than of the footpads. Though she dreaded it, Mary found as she began to tell her of it that she was numb to all feelings and could speak of it all as though she were telling a story she had read in a book.

"And then," she finished, "Lord Leigh learned the truth from Mrs. Herries. How the woman learned it I cannot imagine."

"Well, you say when she questioned you you told her your imaginary employer resided in Wiltenden. I should imagine she has a friend living around here someplace and wrote to inquire about him and you," replied Lady Hyde sensibly. "Naturally, such an unusual event would find its way into her correspondence. These women never have much of interest in their own lives to tell one another."

"Yes. Yes, of course, that must be the way of it. In any event, Lord Leigh said I must leave at once."

"And quite right, too! It must have been disagreeable news to learn from someone else. You should have told him at once when Mrs. Heaven told you who he was," declared Lady Hyde firmly.

"I know I should, but I did so much want to stay with Robin. It was so nice there—so simple. I felt useful. He quite depended upon me—Robin, I mean. He will be unhappy now. I hate thinking that I have caused him to be unhappy."

"But, dear girl, you could not stay there forever. You have your own family and duties."

"I know, Aunt, I know." Mary pushed the hair back from here face with a weary gesture and lay back in her chair. "It was only—only—he is such a dear little boy."

Lady Hyde wisely left her then, saying Mary must rest now. As she went away to her own room, her mind was filled with Mary's story. There seemed to be so much she still did not know. For instance, she could bear to know a great deal more about Lord Leigh. Was

he old, young, handsome, repulsive? Of course, he was
kind, taking in Mary and helping her and taking in his
orphaned nephew. He was also evidently honest and
hardworking, but these were more qualities she had
gathered from Mary's recital of circumstances than from
any description of him she had given. Now Lady Hyde
thought it over, she realized he had figured very little
in her story, only a presence in the background.

Lady Hyde told herself that there was comfort in this,
since it showed he meant very little to Mary. It would
have been dreadful if an impoverished gentleman, titled
or not, had captured Mary's affections. Evidently he had
not attempted any such thing and had behaved very
properly in sending Mary home the instant he learned
her true identity, for which Lady Hyde was grateful. All
the same, she could not banish her uneasiness, nor even
put her finger on its cause.

Mary's feelings remained blessedly numb for the rest
of that day and she prayed they would remain so, but
the next day, when she sat down to write her promised
letter to Robin, she found all of those last days rushing
back to her consciousness and discovered her feelings
were still raw with pain. There also began to find its
way to the surface of her mind an anger she had not
expressed till now. Why had he been so cruel? Surely
her deception had not deserved such rage? She had
meant no harm and had done none. She had done her
job and taken care of Robin to the best of her ability
and loved him dearly as he loved her. Mrs. Heaven and
Betsy had learned to love her and had not condemned
her when they had learned her true identity.

But her anger was no proof against the remembrance
of his voice asking, "What shall I call you? Liar? Actress?" For she could not avoid the fact that she had
been both. She had lied about Sir Paget Peckham and
acted the part of a governess. Then all the other harsh
things he had said would flood back into her mind and
she would give way to the sick feeling of humiliation
she had felt at the time. This in turn would gradually

turn to futile anger that he should have spoken so to her. So for several days she was helplessly in the grip of her seesawing emotions. She moped about silently, causing her aunt a great deal of worry.

However, her normal good-natured optimism succeeded at last in overcoming her mood, and with the resilience of youth she began to recover her spirits. The morning she came down to breakfast in her riding habit her aunt and every servant in the place smiled with relief and felt their spirits rising in response. As she galloped recklessly, day after day, her groom tearing along behind her, her lacerated feelings gradually healed and she began to come to terms with her bad conscience. She had been wrong to tell all those lies in order to gratify her own desire to experience for a short time a life that was not truly her own, but she would not accuse herself of malicious intent, no matter what bitter accusations Lord Leigh chose to make. She had, moreover, proved to herself that she could take care of herself without the constant attendance of scraping and bowing servants, and that she could make friends and attach the honest affections of people like Mrs. Heaven and Betsy and Robin without the assistance of her title and wealth. There was no chance at all that such an experience would ever come her way again, but it could not be taken away from her now she had had it, and she must accept the good things, put the rest behind her, and get on with the life she was born to.

She went back to her old routine at Mallows, riding, driving out with Lady Hyde to pay visits, slipping away sometimes to swim, being kind to Lady Hyde's friends when they came for dinner, and now, added to this, writing her daily letter to Robin. She made him an alphabet book, painting a series of little pictures of a pony, a tree, a dog and cat, and other simple things to illustrate the letters, and stitched the pages together between board covers. She made another to help him with his numbers and tried to find a puzzle or silly verse to end each letter. She urged him to study his letters and learn to write soon so that he could correspond with her.

Mrs. Heaven wrote back perhaps once a week with all the news of Robin and herself and Betsy. She carefully never mentioned Lord Leigh, any more than did Mary.

When Lady Hyde felt things had once more returned to normal, she suggested a dinner party.

"But, dear Aunt, why do you consult me? You have had several dinner parties since I have come home."

"Well, I did not mean just that sort. I thought some young people would be nice for you."

"There are only, as you told me yourself, those three po-faced daughters of the Fortmains. With their mother and the two of us we should be six females and Lord Fortmain. Not a very exciting prospect for any of us, I should think," said Mary wryly.

"I shall invite only Lord and Lady Fortmain and Miss Fortmain. I will explain the problem to Lady Fortmain privately and I am sure she will be understanding."

"Of course she will be. Now we are only four females and Lord Fortmain."

Lady Hyde ruffled up. "Naturally, I do not plan anything so stupid as that. Lord Fortmain has his nephew staying with him. His heir, you know. A most unexceptionable young man. Adrian Fortmain. Quite wealthy in his own right—which is a good thing, since I doubt he will inherit little besides the title and the estate from his uncle—and monstrously attractive, according to Lady Fortmain. Naturally she had hopes that he will take one of her girls, preferably the eldest, Emma, but as she is the least attractive and quite eight-and-twenty, I doubt very seriously if he will. Then I shall invite Lord Dachett—"

"Oh, lovely. I do adore Lord Dachett. He shall hold my hand all evening if he cares to," cried Mary.

"That is a very indecorous remark, Mary," began Lady Hyde with some of her old severity, but then she caught herself and added, "Only your funning, I know, but in your position you must always have a guard upon your tongue. I cannot imagine what Miss Foote would have thought had she heard you.''

''Sorry, Aunt. By the way, what of her at the dinner?''

''I have already explained that she must have a tray in her room that evening, since we are too many women.''

''Well, now we are evening out nicely—only three to four. Perhaps you will have another of your whist cronies.''

''Well, the fact is . . .'' Lady Hyde paused, unusually flustered. ''The fact is I have had such a charming note from Lord St. Hillaire saying he will be staying in the neighborhood next week and requesting permission to call.''

''Oh, no, Aunt, surely you did not—''

''Well, I did, then,'' said Lady Hyde defensively. ''How could I possibly write back to say he would not be welcome here. In fact, I invited him to dinner.''

''Oh, Lord!'' cried Mary, dismayed. ''I wish you had not. Indeed, I wish you had asked me first. It will be so embarrassing.''

''Nonsense. He is a very nice young man. It is just what you need, young people about to cheer you up.''

''If he feels encouraged to propose to me again, I assure you I shall not be very cheerful about it,'' promised Mary darkly.

12

Mary stood talking with Lord Dachett, her hand securely within both his own. She did not mind at all, really, for she was fond of Lord Dachett and had known him most of her life. Apart from this, his hands were warm and dry, the skin worn smooth and silky with age, and somehow comforting.

He was the first of Lady Hyde's guests to arrive and Mary was grateful for his presence, for she was not at all looking forward to the evening. Lord St. Hillaire would undoubtedly pursue his suit for her hand, a suit she was more than ever sure she would again refuse. Then, her previous acquaintance with Miss Fortmain, admittedly brief and sporadic, had not predisposed her to look forward to an evening in her company. She had never met Lord Fortmain, nor, of course, his heir. Lady Fortmain was a pleasent-enough woman, but she was, in Mary's eyes, exclusively Lady Hyde's friend, in the same category as Lord Dachett. To a girl not quite eighteen they all seemed of an immense age.

However, she would not dream of moping or being disagreeable about her aunt's party, which Mary was quite aware had been planned with her own happiness and pleasure in view. It was only a matter of a few hours, after all, and must simply be got through with the best grace possible.

Lord Dachett was rambling on about the improvements the landscape artist was bringing about in his gardens when Lady Hyde, who had been checking the dinner table, returned to the room.

"Well, I believe everything is settled satisfactorily," she said. Then her eyes settled fixedly on Lord Dachett's hands, still enfolding Mary's. He became aware of her stare, patted Mary's hand, and smoothly turned to take Lady Hyde's hand.

"My dear Augusta, I am sure everything is very well indeed. Your arrangements for the comfort of your guests are always perfection," he said, raising Lady Hyde's hand to his lips.

Mary's lips twitched with suppressed amusement as she saw her aunt's expression soften. What a terror with the ladies he must have been in his young days, she thought.

Salcombe announced Lord St. Hillaire, who entered eagerly, his eyes flying at once to Mary. Lady Hyde sailed across the room to greet him, but even as he spoke to her, his eyes constantly returned to Mary. When Lady Hyde released him he hurried across the room to bow over her hand and kiss it fervently, then stood looking at her with a sort of imploring expectancy, very much like a polite, intelligent dog who is sure you will share your cake with him. Mary pulled her hand from his gently and greeted him with a calmly smiling countenance despite her discomfort. She flashed a quick glance at Lord Dachett and caught his slightly raised eyebrow and twinkling eyes as he registered Lord St. Hillaire's ardor.

Blessedly Salcombe announced the Fortmains and she was saved further embarrassment. She went forward with her aunt to greet them. Lord Fortmain was a hearty, red-faced gentleman, his amazing paunch supported by spindly legs that looked totally inadequate for the job. Lady Fortmain gave her a curtsey and her sweet, somewhat cowed, smile. She was faded now, but had clearly been a pretty woman in her day. Her daughter, Miss Emma Fortmain had, unfortunately, not inherited her mother's looks, but resembled more her father, with a short pugged nose and gingery hair. Her manner was haughty as she merely sketched a curtsy and nodded

coldly. Clearly she was not about to allow anyone to
think she was impressed by Mary's title. Mary hoped it
was only shyness and that the girl would warm up as
the evening progressed.

Lord Fortmain now brought forward the gentleman
hovering behind him. "Allow me to present my nephew,
Mr. Adrian Fortmain, to your grace." Mr. Fortmain
stepped forward to bow over Mary's hand and then
turned to be presented to Lady Hyde.

He was slim and very little above Mary's own height.
His blond hair fell over a wide forehead, his features as
finely cut as a woman's. Indeed, he had a profile any
girl would envy, with a small, perfect nose. As he turned
back to Mary, she saw that his eyes were an indeter-
minate hazel-gray in color and seemed to twinkle with
a secret amusement, and that for all the delicacy of his
features, his strong, square jaws denied any effeminacy.

"Come along," said Lady Hyde, "you must all meet
Lord St. Hillaire. Lord Dachett, of course, you all
know, except for Mr. Fortmain."

As they all turned obediently to follow her across the
room, Miss Fortmain put a possessive hand upon her
cousin's arm and smiled up at him. He turned at her
touch, but did not return her smile. With a polite bow
he led her away.

Mary suppressed a smile, for it seemed to her that
Miss Fortmain's open display of ownership did not sit
well with her cousin. Here was a small play to make
the evening more interesting, she thought and continued
to watch them covertly while introductions were made.
Miss Fortmain had, perforce, to release her hold on his
arm while he was introduced, but in a moment dinner
was announced and she confidently took his arm again,
for she well knew it was inevitable that he should take
her in since every other person present took precedence
over them.

Mary sat at the head of the table with Lord St. Hillaire on her right and Lord Dachett on her left. Lady
Hyde sat at the other end with Lord Fortmain on her

right and Mr. Fortmain on her left. Miss Fortmain sat between her cousin and Lord St. Hillaire with her mother across from her between Lord Dachett and her husband.

"Not the best arrangement," Lady Hyde had confided to Mary earlier in the day, "but with so small a company husbands and wives must sometimes be put together." It was Lady Hyde's hope that the intimacy of the party would cause the company to all talk together, with the young people infusing gaiety into the proceedings. Miss Fortmain foiled these plans at once by immediately leaning to her cousin and engaging him in a low-voiced conversation, leaving Lord St. Hillaire free to turn eagerly to Mary to tell her of all he had suffered when she had left London so suddenly, of how dreary the town had become for him in her absence, of his delirious happiness to find on his unexpected visit in the neighborhood that she was in residence at Mallows, and of the unbelievable kindness of Lady Hyde in inviting him to dine tonight. He expatiated upon his happiness in beholding her beauty again as the only anodyne for the terrible unhappiness he had experienced at being apart from her.

Mary listened to all this with acute embarrassment, very much aware of Lord Dachett, his ear cocked politely to Lady Fortmain's soft-voiced inane vagaries, while all the time Mary knew he was not missing a word of Lord St. Hillaire's declarations, highly amused by it all. Not maliciously, Mary knew, but with an incurable curiosity and a delight in the foibles of human beings.

Lady Hyde, murmuring politely to Lord Fortmain's pronouncements, saw all her plans for the evening blasted by that impossible minx, Miss Fortmain, and seethed inwardly. How dare that girl take command of my dinner table—well, really Mary's dinner table—but still . . . And Mary seemed unlikely to take command and set things right. Very well, then!

"Yes, indeed, Lord Fortmain, I could not agree with

you more,'' she said, and turned decisively away from
him. ''Mr. Fortmain, I hope you plan to make a long
stay.''

Though his ear was still mightily engaged by his
cousin, he eagerly accepted this interruption with a
murmured excuse to Miss Fortmain. Before he could
reply, however, Miss Fortmain spoke.

''We have every hope of keeping our cousin for a
month at least, Lady Hyde.''

Mr. Fortmain's brows drew together in a small frown
for an instant before he smoothed it away and said, ''As
my cousin has spoken for me, I am left speechless, my
lady.'' Though it was said lightly and with no hint of
irritability, it was clear to all that he was displeased.
Lady Fortmain stared fixedly into her plate and her husband cleared his throat loudly, while everyone else
avoided one another's eyes. Miss Fortmain flushed a
rather ugly red color and then bravely flashed a toothily
complicit smile at her cousin, as though to declare to
all that they two could confidently speak for each other.

Glad to be diverted from Lord St. Hillaire's ardent
declarations, Mary said, ''May we take that for a com-
mitment, Mr. Fortmain?''

''At your command, your grace,'' he said quickly,
perhaps to prevent his cousin from answering for him
again.

''Then we do command it,'' Mary said lightly.

''It shall be as you desire. But may I hope your com-
mands mean that you have plans in mind for my entertainment?''

''Why—why, certainly we must entertain you, sir.
What is your pleasure?''

''Well, I like to ride and dance and dine pleasantly,
as any other man, I believe.''

''Ah, those are simple requests, I think, though I do
not promise the dancing, for we do not have much of
that here.''

''Why, there is the assembly at Coxton next week,''
cried Miss Fortmain, and then could have bitten out her

tongue, for the last thing she wanted was the Duchess of Runceford queening it at the Coxton assembly, where Miss Fortmain was accustomed to taking precedence over all the unmarried girls in attendance. Apart from this, she had no wish to share her cousin with her grace.

"Why, of course," cried Lady Hyde, "I had forgotten that, Mary. Shall we all go? You will still be in the neighborhood, will you not, Lord St. Hillaire? And as for the riding, I think there can be no problem about that. There are many lovely rides in the district, are there not Mary?"

"Then I will request your grace to show them to me," said Mr. Fortmain, turning to Mary.

"Oh, how delightful," cried Miss Fortmain. "Shall we call for her tomorrow, cousin?"

Mr. Fortmain sat quite unmoving for a half-moment before turning to her with a little, grave bow. Mary thought if it had been directed to her she would have wished the earth to open and swallow her, but Miss Fortmain only gave a little, trilling laugh and patted her cousin's arm. "There," she said, "I knew you would agree with me. Papa can mount you most respectably, I assure you."

The muscles in Mr. Fortmain's square jaw could be seen clinching. Poor man, Mary thought, he is indeed very much put upon. Her mother should speak to the girl and warn her against the game she is playing, for she is bound to lose him if she goes on in this way.

Perhaps Lady Fortmain thought the same, for when the ladies went to the drawing room, leaving the gentlemen to their wine, she led her daughter to a sofa in a far corner of the room and began speaking to her very earnestly in a low voice. That Miss Fortmain did not find her mother's words to her liking was to be seen by the angry tossing of her head and her pouting lips. At last she rose abruptly and flounced away to the pianoforte, where she began to play. When the men joined them she smiled at her cousin and motioned him to join her, but he apparently did not see this, for he went across to Mary quickly and took a chair next to the end of the sofa where she sat.

"Well, sir," said Mary, "you gentlemen completed your business quite expeditiously. I trust the wine was to your liking?"

"It could not have been better, but the port could not compete with other allurements," he replied with a warm look in her eyes.

She flushed slightly but managed to say lightly, "Ah, yes, music hath charms, as has been said."

"Music?" He paused, then very deliberately turned to the pianoforte and as slowly turned back. "So there is. I had not noticed."

"Your cousin plays very well."

"Lord St. Hillaire is one of your London conquests, I presume," he said with a clear intent to change the subject.

"You may presume nothing of the kind," she said reprovingly, "nor must you ask such a question of me."

"I know it was unbelievably rude of me, but I cannot seem to help myself."

"Cannot help yourself being rude? How so, sir?"

"It is jealousy," he said gravely.

She dropped her fan in confusion. He bent to retrieve it and handed it back to her solemnly. She met his eye and saw a twinkle there that caused her to laugh suddenly and he joined her.

This merriment was too much for Miss Fortmain, who ended her piece with a loud chord and rose, crying, "Oh, do share the joke, cousin, so that we may all be amused." She crossed the room as she spoke and stood before them.

Lord St. Hillaire, in polite conversation with Lord Dachett and Lady Fortmain, looked around eagerly, as though he too would be glad to hear.

Mr. Fortmain rose and handed his cousin into the chair he had vacated, saying, "There was no joke, cousin," before turning away to join Lady Hyde and his uncle on the other side of the room.

* * *

In discussing the evening over breakfast the following morning, Lady Hyde and Mary agreed that Miss Fortmain had conducted herself very badly and was hardly likely to hold on to her cousin by such public display. "Lady Fortmain confided in me some time ago that her husband hopes they will make a match of it, but I cannot see why he should do so. He has a great deal of money, will have the title, and is very handsome with it all. He can marry where he likes."

"Well, if she would but be a little less forward, he might like to marry her."

"You are in a very charitable mood this morning, my love. I believe we have been too dull these past weeks. We must do a great deal more entertaining."

At this point Salcombe announced Miss Emma Fortmain, who came rushing into the room upon his heels.

"I made sure you would not mind my pushing myself upon you in this way," Miss Fortmain gushed with ill-advised confidence, not noticing Lady Hyde's affronted look, "for you did say you would like to ride with us this morning. My cousin accompanies me, of course, but he would not come in, silly man."

"Good morning, Miss Fortmain," replied Lady Hyde in chilly accents. "You will excuse our deshabille, but we are not accustomed to receiving visitors at breakfast."

Even Miss Fortmain could not remain impervious to this stern set-down, and she flushed darkly. She recovered in a moment, however, and with a defiant toss of her head cried, "Oh, please do not apologize, dear Lady Hyde, the fault is all mine."

Mary hastily intervened before her aunt could speak. "If you will care to wait, Miss Fortmain, I would very much like to join you. Perhaps your cousin would like to come in and join you in a cup of chocolate while I change?"

"Oh, no, indeed, though I thank you," said Miss Fortmain quickly, not willing to be left alone with Lady

Hyde even for a moment. "I will wait with all the patience in the world, but I much prefer the air on so beautiful a morning."

Mary excused herself to her aunt and went away to change while Miss Fortmain went out to rejoin her cousin, leaving Lady Hyde muttering "Ill-bred jade," and other pleasantries to herself as she sipped her cooling chocolate.

By the time Mary descended, Lord St. Hillaire had joined the waiting riders and presently the foursome cantered off down the drive, Mary and Lord St. Hillaire leading the way. He explained to Mary that he was visiting a bedridden uncle nearby and since the old man slept most of the time and there were no other family or visitors in the house, his time was his own for the most part, and he hoped to spend most of it with her.

For the rest of the week this morning ride became the habit of the four, with three of the party forever maneuvering to get one of the others alone. Miss Fortmain, naturally, determined to have her cousin as her cavalier, while he was equally determined to get Mary apart, as was Lord St. Hillaire. Mary tried to be equally charming to everyone while not seeming to be encouraging to Lord St. Hillaire. She would have preferred Mr. Fortmain's company actually, if they were always to be divided into pairs, for she found him amusing. However, she was loath to rouse Miss Fortmain's ire or cause either gentleman unhappiness by showing a preference, so she allowed events to fall out as they might.

She could not help reaping some amusement, even some gratification, for she was human after all, in the gentlemen's preference for her company, but thought she might have enjoyed herself more alone. One morning she began to think of her rides with Robin on poor old Meg and found, on balance, that she had had more pleasure then than she was having now and, given her choice, would rather be back at Hatchett's End in Lady Leigh's old-fashioned made-over habit with Robin in her lap. This brought back the memory of her first encoun-

ter with Lord Leigh and his men. She caught her breath
as she remembered, for he had been so pleasant to her
and looked at her so—so warmly. Then she remembered
the last look he had given her, so scornful and cold. She
bit her lip and swallowed as she felt tears rising in her
throat.

"A penny for them, your grace," said Mr. Fortmain
quietly.

She started at his voice and her horse shied. When
she had quieted the animal, she said, "Oh, they are not
worth so much, sir. Where—" she looked behind.

"My cousin caught a ribband from her hat on a bough
and Lord St. Hillaire is very kindly helping to disentan-
gle it. I could not let you ride on unaccompanied."

"That was very kind of you," she said, smiling.

"I hope I am always kind. You seemed in such an
abstracted mood that I feared you might incur an injury
by riding into a ditch."

"I hope I should not go so far as that. I was only
enjoying the lovely morning."

"So much so, evidently, that you were oblivious to
Miss Fortmain's little contretemps, despite her
screams."

"Touché." She laughed.

"And am I not to know where your thoughts had
strayed to so deeply?"

"I was remembering another ride with a very little
boy before me in the saddle."

"Oh, dear, that is competition beyond me. One
should never vie with children for a woman's attention."

At this moment Miss Fortmain and Lord St. Hillaire
came hurrying up to join them. Miss Fortmain clearly
not in the best of moods. To placate her Mary dropped
back to speak to Lord St. Hillaire.

In the afternoons Mary wrote her letter to Robin or
worked at small paintings or drawings for the books she
made him, while her aunt occupied the time with her
needlework. It was while engaged in these pursuits one

afternoon that Salcombe announced Miss Emma Fortmain and her two younger sisters.

Miss Fortmain bustled in importantly ahead of her sisters and they all dropped their curtsies to Mary and Lady Hyde. Mary's welcoming smile was only slightly strained. She felt that the mornings spent in Miss Fortmain's company were enough.

Miss Fortmain's eyes were bright and her cheeks pink. She was clearly seething with suppressed excitement. Perhaps her cousin has proposed to her, after all, thought Mary, though it was hard to believe. It seemed to her his politeness to his cousin barely disguised his dislike of her, but she could be wrong. Men could seem to like one very much and then . . . She resolutely pushed the thought below the surface of her mind. This was not the time for brooding on such things.

"You are looking very happy, Miss Fortmain," she said with determined pleasantness. "It must surely be good news to make your eyes so bright."

"Oh, yes . . . I mean, no. Well . . ." Miss Fortmain floundered to a halt in her confusion, then said with seeming inconsequence, "We have just come from paying a call on Mrs. Robeson-Smythe."

"We are not acquainted with Mrs. Robeson-Smythe," said Lady Hyde with stately disapproval.

"Are you not? She is a lovely person, we think, do we not, sisters?" The two younger girls, eyes wide as saucers, nodded in agreement.

"Perhaps we shall make her acquaintance at the assembly," said Mary equably.

"Oh, you are sure to do so. She said she would not miss the chance to meet you after—" Miss Fortmain stopped abruptly as her sisters gasped aloud.

After a suspenseful moment of silence Mary said, "Do go on, Miss Fortmain. You have quite intrigued me, and I am sure you mean to tell us." She knew very well that nothing could have stopped Miss Fortmain from telling. She had clearly come here with every intention on imparting her sensational budget of news.

The color in Miss Fortmain's cheeks deepened and she flung up her head as though challenged. "Well, it was the oddest story I could ever imagine. It seems Mrs. Robeson-Smythe had had a letter from an old bosom bow, a Mrs. Herries." Mary felt her blood grow cold in her veins. "This woman had written to inquire about a governess who claimed to come from this neighborhood and who was taking care of the son of a farmer who is neighbor to Mrs. Herries. It seems this girl had run out into the road half-naked before this farmer and claimed she had been abducted by footpads and had escaped after—well, I cannot repeat what had been done to her—and he, the farmer, took her home with him. And she lived there with him quite alone, as governess to the little boy, they said. She gave her name as Mary Marshall."

Miss Fortmain stopped on this dramatic note and stared at Mary, her breast heaving with breathless excitement. Her two sisters sat clutching each other's hands and watching Mary avidly.

Lady Hyde's eyes were nearly bulging from her head with indignation at the salacious innuendos in Miss Fortmain's account and was on the point of bursting out into rebuttal when Mary spoke.

"What a very shocking story for Mrs. Robeson-Smythe to have repeated to you and your sisters, Miss Fortmain. I feel sure your mother will not be pleased to hear that she had done so. For my own part, I cannot help feeling sorry for my namesake. It is not an uncommon name, I suppose. I must say I would like to hear her version of the story—or even the, ah, farmer's. I doubt they would be so scandalous. Ah, well, perhaps it would not be so interesting to those who like their tales adorned with as much titillating detail as possible and probably add shocking details if they are missing." Miss Fortmain flushed an angry red, but held her tongue. "Now let us speak of pleasanter things. Shall I ring for refreshments, Aunt?"

At this the Misses Fortmain rose as one, declined

refreshments, and departed in a flurry of good-byes and false smiles.

Mary and Lady Hyde stared wordlessly at each other for a long moment.

"That story will be all over the county by nightfall," Lady Hyde said in a doom-laden voice.

"Does it matter, Aunt?"

"Matter? How can you ask such a thing? I cannot understand how you can take this so lightly, Mary. Everyone will hear of it . . . everyone!"

"My dear Aunt, what of it? It is not true—at least this version is not true—and the only person in this county for whom I care knows it is not true."

"You mean Lord St.—",

"I mean you, Aunt. There is no one else within an hour's ride whose opinion of me matters in the least one way or another," said Mary grandly.

"Well, I am sure that is very gratifying, my dear, but still . . . Well, I suppose I must put everyone off for my dinner party before the assembly."

"Why ever should you do that?"

"Well, surely . . . I mean to say you cannot intend to go to the Coxton assembly now?"

"I will go if I have to crawl there on my hands and knees," Mary replied grimly.

13

In the end Lady Hyde decided to cancel her plans for a dinner party before the assembly. "I will not have that lying, ill-bred creature sitting at table with me again," she said in tones that brooked no argument.

"Oh, lying, Aunt? She was just repeating what she heard," replied Mary in protest.

"That is just as bad. She should not have allowed that—that person to tell her such a story, particularly in front of her two younger sisters. It is not a fit story for an unmarried girl to listen to, much less repeat. She will go tattling that story to everyone she meets, and it will lose nothing in the telling, you may be sure. But it will rebound to her discredit, for any well-bred person will take her in disgust."

Mary agreed with every word Lady Hyde said, but she was too sick at heart to discuss it further. The assembly was nearly upon them and she needed every ounce of courage for the dreadful ordeal she knew she must face, since nothing on earth could have persuaded her to avoid it. A Marshall to turn tail and hide herself away in shame? No! She would go and face them down, let come what may.

She had given some thought to what gown she would wear to the ball. Her first thought was to dress simply, lest they think she was flaunting herself—then to be grand, lest they think she was slighting them. Now she settled with a hardened heart on grand. She would wear the celestial-blue gauze with her mother's sapphire-and-diamond necklace and earrings, as well as the diamond tiara. She would hold her hear very high and be smiling and gracious. Let them take her measure!

On the night of the assembly they dined at home with only Lord Dachett to keep them company. Lady Hyde had wanted to invite Lord St. Hillaire, but Mary adamantly refused. "He will fret me to death, Aunt, just when I most want to be calm."

"Why, child, the man is head over ears in love with you—" began Lady Hyde.

"But I am not in love with him. He wearies me with his lovemaking. It is like a tiresome child always tugging at one's sleeve."

Lady Hyde's hopes for an alliance in that direction took a steep dive, for surely no woman could marry a man she felt that way about. Ah, well, she was very young and had several Seasons ahead to find a husband before one need to begin to worry.

So they arrived at the Coxton assembly with only Lord Dachett to attend them. Mary made sure she entered the room ahead of her aunt and Lord Dachett, and it being close to ten o'clock, the room was full. A dance had just finished and the room was loud with talk and laughter, but first a few and then, slowly, all fell silent as they became aware of the dazzling presence in the doorway. They gaped and Mary stared back, smiling and proud. It seemed an eternity to Mary, but it was for less than a moment before Lord St. Hillaire from one side and Adrian Fortmain from the other converged upon her at once and jostled each other to be first to bow over her hand. The throng of people began to murmur together and a veritable buzz arose in the room like several dozen swarms of bees had congregated there.

"Your grace," cried Lord St. Hillaire, who had managed to obtain Mary's hand first. "I feared you had changed your mind and were not coming. I was becoming quite desolate. May I have the honor of leading you out for your first set?"

"Certainly you may, my lord," she said, retrieving her hand from his fervent clasp and turning to Mr. Fortmain. "Good evening, sir. I trust you are enjoying the evening?"

"Not until this moment," he said as he bent to kiss her hand. "And I anticipate even more pleasure if you will grant me the happiness of standing up with you for your second."

"It will be my pleasure also, Mr. Fortmain."

While this was going forward, Lady Hyde said quietly into Lord Dachett's ear, "Point out to me the Robeson-Smythe woman." Lord Dachett obligingly indicated a statuesque red-haired woman across the room in a vivid-green satin gown. Lady Hyde stared at her for a moment. "She paints," she sniffed contemptuously, "as one might have expected."

Emma Fortmain was standing with a group of young women all whispering together, but her eyes never left the group at the door. She had been astonished to see her cousin go immediately to her grace's side, after what she had made sure he had heard, for she knew her father would be incapable of keeping such a story to himself. Her cousin had said nothing about it, but then he had hardly spoken at all in the past few days. He had been up and out when she came down each morning, and had stayed away all day. She had seen him only at dinner, when he had been polite but unforthcoming. No sallies of hers had drawn him from his introspection and she was much puzzled as to what could be bothering him. The abrupt ending of the daily rides was never mentioned, and since he was never there, there had been no need for the elaborate excuse she had concocted for not continuing them. She had been very sure that when he heard the scandalous story about her grace, he would become so disgusted he would turn to his cousin with greater warmth. This had not happened as yet and now he was here positively making a spectacle of himself by groveling at the duchess's feet!

Apart from this, though he had driven here with her and Mama in the same carriage, he had not asked her to stand up for a single set so far. Of course, he had not asked anyone else either, which consoled her some-what. It was also consoling to know that everyone in the room had by now heard the story about "Mary Mar-shall" and that little else would be talked of this eve-ning. Surely her grace would take a great snubbing this evening and learn that her title and her jewels could not command friends.

Miss Fortmain's happiness was short-lived, for even as she was consoling herself, she saw several matrons, including her own mama, going forward to make their curtsies to the duchess, as well as a number of local young men who pressed forward in the hopes of secur-ing a dance with her grace, an opportunity that might not come their way again. Miss Fortmain sniffed her disgust as such pusillanimous behavior. If any of them had an ounce of courage, they would turn their backs on the duchess after hearing such a story.

The music struck up and Lord St. Hillaire took Mary's hand and led her out proudly. He was the only person in the room who had not heard the story. Since it was well-known in the neighborhood that he was courting her grace, and since he was not known personally to anyone in the room, no one had quite dared to repeat the story to him.

Lady Hyde and her little court continued to stand at the entrance in conversation, but she did not miss Mrs. Robeson-Smythe's approach to Miss Fortmain, who was not dancing, and she watched grimly as the two heads bent together in avid conversation. She knew very well what was being discussed, and was waiting her mo-ment. The set ended and Lord St. Hillaire brought Mary back to her aunt. It was then that Miss Fortmain ap-proached across the room in company with Mrs. Robe-son-Smythe. Lady Hyde waited until they were directly before her, all smiles, with Miss Fortmain just opening her mouth to speak before she acted.

Then she took Mary's arm. "Come, my dear. We will find a sofa where we can be comfortable," she said with a cold, unrecognizing stare at the two women as she

turned deliberately away and walked across the room
with a stately tread, followed by Lord Dachett, Lord St.
Hillaire, and Mr. Fortmain.

Very few in the room missed this direct and unmistakable snub, for nearly everyone had been watching the
party at the door. Miss Fortmain and Mrs. Robeson-
Smythe stood rooted in shock, both turning bright red
in the face with embarrassment for all to see, before
they walked on out of the door into the hall.

Mary whispered to her aunt as they walked away, "I
very much hope you will never be my enemy, dear Aunt.
What a dragon you are."

"I hope I know my duty where you are concerned,
my dear. I could never allow you to know such a creature as that. She paints, you know, and I doubt nature
contributed much to the color of her hair. As for Miss
Fortmain, her mother had best look to her. She has a
lamentable want of conduct for a girl not in the first
flush of youth."

Mary felt the laughter in her throat rising irrepressibly and swallowed convusively. She knew she dared not
give way, for if she did so, she might very well become
hysterical. The musicians struck up for the next set and
having seen her aunt comfortably disposed upon a sofa,
Mary gave her hand to Mr. Fortmain and was led onto
the floor.

From the shadows of the hall Miss Fortmain watched,
her teeth grinding together in helpless fury. If only her
papa had come tonight she would go to him at once and
demand that he speak to Mr. Fortmain. Oh, how could
he be so rude to her while he was a guest in her very
own home? She vowed that she would make him pay
for it someday when they were married. Miss Fortmain
had no doubts that they would marry. Had not her papa
and mama as good as promised it to her?

Mr. Fortmain, meanwhile, was saying everything that
was pleasant to Mary in an effort to convey to her that
while he may have heard the story, he did not believe
it. Indeed, he was very angry with his cousin. Lord

Fortmain had not hesitated to tell him the source of the
story about the duchess. Mr. Fortmain had not hesitated
to forcefully express his disapproval of his cousin for
repeating such unfounded gossip. Lord Fortmain had
shown a guilty discomposure at his nephew's reproof,
and had gone at once to berate his wife for the way in
which she brought up her daughters. Poor Lady Fortmain had burst into tears. She knew it must be her fault,
but somehow she had never had the least success in
disciplining Emma. Naturally she had told the girl that
her own credit would suffer if she persisted in repeating
such a story, but Emma had only tossed her head and
looked stubborn.

As he danced with Mary, Mr. Fortmain felt that he
had never known so splendid a young woman. He ad-
mired her for her spirit and courage in coming tonight
to outface the neighborhood, and already he felt the
mood of the room changing. When he had first arrived
tonight everyone had been agog with the scandal and
seemingly ready to turn upon her in a body. If she had
not come, they would have believed the worst. Now the
temperature had changed as wiser heads had second
thoughts on the matter and more and more people were
making a point of paying Lady Hyde their respects as
she sat regally surveying the room. He himself had been
happy to see Lady Hyde snub his cousin and Mrs.
Robeson-Smythe in so public a way, for they had richly
deserved it. He felt he had behaved in a more cowardly
and less gentlemanly way by simply refusing to stand
up with his cousin and making a point of doing so with
the duchess. In fact, he had a second dance with her
before the evening was over, and would have like more,
but he knew Lady Hyde would not have allowed it.

Nor did she allow Lord St. Hillaire more than two,
and she was much gratified to note that her niece stood
up for every set. however, seeing that Mary was on the
very edge of her endurance, she stood up decisively
before the last set but one and announced that they must
go. Mary rose at once, more grateful than she could

imagine being to leave dancing, which she adored. However, the effort needed to stand tall and smile unconcernedly, for the last two hours had taken away all the pleasure of dancing and given her a headache besides. She wanted only to be alone now and went directly to her bed when they finally reached Mallows. She longed for sleep, but her thoughts raced around and around and a band of pain tightened about her head. She had again told a lie. She had not actually denied the story as false, but she had allowed Miss Fortmain to see it as a denial. If she had had the courage to tell the true story . . . But the story Miss Fortmain had told had so much that was true in it that she knew her own version would never have been believed. No, it was best this way, though she wondered what Charles Leigh would think of her if he could know. Would he despise her even more for her cowardice?

After a tense and silent ride Mr. Fortmain went straight to his room also, while an indignant Miss Fortmain flounced in upon her hapless father in his library, trailed by her fearful mother, to lay before him all her humiliations in a stormy session of rage and tears. As a result Mr. Fortmain received a note from his uncle before he slept requesting him to attend him in his library after breakfast the following morning.

When his uncle rose from the table the next morning, Adrian Fortmain promptly rose and followed him out of the room.

"Sit down, my boy, sit down," cried Lord Fortmain jovially. "Might as well be comfortable, I always say. Find that bay to your liking, do you?"

"He is a very fine animal, sir. I am grateful to you for allowing me to ride him. What did you want to speak to me about?"

"Well, well, a trifle, really. Wanted to make sure there was no quarrel between you and Emma. Headstrong girl, y'know, but good at heart. Means no harm, y'know."

"Perhaps not. Nevertheless, to my mind she has done harm by repeating that malicious tale."

"Now, now, my boy, women will tittle-tattle, and no doubt the story would have come out even if Emma had held her tongue. Have to learn to understand women and not take their gossip seriously if you want to get along with 'em. Point is, you see, the poor little girl was upset last night. Not quite the thing, you know, not to stand up with her at the assembly. Her cousin—staying in the house and all. Looked bad. Surprised at you, must admit."

"I am sorry to have incurred your displeasure, sir, but I could not countenance her behavior by dancing with her as though nothing had happened," said Mr. Fortmain stiffly.

"Well, well, must patch it up between you. A few sweet words and all's forgotten, eh?"

"I do not feel I have anything to apologize for, Uncle. In fact, I was going to tell you today in any case that I must leave. I have been away from my own affairs long enough."

"What's this, what's this? Surely you will make a longer visit? Oh, this will never do, never do! All over Emma's little silliness. It would be cruel. Why, she has set her heart—I meant to say—well, my boy, it has always been my hope you and she would, ah, make a match of it."

"I am sorry to disappoint you, sir, but I am afraid such has never been my intention. Nor do I believe I have ever indicated any such intention."

"Perhaps one of the younger girls—"

"No," said Adrian Fortmain firmly. "My heart has already been given, Uncle."

Now, it happened that there was a young woman with whom he had grown up whom he was half-inclined to believe himself in love with, but since he had met Mary, he was no longer sure. He was more than a little in love with her, and with any encouragement at all from her he would declare himself at once, though he called him-

self a fool for imagining she would be allowed to throw
herself away upon a mere Mr. Fortmain. The fact remained, however, that he was glad to be truthful to his
uncle; besides, it brought a complete end to this very
distressing conversation. Poor Lord Fortmain was left
with the dreadful task of informing his daughter of this
unhappy news, a task he could not look forward to with
any equanimity.

Mr. Fortmain did leave his relatives on the next day
after a final call upon Mary to bid her farewell and
obtain her permission to write to her.

Mary found she was sorry to see him go, for she had
grown to like him very well. She could not blame him,
however, for wanting to escape from his cousin and her
designs upon him. She agreed that he might write,
"though you will find correspondence with me a bore,
I very much fear. Very little happens here, you see."

They shook hands and he went away. Mary had just
settled down to write her letter to Robin when Lord St.
Hillaire called to beg her to come riding. She de-
murred, but Lady Hyde declared it would do her all the
good in the world, and at last she allowed herself to be
persuaded and went away to change into her habit. Being blithely unaware of any problems, Lord St. Hillaire
talked quite cheerfully about the pleasures of the previous evening, his joy at dancing with her once more,
how jolly the company and how fine the musicians.

When they returned, Lady Hyde invited him to stay
for dinner and afterward he sang, in a surprisingly
pleasant light tenor, while Mary played his accompa-
niment. Mary behaved quite warmly to him and Lady
Hyde's hopes began to rise again. Perhaps, after all . . .

He came for the next three days to ride and dine and
inevitably began to make love to Mary again, and on
the last day of his stay he renewed his proposal.

"You do me much honor, sir, but I must again say
no."

"Ah, I have asked you again too soon—"

"No, it is not that. I should never have agreed to

allow you to speak to me again on the matter. I can never marry you, Lord St. Hillaire, though I hope we may always remain friends. I shall value your friendship.''

Lord St. Hillaire was desolate but had to accept it, being too much a gentleman to plague her with further protestations. He rode away brokenhearted.

Mary told her aunt about it so that she would have no further illusions in the matter. Lady Hyde accepted her decision with a sigh of regret. Such a very suitable young man, she thought sadly, so steady and sensible, wealthy and well-connected, and the best blood in England in his veins.

After this another lull descended upon Mallows. Mary, not without reason, was disinclined for society, though she still consented to make morning calls with her aunt, dine out, of have guests to dinner, but only with her aunt's oldest cronies whom she had known from childhood. She also rode, went for walks, swam in the pond on hot days, and wrote to Robin or painted pictures for his little books, and several eventless weeks passed.

14

"**W**ill you like to hear me read from my book, Uncle Charles?" piped Robin, who had come to the table with Mary's latest book and placed it carefully beside his plate.

Charles looked up startled, for Robin was usually silent in his presence. "Can you read?" Robin nodded with a shy smile. "Let us hear you, then, by all means. Bring your book here."

Robin jumped down from his chair at once and carried his book around the table to his uncle. Mrs. Heaven and Betsy exchanged worried looks but did not speak. Charles took the book, which was entitled *Robin's Reader*, in hand lettering. On the first page was a watercolor of a little boy seated upon a horse and beneath it the words *"Robin likes to ride Old Meg"* in large, simple, hand-printed letters.

Charles cast a puzzled look at Mrs. Heaven, who must have made this book for the boy. He had no idea she was so skilled an artist. Before anyone could speak, however, Robin began to read, a pudgy, dimpled finger beneath each word, as he carefully and slowly pronounced each word beneath the picture. Then he turned the page to a picture of a little boy paddling in a pond with the message, *"Robin likes to swim in the water."* There were but five pages in all, each depicting Robin in various activities and all of which Robin read without mistake.

Charles was impressed and praised the boy highly for his accomplishment. When Betsy had taken him out and

Mrs. Heaven was clearing the table, he spoke to her good-humoredly.''I never suspected you had so much talent as an artist, Mrs. Heaven.''

''Oh, sir, 'twas never me did the book,'' she blurted out before she could stop herself, she was so taken by surprise that he should think she was capable of it.

''Not you? Who, then? Never tell me it was Betsy,'' he asked with a grin.

Mrs. Heaven continued stacking plates, wishing she knew what it would be best to say. ''Well, sir, he is sent the books. He has several of them and has made progress in his reading and can print the entire alphabet without copying from anything. Oh, it's a clever boy, for sure,'' she equivocated.

''Yes, I can see that he is, but you have not answered my question, Mrs. Heaven. Who sends him the books?''

''Well, sir, 'tis her grace that sends them.''

Charles' brows drew together ominously, but he rose from the table and left the house without another word. In truth, he had known all along in his heart who must have made the books. It could have been no one else, but he had not wanted to acknowledge it, had hoped to hear differently. His head felt as though it were boiling as all the thoughts and emotions released so suddenly whirled and battered their way through his mind.

After that last devasting scene with her, Charles had sworn he would not allow any further thoughts of her to enter his mind. He was a strong-willed man and for the most part he had succeeded in his vow. Sometimes, however, her face would appear clearly before his eyes, taking him by surprise and causing his heart to pound and a sick sort of languor to invade his whole body. He would battle it with all his might and at last conquer it, assuring himself he would not allow it to happen to him again. He did not attempt to deny to himself that he was still in love with the girl, but he was determined to cure himself of it, and was sure that he would eventually succeed. He willed it to be so.

When the first white heat of his rage at her had cooled,

he had acknowledged to himself that some of his accusations against her had been cruel and unjust. No one who had seen her scratched and bruised body, her bleeding wrists, could seriously believe she had been playing at some masquerade. The fact remained, however, that she had deceived him. His pride still smarted from the knowledge that he had made a fool of himself, if only in his thoughts, because he had believed the story she had told him.

Now, after all the heartsick agony he had endured to cut her out of his life, she was making her existence vivid to him once more with these books. She must have been sending them to Robin since she had left, which proved that she was truly fond of the child and felt responsible for his welfare, but he did not want to know these things about her! He must instruct Mrs. Heaven to write and tell her not to send any more. She had no right to intrude herself into his life again.

All the afternoon, as he worked, his thoughts circled endlessly around this new problem, but by evening, when he was at last returning home for the day, he knew he could not do such a thing. He decided, wearily, that it was not fair to the boy to deprive him of those delightful and instructive little books, or of the love and tenderness for Robin they expressed. God knew the poor child was deprived of enough in his young life. No, he could not prohibit the books, but he himself must ignore them—pretend they did not exist, just as he tried to pretend she did not, and eventually he would succeed. He must!

The only other problem that plagued him in his usual life of hard work was the squire's daughter, who had developed a habit of appearing frequently on horseback to take him from his work. She always seemed to know where to find him, and he came to dread her appearances, aware of the sly exchange of glances between his men. He could not think of a way to discourage her. He could not, for the squire's sake, be rude to her or forbid her to trespass on his land.

Miss Herries was totally unaware of his feelings. In fact, she was beginning to feel great confidence in her powers, for he always left his work at once to come talk to her when she rode up and he was always unfailingly courteous. She felt sure he was beginning to look forward to her little casual visits. She saw him, of course, when they exchanged dinner parties, but that was only for two evenings each month. She had decided to remedy this situation by her rides. Now she began to feel she must find some way to show her interest in an even more positive way, and she remembered the child. He was still quite a small boy, so he would be no trouble.

One day she ordered the carriage brought around without consulting either of her parents and had herself driven to Hatchett's End. When Mrs. Heaven answered the door, she could only stare speechless in her surprise.

"Well, am I to be kept standing on the doorstep, Mrs. Heaven?" demanded Miss Herries haughtily.

"Oh—oh, do come in, m'lady. I was that surprised I lost my wits." She ushered Miss Herries into the drawing room.

"Have the child dressed. I have come to take him for a ride."

"The child?"

"You have a child here, I believe? Lord Leigh's nephew? Please dress him suitably and bring him to me at once."

"But, m'lady, I don't think . . . I mean, the master—"

"Please do as I say. I think you will find Lord Leigh will be delighted for his nephew to be entertained."

After a lifetime of taking orders from quality Mrs. Heaven could not think of disobeying now, though she was much disturbed. She fetched Robin from the stables, where he was feeding Old Meg with a carrot, and hurried him upstairs.

"But I don't want to change my clothes," he pro-

tested. "Why must I? It is not nearly time for Uncle
Charles to come to dinner."

"There is a young lady come to take you for a drive
in her carriage. Won't that be nice for you? Come along
quickly now."

"What young lady? Do I know her?"

"No, but she is a friend of your uncle's and means
to be kind to you."

"I do not want to be kinded to," he muttered darkly,
and when she tried to take his hand to lead him from
the room, he pulled away. "I will not go."

"Robin, dear, you must come downstairs." She lifted
him into her arms. "Just make your bow and thank her
nicely and say you would rather not," she whispered
desperately as she carried him down to the drawing
room.

"Why, what is this?" cried Miss Herries. "Such a
great boy being carried about like a baby. Put him down
at once, Mrs. Heaven."

Robin was set on his feet, but one arm clamped itself
about Mrs. Heaven's knee and his head was buried in
her skirt. "Robin, go and make your bow to Miss Herries," Mrs. Heaven demanded sternly.

Reluctantly he released her knee and advanced two
steps and bowed.

Miss Herries reached out, grasped his arm and pulled
him to her. "Now, there! What a delightful child it is.
Give me a kiss, darling."

"No," he replied succinctly.

"Sauce!" she reproved roguishly. "We must teach
you better manners. Come along now." She rose and
began to lead him to the door, but he dug in his heels
and struggled to release his arm. She paid no attention,
but towed him out of the room, out the front door and
down the steps. Robin began to scream his protests
against such treatment, which she also ignored.

"Forgive me, m'lady," said Mrs. Heaven, "but I really think another time will be better, when he's more
prepared like."

"Nonsense. Pay no attention to him. He will forget all about it in a moment." And with that Miss Herries lifted Robin into the carriage.

"I really don't think this is for the best—" began Mrs. Heaven as Robin began crying and calling her name piteously. Mrs. Heaven reached out for him.

"Please do not concern yourself, Mrs. Heaven. Drive on," she ordered the coachman, and Robin was driven away, his shrieks and cries tearing at Mrs. Heaven's heart.

At last they died away and Mrs. Heaven shuddered. It was wrong, that's what it was. She had no right, no matter if she is to be mistress here someday. Oh, what must I do, what must I do? She stood there indecisively for a moment, wringing her hands helplessly. Then Betsy came running out.

"What's to do, Mrs. Heaven? I thought I heard young master crying out."

Mrs. Heaven woke from her shock. "Young Betsy, do you run as fast as you can go and fetch his lordship. He's working in that field south of the pond. Go on now, quick as you can. Tell him it's about Robin."

Betsy lifted her skirts above her knees and hared off around the house. Mrs. Heaven went to the stables and ordered Scraggs to saddle master's bay and bring it around at once.

Betsy ran across the fields, and as she espied the men, she shrilled out, "Master, master, you're to come at once. 'Tis Master Robin."

Charles straightened abruptly and stood staring a moment before he began striding quickly toward her. "What is it? What has happened?" he shouted as he neared her.

"I don't know, Master. 'Twas young master a-screamin' and then Mrs. Heaven tellin' me to fetch you quick as quick."

Charles set off for the house at a dead run. Not the boy, he prayed silently, don't let anything have happened to that boy after I promised my brother to take care of him. The run seemed to take forever, but he came in sight of the house at last and saw Mrs. Heaven coming along to meet him.

"What has happened?" he cried.

"Oh, my lord, forgive me, but I didn't know what to do to stop her. She would take him, though he cried out so pitiful to me and—"

"Who took him? What are you talking about?"

"That Miss Herries, sir. Said she wanted to take him for a ride in her carriage. He said he didn't want to go and began to cry, but she dragged him away. I couldn't stop her. She wouldn't listen to me, and him shrieking so 'twould break your heart."

"Which way?" he demanded tersely.

"They turned left out of the drive. I've had your horse saddled."

They had arrived by now at the front of the house. Without another word Charles leapt into the saddle and galloped away, grinding his teeth in rage that anyone should dare to treat a Leigh in such a fashion. By God, he'd like to shake that interfering baggage until her brains rattled for her highhandedness. How dare she take it upon herself to take his nephew in such a way without so much as a by-your-leave?

Muttering imprecations, he galloped for at least a mile before he saw the carriage coming toward him; he pulled up in the middle of the road to wait for the carriage to stop. He jumped down and strode up to the door where Miss Herries was staring out at him somewhat apprehensively. She decided she must make the best of this encounter and flashed him her most ravishing smile.

"Well met, sir," she cried. "We were just returning from our ride. Robin was a naughty boy, I fear, but—"

Charles wrenched open the carriage door and saw Robin cowering in a corner sobbing hopelessly. Charles lifted him out. When Robin saw who it was, he flung his arms about his uncle's neck, wrapped his legs about his waist, and dug his face into Charles' shoulder, his body still shaking with sobs.

Miss Herries chattered on, but Charles remained grimly silent, afraid to speak lest he say things no gentleman could say before a lady. He stalked back to his horse and managed to swing himself into the saddle with Robin still clinging to him like a limpet. They rode away, Charles holding the small shaking body hard against his own.

Mrs. Heaven was waiting on the steps and Charles pulled Robin gently away from him and handed him down into Mrs. Heaven's outstretched arms. Robin fastened himself to her and she had turned to carry him into the house when suddenly his little body went limp and his head fell back. Mrs. Heaven cried out.

"What is it?" Charles asked.

"Merciful heavens! He's—he's fainted, I think."

"Oh, my God! Put him to bed and try to revive him. I am going for the doctor."

"I really don't think you need—" began Mrs. Heaven, but it was too late, Lord Leigh was already halfway down the drive.

By the time he returned with Dr. Pilgrim, Robin was conscious. He cowered away when the stranger entered his room, but with his uncle and Mrs. Heaven soothing him, he at last allowed the doctor to examine him.

The doctor was sanguine. "Worn out with all the crying and excitement. He'll be all right after a good night's sleep."

Robin was not, however. By morning he was running a temperature, and by the time Charles came in for his meal, it had risen alarmingly. Charles again went for the doctor.

When Dr. Pilgrim came down to Charles, he looked grave. "It is a brain fever. Evidently he suffered a severe shock and it was too much for so delicate and undeveloped a nervous system. From what you told me yesterday and Mrs. Heaven today I think it is probable that he imagined he was being taken away from here permanently by a stranger. Mrs. Heaven tells me it is only a few months since he lost his parents and home.''

''What shall we do?''

''He will need a great deal of care, but I think we can rely on Mrs. Heaven for that. I suppose this Mary he calls for was his old nurse. Is it possible to bring her here? It would help, I believe.''

Charles flushed and turned away. ''No. She is not his nurse. It is not possible to bring her here.''

''Too bad. Well, we must do the best we can. I will come again in the morning. Good day to you, Lord Leigh.'

At the dinner table on the day of Miss Herries's abortive attempt to entertain Lord Leigh's nephew, she waxed indignantly upon the subject to her parents. ''After all, the poor child has no one to pay any attention to him. One would have thought Lord Leigh would be grateful that I was interested enough to—''

Her papa, whose thoughts, as usual, had strayed, was caught by the name ''Lord Leigh,'' and interrupted her. ''One moment. What were you saying about Lord Leigh?''

''Really, Papa, I think you might do me the courtesy of attending to me,'' she said pettishly and then proceeded to repeat the story of her morning's adventure. ''And a more ill-bred brat I have never met. Screaming and crying no matter what I said. He kicked me quite violently when I tried to take him in my lap. I slapped his face for it, thought,'' she finished, satisfaction evident in her voice.

''You did what?'' thundered the usually mild-spoken squire. ''Of all the dunderheaded behavior! No wonder Lord Leigh was rude to you. It is a wonder he did not box your ear.''

''Papa!'' cried Miss Herries, outraged.

''You richly deserve any treatment you received. Mrs. Herries, I must tell you that your daughter does not have a grain of sense, nor a trace of sensibility. You had best

look to her conduct!'' With that he threw down his napkin and stomped out of the room.

Miss Herries and her mother looked at each other in
genuine bewilderment. Then Miss Herries began to cry
and her mother rushed around the table to her darling,
misunderstood daughter.

The next morning Squire Harris rode to Hatchett's
End to make what apology he could. The doctor's carriage was just leaving.

"My dear Lord Leigh,'' cried the squire, "was that
the doctor? I do hope the boy had taken no harm from
this—this bit of unthinking stupidity on my daughter's
part.''

"The doctor says it is a brain fever brought on by the
shock,'' replied Charles starkly.

"Oh, dear lord,'' whispered Squire Herries in a
shaken voice. "I cannot begin to express my grief that
this should have come about through one of my family.
It must have been because she slapped him. She lost her
temper, I fear, when he kicked her.''

Lord Leigh seemed to visibly swell, and his face
turned red. He turned away abruptly and walked to the
window, where he stood silently for some time trying
to regain control of his temper. At last he turned about.

"She was a complete stranger to him. He told her he
did not want to go, but was carried away by force. By
force, sir!'' he cried, his temper slipping out of control
again. He swallowed. "He is only recently orphaned,
as you know. He lost his home and all that he had ever
known. He was just beginning to feel safe here. He
thought he was being taken away from all he had left
that was familiar to him.''

"My dear friend. if I may continue to call you so, I
could not regret this more. Is there anything at all we
can do?''

Between them hovered the words, *"You* have done
enough,'' but Charles only said, "No. I thank you,''
and held out his hand to indicate that between the two
of them, at least, friendship still existed. Squire Herries

went sadly away. Charles, after consulting with Mrs. Heaven, went out to his work.

For all the next day the temperature continued and Robin was often delirious, speaking to his mama, reliving his terrible experience with Miss Herries, and calling repeatedly for Mary, Mary, Mary, until Mrs. Heaven could bear it no longer. She called Betsy and told her to fetch her brother. He was to ride with a message to the Duchess of Runceford at once. Robin's well-being was worth more than Lord Leigh's feelings. Lord Leigh would get over it, but Robin might not. Besides, there was no reason for Lord Leigh to even know she was in the house if they managed all carefully.

15

"There is a, ah, person arrived, your grace, who insists upon seeing you personally to deliver a message from a Mrs. Heaven," announced Salcombe, barely able to conceal his astonishment at such cheek on the part of a mere scruffy farm boy mounted upon a disreputable-looking horse who had refused to be dismissed.

Mary, who had been sketching pictures for a book for Robin, sprang to her feet, pencils and drawing paper scattering from her lap over the carpet. "What? Where is he? I will see him at once."

She rushed out of the room with Salcombe following at a more stately pace, leaving Lady Hyde staring after her with apprehension. Letters were one thing, but the sending of messages boded no good. She was still staring at the door when Mary came hurrying back into the room and Lady Hyde saw at once that her prognostication had proved right just from the look on Mary's face.

"It is Robin, Aunt. He is very ill. I must go to him at once!"

"Mary, my dear, please sit down and calm yourself. You are behaving hysterically," replied Lady Hyde soothingly, attempting to take control of the situation before it became out of hand.

"I am not in the least hysterical. I am telling you that Robin is very ill and calls for me constantly. I must go to him."

"Now, Mary, this is quite ridiculous. Of course I

cannot allow you to go haring off about the country simply because—''

''Aunt. I must go. I am sorry to disagree with you, but I am going to Robin and I am going now!'' This was said quietly but with such steely determination that Lady Hyde knew she could not stop her. With or without her aunt's consent Mary would go. And what could Lady Hyde do? Lock her in her room? Such a remedy was impossible. One simply did not lock the Duchess of Runceford in her own room in her own house when she was nearly eighteen years old and had made her come-out in London. Lady Hyde seemed to wilt back into her chair in defeat while Mary waited politely for her to speak.

''Oh, child, child,'' cried Lady Hyde plaintively, ''I cannot think what has come over you. You were used to be such a biddable sort of girl, now you are forever running away somewhere. I cannot think where I have failed in raising you that you have developed this dreadful urge to go tearing off without any thought for the consequences. Only to think of those dreadful footpads! I still have nightmares about that, and it was a result of your going away against my wishes. I knew no good could come of anything to do with that Maud Bryce. And now this!'' Mary remained silent, only looking at her aunt steadily and at last Lady Hyde could hold out no longer. ''You will take Watts?''

Mary softened at once. ''Yes, darling Aunt. I will take Watts. I am sorry to cause you worry, but it will all be all right, you will see. He is such a small boy and so alone and he calls for me. You would not be so hard-hearted as to ignore that if it were you he called for. I will only stay until the crisis is over, I promise. Probably no more than a day or two. I shall be back before you even have time to miss me.'' She came to kiss her aunt's cheek and then hurried away to call Watts to pack a case for her and to order the small carriage to be brought around at once.

By ten o'clock they were on the road with the day-

long drive before them. Mary sat stiffly as the carriage
jolted along at a spanking pace. She was so tense she
could barely bring herself to relax against the velvet
squabs. Watts sat opposite her, trying not to think about
footpads. Her previous experience had left an indelible
impression upon her mind.

They seemed to have been driving forever and every
halt to bate the horses or take refreshments caused Mary
to fidget with impatience. She was in a dreadful fear
that they might not arrive at a time when Lord Leigh
was away from the house. Mrs. Heaven, though not
requesting this directly, had hinted discreetly that it
might be for the best. Lord Leigh, she wrote, need never
know of her presence in the house unless she chose to
make herself known to him. Mary had eagerly agreed
to this plan in the brief letter she had sent speeding back
with Betsy's brother. She had no desire at all to meet
Charles Leigh's cold eyes again.

Eventually they came to Hatchett's End near six in
the evening. There would be several more hours of daylight, it being mid-summer, and Lord Leigh always
worked until darkness fell, so their arrival went unob-
served by all but Mrs. Heaven and Betsy, who came out
to greet them at once. Storrs and George drove away to
find accommodation in the village while Watts was taken
off to the back of the house by Betsy. After a brief embrace Mary and Mrs. Heaven hurried upstairs, Mary
not even pausing to remove her bonnet.

Robin was in the old room that she had shared with
him, and as they entered, he was moving his head restlessly from side to side on the pillows and muttering to
himself. Mary threw herself down beside the bed and
put her hand on his burning forehead.

"Darling Robin, here I am," she whispered.

"Take me back. I do not care to go—Mary, Mary—I
want to go home—Mary, Mary—" he muttered piti-
fully.

"Yes, I am here, darling. I am here!"

His head stopped moving and after a moment he

slowly opened his eyes. He looked into her face with a little frown of concentration. "Is it—are you really here?"

"I am really here. I have come to help Mrs. Heaven take care of you. You must sleep now and get well."

"Hold my hand," he commanded, and his eyes closed as he sank back into his feverish dreams.

Holding his hand with one of her own, Mary rose and untied her bonnet and removed it and shrugged off her traveling cloak from her shoulders. Mrs. Heaven brought up a chair and Mary sat down close to the bedside. "Poor mite, he is so very hot. Could you ask Watts to bring up a basin of cold water, Mrs. Heaven. I will try bathing his face and arms. Perhaps it will make him more comfortable."

"Well, of course, the doctor did not say—but there, you shall have anything you want, dearest Mary," said Mrs. Heaven, and hurried away.

Watts had carried up several basins of cold water before Mrs. Heaven said Lord Leigh would be coming in from the fields at any moment and it would be best if Watts retired for the night to the room they had prepared for her. Watts protested. "I must stay with her grace. And who is to undress her for bed, I should like to know?"

"Please go along at once, Watts. It would not do for you to be seen flitting about the halls. I shall have Mrs. Heaven to help me if I need help, and I shall not leave this room tonight, so there is no question of needing to be prepared for bed."

All that night, the next day, and all the following night Mary kept her station beside the bed. If she felt sleep overcoming her, she would rest her head on the side of the bed to doze, but always woke instantly if Robin stirred. She bathed his fevered brow and held his hand as he slept, only agreeing to leave him for a few short moments from time to time to stretch her weary muscles and refresh herself.

It was late on the second evening that the fever broke

at last and the sheets had to be changed twice before he
at last fell into a sweet, restorative sleep, pale and thin,
but cool and his restless muttering and movements
stilled at last.

During this time Charles had questioned Mrs. Heaven
closely about his nephew's progress as well as hearing
reports from Dr. Pilgrim, who came every morning.
Naturally, Mary was out of sight when the doctor came.
He was able to tell Lord Leigh that the fever seemed to
be running its course with no complications, and he
praised Mrs. Heaven's nursing. Whenever Charles proposed going up to look in on his nephew, Mrs. Heaven
had put him off with various excuses: it was better not
to disturb him, or he had just fallen asleep after a fretful
hour.

On the night that the fever broke Charles came in late
for his supper and inquired as usual for Robin. Mrs.
Heaven was able to reassure him joyfully that Robin was
on the mend now and would soon recover. He grinned
with relief and sat down to his supper while she returned to the kitchen. When he had finished and turned
his chair away to face the low-burning fire, he sat contentedly for awhile, giving thanks silently for his nephew's recovery. Poor child, he thought, ill and mother-
less. I must take more time for Robin from now on.

He rose at last to go to his bed, treading quietly up
the stairs not to wake the boy, and on an impulse decided just to look in the door of the boy's room to reassure himself. He reached Robin's room quietly and
softly opened the door.

He stood there for a moment while his brain attempted to admit the inadmissible, and he slowly went
rigid with shock. She was here! Becoming aware of a
presence behind her, Mary turned to smile over her
shoulder at, she thought, Mrs. Heaven. Her eyes widened slowly and her smile faded.

They stared at each other aghast while a long silent
moment passed, each trying to adjust their minds to this

impossible position. At last he motioned with his head, indicating that she should leave the room. She turned back to the bed, slowly released her hand from Robin's, then waited another moment to be sure he would not wake. She then stood up and walked out of the room, her head well up, not looking at Charles Leigh. He followed, closing the door quietly behind them.

Without questions Mary trod at a stately pace down the stairs and into the dining room. He followed stiffly behind, his anger slowly building into righteousness as he realized that she had been smuggled into his house with the help of his servants, specifically Mrs. Heaven. It was bad enough that this impertinent girl had dared to come here again without applying to him for permission, without being forced to realize the treachery of his own servants.

Apart from this was the utter chaos of his feelings for her, roused anew by just the sight of her. During her absence his fury at her lies had helped him hold his feelings in abeyance for the most part, and he was beginning to congratulate himself on his vow to forget her. He now realized he had been premature. However, he was certainly not going to allow those feelings to gain the upper hand with him now, and he stoked up his anger while at the same time cautioning himself not to allow himself to lose his temper. Any display of emotion was not only beneath his dignity, but might possible be too revealing.

Mary was making resolutions also, mostly that she would not allow him to intimidate her anymore, though her pulses pounded at the thought that again he had caught her in the act of deceiving him. It was no doubt true it had been wrong of her to come into his house in such a way, but if she had requested permission, he would have refused it, and she had had to see Robin. That was what she must keep well in the front of her mind: she had come to help Robin, who was more important than his uncle's displeasure. She would simply face that displeasure with a calm dignity and firmness.

He spoke at last. "Perhaps I may know to what we owe the pleasure of this visit, your grace?"

"Naturally I came because of Robin. He has been very ill."

"I assure you that I have been very much aware of that, your grace. I have been in consultation with the doctor every day, and he has assured me that all was going well."

"If you had tended him yourself you would not have been so sanguine about that diagnosis," she replied with an edge of steel in her voice.

"Am I to understand your grace is as advanced in medicine as you are in other arts," he inquired, allowing a tinge of sarcasm to show.

"I believe I know what any woman knows of illness," she said loftily.

"I think, your grace, that Mrs. Heaven might claim as much, perhaps even more, due to her more advanced years."

"No doubt, but he was crying for me continuously."

"I believe I assured your grace before that I was perfectly capable of looking after my own. Your grace is too condescending in interesting herself in my concerns."

"Must you say your grace in every breath?" she flashed out irritably.

"It is your title, I believe. I was only too mortified to have omitted using it when first we met."

"And no doubt, if you had known it, you would have been just as pompous and disagreeable then as you are being now," she cried, forgetting her resolves.

"There is an easy remedy for your complaint if it distresses you so much, your grace. You may leave my house," he ground out, forgetting his own resolves.

"Do you think I am so callous that I could just turn my back on that ailing child?"

"No doubt this comes under the same category as carrying soup to your cottagers and other dependents when they are ill? Well, I am sure we are all most grateful for the thought, but I have no need for your Lady Bountiful charity.''

''You are a heartless beast,'' she cried furiously, and her hand flashed out and slapped his cheek stingingly.

He went white with rage, the print of her hand standing out in vivid red on his cheek. He bowed. ''We are now to be enacted a Cheltenham tragedy, I see, having been treated to your comedic talents on your previous visit,'' he said stiffly.

''How—how d-dare you s-speak to me so—'' she gasped, stuttering with rage.

''No, I am sure you are unused to hearing the word with no bark on it,'' he snapped. ''Well, I am not one of your London puffs, tiptoeing around you with smirks and compliments. I speak as I find. And I have had only lies and deceit from you, your grace!''

Beside herself, her hand flashed out again, but this time he was prepared and caught it in midair, and just as quickly caught her left hand as it was launched. He twisted both her hands behind her back and held them there, and then lost his head completely in her proximity. Her breast was heaving against his own and her lips were not an inch from his. Releasing her hands, he snatched her into his arms and kissed her. His kiss was not gentle. It expressed all his anger and frustrated love for her, and was rough and demanding. She struggled frantically to get her arms between them to push him away.

Then, gradually she ceased to struggle and her lips softened. His kiss became more gentle, probing, and asking rather than demanding, and she answered. Her arms somehow did come between them, but instead of pushing him away, they crept up around his neck to caress the back of his head.

They lost all consciousness of self and time, being only two bodies urgent to be closer. His hand came up to touch her face, her neck, and she allowed it freedom to go where it would, quivering as she welcomed it.

Then suddenly he pushed her away so violently she staggered. "My God! What am I doing?" he gasped.

She did not answer, only staring at him bemusedly, brought too suddenly back to reality to understand anything.

"Forgive me," he said hoarsely, running a hand distractedly through his hair. "I must be mad," he muttered, then turned and stumbled out of the room.

She heard his footsteps cross the hall and the front door opening and closing, and then she was alone. Her knees gave way and she sank slowly to the floor. She did not faint, but was too dazed to think clearly. Then, as memory returned, she bent over and put her face in her hands in despair. The violence of his rejection was what she remembered. Now he despised her completely. She had behaved like one of those loose London women he had accused her of being. Oh, God, she must go away at once!

She dragged herself to her feet and up the stairs, meaning to summon Watts and leave now, even if they had to walk to the village carrying their boxes. When she reached her room, however, she sank in exhaustion onto her bed and knew she had no energy left for such a project.

She forced herself to her feet after a while and went to Robin's room. He was sleeping peacefully, Watts beside him. "Oh, your grace," whispered Watts, rising to curtsy, "I—I heard such loud angry voices I was frightened and came in here. Are you all right?"

"Yes, Watts," said Mary, finding from somewhere the strength to appear calm. "We must leave in the morning very early. Will you go down and ask Mrs. Heaven to send someone into the village with a message to Storrs to have the carriage at the front door by seven?"

"Yes, your grace, but not before I put you into your bed," said Watts firmly. "You look that tired you could drop."

She urged Mary out of the room and, scolding all the

while, got her out of her clothes and into bed. Then she blew out the candle and went away to find Mrs. Heaven.

Mary sank into blackness, her mind happy to escape, exhausted by her days and nights of nursing and the too many rapid changes of extreme emotion in the past hour.

It seemed only moments before Watts was calling her softly out of sleep. " 'Tis gone five, your grace. You'll want time for the boy and your breakfast before the carriage comes."

Mary came awake reluctantly and it was a full minute before memory came rushing back and she closed her eyes again. Surely she had only dreamed it? But even as she thought this, she knew it was no dream. It had actually happened. The bitter quarrel, her physical attack upon him, then his arms . . . Oh, how could she have struck him? She had never struck anyone in her life. In fact, she could not remember ever being really angry with anyone in all her life. Any more than she had ever known those other feelings he had aroused in her.

But she could not bear the memory of that now, She must not. Already her knees were beginning to tremble. She threw back the coverlet and stepped hurriedly out of bed.

"I will wear the blue traveling dress, Watts. Did you bring hot water? Good." She bustled about washing and dressing, assisted by Watts. "Is the child still sleeping?"

"Yes, your grace. You go along now and have a bite of breakfast. I'll stay with the boy till you come up."

Mary went slowly down the back stairs into the kitchen. Mrs. Heaven turned from the stove and they looked at each other silently, for a moment. Then Mary made a little, helpless gesture with her hands, as though to say she could not have prevented what had happened, and her eyes filled with tears.

Mrs. Heaven rushed across the room and gathered her close. "There, there, darlin'. Never you mind. He'll get over it and Robin's well, that's the important thing.

His lordship doesn't mean all he says. He has so much responsibility on his shoulders, poor man, and works so hard. And he was that upset about Robin you wouldn't believe.''

''Yes—yes—well, I must leave. I—will take a cup of chocolate and then go up to say good-bye to Robin. I hope he will not have a relapse—but I cannot stay, Mrs. Heaven.''

''I know, love, I know. Of course you must go. Don't you worry yourself about Robin, either. He's going to be all right for sure now. You just explain to him that you must go and he'll understand. He's as clever as a roomful of monkeys, that one.''

Mary took what comfort she could from Mrs. Heaven's words and managed to force down some toast and a few swallows of chocolate. Then she rose, saying she must go up. She wanted to be there when Robin woke. Mrs. Heaven said she would send up a breakfast tray for him shortly. ''I've sent Betsy out to find a nice, fresh-layed brown egg for his breakfast. You must see he eats it all up. He needs building up now.''

Mary found him still sleeping, dark shadows still staining the delicate skin below his eyes, but a faint tint of healthy rose in his cheeks. Watts rose from the seat by the bed.

''Such a pretty child, eh, your grace? And sleeping so sweetly.''

''Yes, Watts, he is. Have you finished the packing?''

''Only your bed gown and brushes to go in. I'll take the boxes down in a moment.''

She left and Mary sat down by the bed. Presently Robin stirred and woke. He smiled sleepily. ''You are up so early, Mary. Where did you get that dress?''

''I wore it when I came, darling.''

''When you came?'' He looked puzzled. Clearly he had forgotten that she had ever gone away. This was just one of their usual mornings.

''You have forgotten that I went away before. Then you became ill and Mrs. Heaven sent for me to come help nurse you, and now you are all well again and I must go home again.''

"I was very ill?" He pondered this for a moment. "You went away," he said at last, accusingly.

"Yes, I had to go home."

"Why?"

"Because I do not live here. You live here with your Uncle Charles, but my home is in another place and I must go back to it now you are well."

"What if I become ill again?"

"Then I will come to you again," she promised rashly, feeling in her heart that she might possibly never be able to come again. But I will, I will, she cried silently. If he needs me I will come no matter what.

Betsy entered then with a tray and Mary began coaxing him to eat his egg. She told him all about Mallows and her mare and of swimming in the pond, and managed to get most of the boiled egg into him before he pushed her hand away. "No more, Mary, I feel too tired."

"Of course you do, darling. That is because you have had a fever. That takes away your strength. You must sleep and rest a lot, and in several days you will be wanting to be up and running about, you will see."

"Will you be here when I wake up?"

"No, my love, I must go home. I promised my aunt, you see. Now, may I have a nice kiss before you close your eyes?"

"No, I shan't kiss you and I shan't close my eyes either." he said weakly rebellious.

Mary felt her throat tighten, but she swallowed down the rising tears. It would never do to leave him crying. She bent to kiss his cheek, so deliciously cool now, and rose. "That is all right, darling, you needn't. I know how you feel. I will write you tomorrow. I promise. Good-bye, for now."

She turned to the door, but before she reached it, he called out to her, "Mary! I have something for you."

Forcing a smile, she turned. "Have you, darling? What is it?"

"I have a hug," he said, holding out his arms.

She rushed back and took him up against her. His arms went around her neck and he kissed her passionately.

She held him close for a long, sweet moment, then laid him back against his pillows and tucked his coverlet around him. "Thank you, dear Robin. It was the best present I have ever had. Now you will sleep, I know. Learn to write very soon so you can send me a letter. Good-bye, my darling."

Even as she watched, his eyelids fluttered down. She turned to tiptoe away her eyes blinded by tears he must not see.

16

Lady Hyde was appalled by Mary's state when she returned to Mallows. It was not that she behaved irrationally, or that she said anything out of the way; it was more that everything she did seemed the result of effort. There was an artificiality about her every word and gesture that seemed to cover some dreadfulness that she hid carefully away, even from herself. And then, the blank emptiness of her eyes! It would, thought her aunt, have been better if she had raved and cried.

Lady Hyde had inquired immediately about the little boy and been assured that he was now recovering. Mary told her the reasons for his illness and Lady Hyde had been horrified by Miss Herries' conduct, but beyond that Mary did not go. She did not mention Lord Leigh's name, and when Lady Hyde did, Mary went very still—exactly, thought Lady Hyde, like an animal confronted with danger. After a moment, as though her aunt had not spoken, Mary went on to describe Robin's sweet farewell. Lady Hyde surmised from this that her niece would not, or could not, speak of Lord Leigh, and held her peace.

What, however, could have happened? She had understood that he had been perturbed by Mary's previous deception in claiming to be a mere Mary Marshall. Was it possible that he had been, in fact, very angry, and was so still, and had been, on this visit, very cold to Mary? That would, of course, have been unpleasant, but Mary was not the sort of person who became completely unstrung by such situations. Look at how she had handled the problem caused by Emma Fortmain and Mrs. Robeson-Smythe.

Of course, Mary's youth had precluded a great many social unpleasantnesses for her so far, but Lady Hyde had always felt that Mary's normal equitable nature and common sense, combined with the Marshall pride, would carry her through the worst of life's little contretemps. She could not picture Mary in a flaming temper, nor sinking into a black depression, but though she was not imaginative, Lady Hyde did have a sensitivity in regards to her niece, having been with her nearly every waking moment for fourteen years, and was now aware that something quite extraordinarily hurtful had occurred during Mary's short stay at Hatchett's End.

Naturally all of these thoughts did not occur to Lady Hyde at once, but accumulated as the days passed and Mary did not change. She went about her usual occupations, riding, walking, painting and sketching, determinedly making conversation with her aunt and any of her aunt's friends who called. Lady Hyde, however, saw that the old Mary was no longer involved in these things. They were more or less imitations, a recital of lessons learned by rote.

Clearly more than an open unfriendliness had been expressed at Hatchett's End, and naturally, whatever it was had been expressed by Lord Leigh. Was it possible he had been outright rude, or even abusive? No, surely not, for Lord Leigh was a gentleman, after all, and young enough to have had several recent London Seasons, not an old curmudgeon suffering from gout and indigestion who no longer cared whom he insulted.

Then Lady Hyde had a thought that made her feel quite ill for a moment: could the man have made improper advances? She shuddered away from the thought. It could not be! A man who took in his orphaned nephew and worked with his own hands to restore the honor of his family? Such a man could not behave so.

In any case, no such treatment, whether abusiveness or the other, could have turned Mary into an automaton.

She was, after all, a Marshall, and would stand up firmly against anyone who dared to take liberties with her honor or dignity.

Unless—unless she had formed an attachment for him! The thought leapt unbidden and unwelcome into Lady Hyde's mind, and though she fought it, it would not be banished. It would be catastrophic! A penniless earl whose father and brother had gambled away a family fortune! Not that Mary had any need to hold out for a wealthy husband, but still . . . And then the man evidently did not like Mary, or at least disapproved of her, which meant there could be no hope. With the Marshall penchant for giving their hearts for all time, this could only mean disaster. Look at her own brother, Mary's father. Despite Lady Hyde's disclaimers, she knew very well her brother had lost his will to live when he lost his wife. And she herself, a wife at one-and-twenty and a widow at four-and-twenty and never even contemplating remarriage in all these years.

No, no, this must not be allowed to be, she thought, near panic. I must prevent it, somehow. I will take her away—somewhere gay. For the life of her, however, she could not think of where that could be. Then one morning she had a letter from and old friend in Bath, filled with news of parties and balls and concerts and plays. The very thing that was needed! Yes, she would take Mary there as soon as possible.

"Mary," she cried, "let us go away from Mallows for a time. It is so exceedingly dull here now."

"It is pleasant enough, Aunt."

"So is blancmange pleasant, but it is also dull," said Lady Hyde tartly. "I, for one, long for some company, some new faces. Shall we go away? Someplace like Bath? There will be so many people there now, and there are lovely shops and libraries, and, well, many entertainments. Oh, I do think it would do us the world of good."

"As you like, Aunt," replied Mary indifferently.

Lady Hyde bustled away at once to summon the steward, Mr. Shrubsole, to her private sitting room. There she issued orders for him to go today to Bath, "Yes, Mr. Shrubsole, today, at once! We require a house, I think—I do not care for lodgings—say, for a month. I need not tell you it must be in the first style of elegance and in the best part of town. Nothing on top of one of those dreadful hilly streets. We shall need staff, of course—maids, footmen—I shall take Cook and Salcombe from here. And all must be ready no later than a week from today."

When he was gone, she sat on, considering what else must be attended to. Watts was summoned as well as her own abigail to receive orders for assembling the wardrobes. Then she considered the problems of Mr. Goodenow and Miss Foote. There was really no need for them to be taken to Bath—but then she relented about Miss Foote. Poor soul, she had little-enough excitement in her life and she would adore Bath, and she would be no trouble to anyone. There was no need for Mr. Goodenow, however. There was the Laura Chapel to attend in Bath, so his services would not be needed, and he was such a boring man, only interested in his meals.

She summoned Salcombe, Cook, and Miss Foote to inform them of the impending removal to Bath. "You will all travel there the day before her grace and myself to make sure everything is in order before we arrive," she pronounced, and dismissed them. She then dashed off a letter to her friend in Bath to apprise her of the visit, and after some hesitation a more thoughtful letter to Mr. Adrian Fortmain.

There was a great deal of bustling about at Mallows for the next week as all the preparations were put in train. Mary remained indifferent—indeed, nearly oblivious. She was much too inwardly occupied to be interested in anything else. Her first numbness had given away after some days at home to a dull pain, as though deep inside she had sustained a fatal wound that still bled. It took some time for her to acknowledge the pain, and still more to realize its cause. This did not occur to her in a blinding revelation, but as a gradual acceptance of knowledge, almost as one slowly learns a foreign language.

She was in love with Charles Leigh—had, perhaps, been in love with him since she had first come to know him well, in those intimate meetings after his supper when she had taken tea with him.

She loved a man who despised her wholeheartedly, even more now than before, since she had allowed him such a great freedom with her person. No well-brought-up young lady would have given way to him so quickly—or at all! She still did not understand what had happened to her to cause her to behave so badly. She had first been in the grip of a greater anger than she had ever experienced, and then, within the space of a moment, she was in his arms and feeling emotions even more unimaginable. At least she had heard of anger, even if she had never truly felt it. The other thing—the feeling of one's bones melting, of actually feeling one's blood rushing through one's veins, of the total rapture in the experience of such closeness to another human being—these were all too exotic to even have been imagined before. Had other people felt as she had, or was it something wicked that good people were never subjected to? Should she pray for forgiveness? If there were only someone to consult . . . But there was no one but her aunt, and she knew she would never have the courage to confess such feelings to Lady Hyde.

If it were wickedness, then she had compounded it many times over, for she could not prevent herself from remembering it, experiencing it, again and again, and always the memory was accompanied by the same melting feelings, the rapture she had felt in his arms. It was only in those few ecstatic seconds of memory that the pain eased. In spite of that momentary relief, however, she hoped very much that those feelings would fade and be lost, for she felt there could be no recovery until they had. Not that she would ever be able to stop loving Charles Leigh. Though she had never loved before, she sensed somehow that her love for him would never release her to love anyone else.

Charles had not escaped suffering either, for, on top of his love for her, he now had quilt gnawing away at his conscience. Never in his wildest imaginings would it have occurred to him that he could behave to a lady, or even someone not a lady, the way he had behaved to Mary Marshall. No, not just Mary Marshall, but to the Duchess of Runceford! Only a princess of the blood could have been worse!

And what was he to do about it? He had stumbled out of the house that fatal night, hardly aware of what he was doing nor where he was going. He had walked the night through, but no solution had presented itself to him. The thought of confronting her in the morning with an apology was unthinkable. Not that he did not want to apologize, but he simply felt that face to face with her he would not be able to form the words. He had returned to the house while she still slept, to have his breakfast and escape to the fields, feeling not only an ungentlemanly swine but a coward as well.

Since her departure the days had passed while he attempted to compose a letter of apology to her, but everything he wrote sounded stupid and pompous, for he could only address her as your grace. To apologize for treating her as an accredited rakehell treated a kitchen maid while addressing her thus seemed impossible. He tore at his hair in frustration after every attempt and always ended up ripping the paper to shreds and throwing it angrily onto the fire.

"Damnation!" he roared aloud one night at another failed attempt. "Why must she be a duchess, of all things on earth?"

Yes, there was the fence he could not take, no matter how much he loved her. He could not go, hat in hand, with an honorable proposal of marriage, as he would have to any other girl after taking the liberty of kissing her. She was a duchess! She, her relatives, and everyone on earth would think he was only after her money to repair his own estates, and after the rank and power that would come to him from her title. He saw now that all his anger at her was the result of learning of her title after falling in love with her. The scaldingly hurtful things he had said to her were the result of realizing he could never have her. He might as well expect to be given the hand of Princess Charlotte in marriage.

He had only one solace, and that was in Robin. He had kept his resolve to spend more time with the boy, hearing his lessons every day after dinner, and several times taking him out to the fields with him. On Sundays he took him for rides, sitting up before him on the saddle, or to the pond to fish. Robin blossomed with this attention and chattered away confidently to his uncle about everything, including any news in his letters from Mary. It was thus that Charles learned of Mary's stay in Bath.

There was no comfort for him in these reports of Mary's doings. It was like probing a sore tooth with one's tongue, but he could not bring himself to cut the boy off. Alone at night, he tormented himself with pictures of her dancing and flirting with the cream of the *ton* in Bath.

On one of his Sunday rides with Robin he met the Herries in their carriage. He bowed and lifted his hat, but Robin, after sighting Miss Herries, scrambled about in the saddle to throw his arms about his uncle's neck in a stranglehold, his little body trembling with fright. Charles rode on quickly.

Miss Herries was indignant. "Of all the stupidly babyish things I ever saw! He should not be indulged in that way. Behaving as though he saw an ogre! Lord Leigh spoils the child and has become very rude himself. Not even speaking, for heaven's sake!" Her papa told her shortly that she had brought it all on her own head and he wanted to hear no more about it, and Miss Herries told him he was a cruel papa who did not care what became of her and never took her side in anything.

* * *

Miss Fortmain was also being indignant at about the same time. She was sitting with her mama when her two younger sisters came in and informed her slyly that their cousin, Adrian Fortmain, was visiting in Bath. They enjoyed their sister's consternation at this news. They knew, as everyone in the neighborhood knew, that the Duchess of Runceford and her aunt and household had removed to Bath and that the news of Adrian being there also would torment Emma. She deserved it, they thought, for she had always been unkind to them from the nursery on, pinching and slapping them when no one was by to see, and running to Nurse or Mama with tales that inevitably resulted in punishment for them.

To Adrian Fortmain, Lady Hyde's news came with such exquisite pleasure it was nearly painful. He had received no answers to the two letters he had written Mary since returning to his home, and he had begun to despair. He was no longer in any doubt at all about his feelings for her. He loved her entirely. The young lady he had thought for years he would someday give his heart to had faded to nothingness in comparison.

Mary's unresponsiveness had only whetted his feelings, until he had begun to feel that he must return and be near her, if if meant staying in an inn nearby. But then he knew that word would instantly reach his uncle's ears, and little as he felt for the man, he had no inclination to insult him in such a way, for he knew his uncle would feel it so. Then, in desperation, he had even considered going to stay again with his uncle just on the chance of being able to see Mary occasionally, but then he thought of his Cousin Emma and knew he could not do it. The problem had seemed insoluble until he received Lady Hyde's letter. There could be no mistaking her intention in writing it. She wanted him to come to Bath. In intimating so much, she said a great deal more: that she approved of his suit and would support it. He wasted no time in setting off for Bath, his hopes very high indeed.

Bath itself was in a state of mild hysteria over the impending visit of the Duchess of Runceford. Word had spread rapidly after Mr. Shrubsole's appearance, not only over the town itself but all over England as friends had written friends, and many people who turned up their noses at Bath as a fusty old place filled with fusty old people decided that a course of waters would do them all the good in the world. Once it became known which house had been taken for her grace, there was a continual parade of residents and visitors past the mansion on Laura Place only to stare at the house. The more enterprising ladies left their cards to await the illustrious arrival. Those who had caught glimpses of her at the play or in the stores of London became fonts of information, and Mary's reputation for beauty and elegance grew with every telling, while those who had actually been introduced to her found their popularity increased a dozenfold as they were besieged with requests for introductions for themselves. The town literally hummed with anticipation.

17

The Duchess of Runceford entered Bath with all the panoply its citizens could have desired. The elegant traveling coach, the ducal arms emblazoned on the doors, with Storrs and George up, two grooms perched behind, and no less than six outriders, all in the Runceford livery of blue and buff, was just as hoped for.

Since the town was packed with visitors, not a few were privileged to view this gratifying spectacle, and little else was discussed for the rest of the day. The general consensus was that the duchess seemed haughty, staring straight before her, totally uninterested in looking about her at the town she had never before visited. Most of them did not even notice Lady Hyde beside her. If they had, they would have seen that she showed the liveliest interest in everything and even espied several old acquaintances to bow to.

They swept up before an imposing mansion on Laura Place, and on the doorstep, almost before the wheels stopped turning, was a twittering Miss Foote, Salcombe hovering behind, keeping a sharp eye on three new footmen lined up next to him. Mary smiled briefly at Miss Foote and Salcombe and entered the house, with Lady Hyde behind her dispensing orders and counterorders and creating much confusion.

"Hand out her grace's jewel case. No, not that one, fool, the black one. Watts—where is Watts? Oh, you are here. Well, don't just stand there, girl. Take the case and show her grace up to her room at once. Salcombe, can you please ask those footmen to stop stumbling about getting in everyone's way?''

In the hall she glanced briefly at the brimming tray of cards and invitations. ''I shall have a look at those tomorrow. Ah, Mr. Shrubsole,'' she said to the steward as he came forward to greet her, ''very nice, very nice indeed. Just what I had in mind. You must have had a great deal of difficulty procuring it.''

''None at all, your ladyship, I assure you.''

''But the town seemed very full when we came through.''

''It was not so a week ago, your ladyship,'' he replied with a smile.

''How extraordinary. Have all these visitors arrived within the week, then?''

''Er, not quite a week, my lady. Say in the past five days. Since the day after I took this house, to be exact.''

''Do you mean to say . . . ?''

''Yes, my lady. Word got about, you see. Residents wrote to their friends, that sort of thing. The town is filled with people come just to get a glimpse of her grace, as well as fortune-hunters by the score. I know I need not warn your ladyship to be very careful who her grace is allowed to meet?''

''I hope I know my duty, Mr. Shrubsole,'' she replied repressively.

''Just so, your ladyship. Will there be anything else?''

''Not for the moment. I had thought to send you back to Mallows straightaway, but perhaps it will be as well for you to remain here for some days until we are settled properly.''

''Very good, your ladyship.'' Mr. Shrubsole bowed and melted away and Lady Hyde turned to Salcombe, just coming in from overseeing the unloading of the carriage.

''Well, Salcombe, are there any problems?''

''Cook has expressed some displeasure with the, er, arrangements in the kitchen, my lady, and also with one of the new kitchen maids.''

"Tell her she must just make the best of it. As for the kitchen maid, if she does not suit, get rid of her and find another, for heaven's sake. Must I be bothered with such things?"

"Very good, my lady."

"We shall dine alone tonight, and we will not be receiving visitors today or tomorrow."

"Very good, my lady."

Lady Hyde, accompanied by Miss Foote, then made a tour of the lower rooms before proceeding upstairs, well-satisfied with all her arrangements. After a very comfortable night, she sailed into the breakfast room on the following morning filled with energy. Miss Foote was there to greet her.

"Good morning, Miss Foote. Her grace is not down yet, I see."

"No, my lady, but she was very tired, perhaps, after the long journey. I myself felt quite fatigued when—"

"Pooh! Not so very long a journey as that. I scarcely noticed it myself, but then, I do not believe young people today have so much stamina as we had. Ah, there you are my dear. I hope you slept well?"

"Good morning, Aunt. Good morning, Miss Foote. Very well, I thank you," said Mary, seating herself at the table.

Lady Hyde was busily sorting through the large pile of visiting cards and invitations that had awaited their arrival. "Heavens, how very gay they are in Bath, to be sure," she exclaimed in gratified tones. "We shall be very busy, Mary, if we accept even half of these. I had thought Brighton was the fashionable place to be, now the Prince Regent has taken it up so, but it seems to me half the *ton* must be here."

"Must we accept all of those invitations?"

"Oh, dear me, no. I shall only accept from people I know. Lady Besborough and Lady Graves' musical evenings. Mrs. Frobisher-Coke's dinner and also Lady Cannon's. Then Lady Parrish is making up a party to go to Sydney Gardens. That should be amusing. The

rest are from strangers. Rather pushing, perhaps, but
we shall see. Now, when you have finished your breakfast, we will walk to the Pump Room. Everyone walks
here, or takes chairs. But it is so near, there is no reason
not to have the exercise.''

''The Pump Room? But whatever for?''

''Why, to drink the waters, child. Everyone must
drink the waters in Bath. Besides, that is where everyone goes in the mornings. It is what one does in Bath.''

''Oh,'' was Mary's only comment to this. She did
not demur, however, when her aunt suggested that she
change into a walking dress, and at eleven o'clock the
two ladies emerged from the front door of Laura Place
and proceeded toward the Pump Room, followed by
Miss Foote carrying extra shawls and two umbrellas in
case of rain.

The room was thronged with people, many sitting on
the benches provided, dutifully sipping their glass of
water, but the mass strolled about the room in animated
conversation. An instant hush fell over the room as Mary
and Lady Hyde entered, but then the volume of noise
rose by many decibels as everyone bent toward their
neighbors to discuss the duchess's looks and dress.

Lady Graves and Mrs. Frobisher-Coke came hurrying
forward importantly, trailed by two fashionably dressed
young men. ''My dear Augusta!'' cried Lady Graves.
She and Mrs. Frobisher-Coke swept curtsies to the
duchess, murmuring their pleasure at meeting her again.

Mary murmured back. She vaguely remembered the
women from London.

''I am sure, your grace remembers my nephew, Henry
Cooms,'' said Lady Graves.

Mr. Graves bowed profoundly.

Mrs. Frobisher-Coke's son, Sylvester, was more enterprising when his turn came. He reached for Mary's
hand and pressed a kiss onto it as he bowed and rose
to smile warmly into her eyes. ''I cannot hope that you
remember the dance you so graciously awarded me at
the Brumbie's ball last season, your grace. A matter of

small moment to you, I am sure, but a moment I shall never forget, I assure you.''

Mary gently removed her hand from his grasp and said something noncommittal. Lady Hyde and the two older ladies had a great many bits of information to exchange about mutual friends, and the party strolled along together. The young gentlemen fetched glasses of water for Mary and her aunt and then took their places on either side of her and followed their elders around the room. As they progressed, Lady Hyde greeted other ladies who came forward to claim acquaintance and to be seen making their curtsies to the young duchess, who smiled graciously on everyone as required and tried to sip her water without making unbecoming expressions of distaste.

She couldn't help wondering what on earth could have persuaded her aunt that it would be a good thing to come to Bath. All these antiquated old gossips and boring callow young men—and all those many more miles separating her from Charles Leigh, she admitted to herself. Not that it would have mattered in the least if she had been encamped on his very doorstep. He would still despise her. This thought, which she had been holding at bay for days now, brought on such a fit of the dismals that it was all she could do to keep her countenance until Lady Hyde at last announced that they must leave now.

''Really,'' said Lady Hyde as they made their way home, ''poor dear Lady Graves and Mrs. Frobisher-Coke are so very obvious. They clearly sent for those young men the moment they heard you were to be here.''

''They are only boys! Surely those women could not think—''

''They are of an age with you, my dear.''

''But still they are only green boys.''

This being indisputable, Lady Hyde wisely held her peace. Instead, she silently speculated on when she might hope to see Mr. Fortmain. At least he was no green boy. She had made sure he would be here before them and had been much surprised, and not a little annoyed, not to encounter him, as she had planned, in the Pump Room this very morning. Could she have been mistaken in his ardor?

"Why—why, there is Mr. Fortmain," exclaimed Mary.

Lady Hyde looked up and there indeed was Adrian Fortmain approaching them. He removed his hat and bowed.

"Good morning, your grace. Good morning, Lady Hyde. Since you are coming away, I presume you have already visited the Pump Room and taken your obligatory glass of water?"

"Indeed we have, Mr. Fortmain. We are not slugabeds. Why the day is half over."

"Oh, dear, I am sorry to have missed it."

"You should be grateful," said Mary with a little moue of distaste.

He laughed. "Yes, I have heard of it, but its curative powers are formidable, I am told."

"I think it depends upon what ails you," retorted Mary with more spirit that her aunt had heard her use since she had returned from Hatchett's End. She congratulated herself on her foresight in writing to Mr. Fortmain. There was nothing like an ardent admirer waiting upon one to cure any unhappiness one might feel at the disapprobation of another. Not that she supposed for a moment that Lord Leigh could be classified as Mary's admirer from all she had heard, but still . . .

"Do you make a long stay in Bath, Mr. Fortmain?" Mary asked.

"Well, that depends . . ." he said, and then paused.

"Upon what ails you," she said with a smile.

"Exactly so," he said, bending upon her such a particular look she colored slightly.

Mr. Fortmain accompanied them back to Laura Place, declined to remain for a cold luncheon, but accepted their invitation to return to take dinner with them and

accompany them to the Lower Rooms, where dancing
was to be held that evening.

"Oh, Aunt, dancing?" protested Mary when they
were alone.

"Why not, I should like to know? You adore dancing."

"My mood now, however, is not quite in tune with
dancing."

"Nonsense! That is exactly why you should do so—
to shake you out of this mood. It is the very thing!"

Mary was not at all sure that it was, but she disliked
disagreeing with her aunt over so small an issue. After
all, what did it matter? And perhaps it would help her
to forget.

So Adrian Fortmain came to dinner and escorted the
ladies to the assembly in the Lower Rooms. Their entrance caused a swelling excitement to spread over the
guests assembled. Mr. King, the master of ceremonies,
came hurrying forward to welcome them and lead them,
with many bows and protestations of the honor, to a
sofa.

Mary stood up twice with Mr. Fortmain and several
times with other young gentlemen who were brought up
by relatives to be introduced and try their hand at winning a duchess. She did not enjoy dancing with these
young men, for she found them either overconfident or
tongue-tied, but she did enjoy dancing with Adrian
Fortmain, whose manner was polished just enough to
make her comfortable and whose conversation was
lighthearted and witty. And she did find that for those
few moments she forgot the oppression hanging over
her.

Lady Hyde watched complacently and felt that she
had hit upon the very thing in bringing Mary here and
making sure that Mr. Fortmain came also. As she stood
up with him, Mary's countenance was quite animated,
her eyes bright, the color in her cheeks matching exactly
the blossom pink of her gown. Lady Hyde was convinced now that her worst fears concerning Charles

Leigh had been mere fantasies. No doubt he had been cold and disapproving and Mary's nose had been put out of joint by his treatment and she had been sulking as a result. A girl in Mary's position, after all, rarely encountered disapproval head-on and would be too green to know how to handle such treatment. A little flirtation with Adrian Fortmain as well as the admiration of several other young men while they were in Bath, then the Season would be upon them again and they would return to London. By that time Charles Leigh's unpleasantness would be forgotten.

The dancing in the Lower Rooms ended at eleven and Mary declared herself ready for bed as soon as Mr. Fortmain bade them good night. Lady Hyde was looking forward to bed also. As she sank into her pillows, she had time for only one long self-satisfied sigh before she fell asleep.

It was some hours later when some continuous sound pulled her relentlessly from sleep. She tried to tell herself it was but part of some dream she had been having, and turned over impatiently, snuggling the covers comfortably about her shoulders. The sound followed her, however, and prevented sleep from returning. At last she turned upon her back and lay listening intently. Yes, she thought at last, it is very definitely someone crying, unless the house were haunted. That daunting thought sent a chill of fear over her, but in a moment she fearlessly sat up, lit her candle, and felt about for her slippers. She studied her little pocket watch on the bedside table and found it was close to three in the morning. What an hour to begin crying and no doubt waking the whole household, she thought crossly, shrugging herself into her dressing gown. One of the maids perhaps, but then how could she hear it so clearly? The maids were upstairs. She took up her candle and stumped out into the hall.

The sound of sobbing was clearer now and its direction unmistakable. It was coming from Mary's room, directly across the hall from her own. She crossed to

the door and applied her ear to the panel. Yes, it was
Mary. Without hesitation Lady Hyde opened the door
and crossed to the bed. "Mary, my dear, whatever is
the matter," she said anxiously, holding the candle
higher to light up the bed.

Mary lay on her side, her eyes closed, tears streaming
down into the pillow, which was already soaked.

"Mary, Mary, tell me what this is all about?" demanded Lady Hyde, plumping down upon the side of
the bed and depositing the candle on the table. Mary
made no response to her aunt's voice or to the distur-
bance created as the heavy body of her aunt sat down.
Lady Hyde studied her for a long moment, puzzled. It
slowly became apparent to her that Mary was asleep.
Dear Lord! The child was crying heartbrokenly in her
sleep! Lady Hyde could not decide for a moment what
it would be best to do, but it became too painful to
herself to listen to such an outpouring of unhappiness,
even it was only caused by a bad dream. It would be
better, surely, to wake her from it. She put out a hand
and shook Mary's shoulder.

"Mary. Mary, dearest child, wake up now, wake up.
It is only a bad dream. Wake up, dearest."

Mary came awake with a gasp, her dark-green eyes
wide and shimmering in their pools of tears. With a
moan she threw herself upon her aunt, her arms about
Lady Hyde's neck, crying more piteously than ever.

"Dearest, please control yourself," begged Lady
Hyde, holding her close. "It was only a bad dream. It
is all over now."

"Y-yes, all over. All o-over. He c-could never love
me n-now. Oh, what s-shall I d-do? W-what shall I do?"

Lady Hyde felt the hairs on her scalp rise in forebod-
ing at these words. "Mary, darling, please calm yourself. You cannot know what you are saying. It was only
a dream."

"Yes. He was there and I kept trying to explain, but
he—he turned away. He is disgusted with me. First the
lying to him and then the other. Oh, why did I let him?"

Frantic now, Lady Hyde hardly dared believe her ears. Could the child still be asleep? What dreadful admissions were these? Surely she could not mean she had . . . they had . . . ? "Mary, what happened? Please tell me everything so that I will know what must best be done," she said gently, caressing the damp curls away from Mary's wet face.

And slowly a much-tangled tale was recited, interrupted by frequent bouts of speechless weeping: the first stay at Hatchett's End, the intimate evenings over the teacups, her admiration for the hardworking earl. Then how she had missed him when she had been forced to leave and come home, and how they had met and quarreled on the second visit, how she had struck him and then found herself in his arms and had responded to his lovemaking. Then, worst of all, how he had pushed her away in disgust and left her and she had realized how very much in love with him she was, and had been for longer than she had known.

Lady Hyde listened in horrified silence, her hand automatically smoothing the soft hair away from Mary's face. When the halting narrative at last came to an end, she could only whisper, "Oh, dear God." She held Mary close and rocked her back and forth as one comforts a child. It was not so terrible as she had thought when Mary first woke and uttered those fearful words. The very worst had not happened, and yet the situation was as bad as it could be. Lady Hyde's fears were realized. The child had given her heart to an impossible man: impoverished, bitter, no doubt, at the empty inheritance left him by his wastrel relatives, rigidly moral and judgmental, and clearly not the least in love with Mary.

"Mary, dearest," she began tentatively, "nothing is more fatal to happiness than for a woman to allow herself to form an attachment before she is sure of a gentleman's feelings."

"I did not allow it—it simply was there," whispered Mary, with the long, shuddering sigh of receding sobs.

"Yes, yes, I understand, but when one realizes it is hopeless, one must take control of one's feelings or there can never be any happiness."

"I have tried—I know I must—ever since I came back. I try not to think of him, I don't want to, but then I dream of him, like tonight. Oh, Aunt, I do love him so much."

"Yes, I see that you do, but you must make up your mind that what cannot be must be done without. It is hard to believe, I know, but these feelings will fade without nurture, if you give it time and work at it very hard, as surely as a flower, untended, will die. You must look to someone else for your happiness, determined to have it."

"But how can I? I could never give my heart to anyone else now."

"Give your hand and your heart will follow, you may be sure. Once married, with a family of your own about you, and you will find you love your husband as thoroughly as possible."

"Oh, no! I could never, never—" Mary protested wildly, the tears starting to roll down her cheeks.

"Then you condemn yourself to an empty life," replied her aunt remorselessly. "The Runceford title is to die out. Your father's trust that your own son would inherit it is to be forgotten."

"Oh, please, Aunt, do not—"

"I must. You should realize all these things now. It is not too late to change, if you will it to be so. It is not as thought you had been through a long courtship. One kiss was exchanged when passions were roused by anger, and naturally, for an inexperienced girl like you it would have a profound effect, but you are allowing it to take over your every thought, waking and sleeping. You must fight this thing, Mary. You owe it to yourself and to your poor father to look elsewhere for love and to marry."

This forceful speech touched Mary. She sat up and asked for a handkerchief. Lady Hyde brought one out from her pocket and handed it to her. She was wise enough to say no more.

Mary blew her nose and mopped her wet face and for long moments did not speak. At last she said, ''I suppose I am very foolish.''

''No, no, my dearest child. You are only young. Everyone must go through these unhappy experiences in order to grow. You will come about, I know. You are a Marshall, after all.''

''Yes, I will come about. I must.''

''And you will. Just concentrate upon those about you and you will find someone else who attracts you. There is Mr. Fortmain, and next Season in London someone equally delightful may appear and you will find this was all just a green girl's first infatuation.''

''Yes, Aunt. Thank you. I will sleep now, I think.''

Lady Hyde kissed her tenderly, took up her candle, and left the room. As she climbed wearily back into her bed, she prayed silently that her last words to her niece might indeed be true, though she could not be easy about every argument she had used. Had it not been unkind to throw her duty in her face in such a way? But sometimes one is forced to be cruel to be kind, and anything that stopped this infatuation before it took a real hold on the girl's heart would be vindicated in the end if the girl found herself at last able to give her heart where it was wanted, and achieved happiness with another man. It was all very well saying the Marshalls had a propensity for giving their hearts once and for all time, as had she herself and the dear duke, bless him, but she had had, at least, four years of requited love, and her brother his adoring wife and child. Poor Mary had had nothing yet, and would have nothing if she persisted in this foolishness. Yes, it was much better to stamp it out now, but still . . .

18

Mary fell into deep, seemingly dreamless, sleep and woke late. For a few moments she stared blankly around her, unable to remember where she was in the unfamiliar room. Then everything flooded back into her mind and the old oppression fell upon her spirits. She allowed it to have its way with her for a time, but then Watts came in, followed by a maid carrying a tray with Mary's morning chocolate, and she had to sit up. This brought about a change in her drifting thoughts. This will never do, she thought. Aunt is right. I have been handed a sacred trust by Papa and I cannot allow myself to mope around crying for the moon as I have been doing. I must get on with my life and forget Charles Leigh. I must marry and produce the next Duke of Runceford!

It was not necessary for her to run through the list of all the men she had met who could possibly be considered. So far there was only Adrian Fortmain, the only man she liked and enjoyed being with. But could she marry him? Her whole self shrank from the thought, but she knew very well she would react in the same way to everyone except . . . She resolutely turned her mind away from his name. No more of that—ever again.

Very well, then, she would, for now, concentrate upon being more open to Mr. Fortmain and hope that she might develop an attachment for him. To await some future gallant to sweep her off her feet was ridiculous. It was too late for that. She knew very well that her heart had been irretrievably given already, but if Adrian Fortmain was willing to accept her in that knowledge, she could hope that real affection and caring would grow after marriage, as her aunt had said it would.

She practiced a variety of pleasant expressions in the mirror before she went down to breakfast, and when she met Lady Hyde's somewhat apprehensive expression, she was able to flash her a bright smile, which reassured her aunt completely.

She's come about, thought Lady Hyde triumphantly. I should never have doubted that Marshall spirit.

Later they dressed and set off for the Pump Room, where they found Adrian Fortmain lingering near the door, obviously awaiting their arrival. Mary gave him one of her new, determined smiles and he responded with one so radiantly spontaneous she felt ashamed.

"I was determined to be beforehand today," he said, "after being called a sluggard yesterday."

"Now, now, sir, you took me up too sharp," chided Lady Hyde gaily. "I hope I was not so rude?"

"I am sure you could not be," he said gallantly.

"Then you have forgotten a certain assembly at home," retorted Mary with a sidelong glance at her aunt.

"Cheek," responded Lady Hyde mildly. "Shall we take a glass of the waters?"

"I will take one, but I will not drink it," said Mary.

"But, child, it is really so good for . . . Ah, good morning, Lady Besborough."

Lady Besborough curtsied to Mary, bowed to Lady Hyde, and turned an inquiring look upon Mr. Fortmain.

"Oh, yes, do allow me to present Mr. Adrian Fortmain to you, Lady Besborough. He is an old friend from Mallows. His relatives are our neighbors."

"Ah, those Fortmains. You will be the heir," stated Lady Besborough, who did not believe in beating about the bush. Adrian bowed in acknowledgment. "Perhaps you will care to come to my musical evening tomorrow, Mr. Fortmain? At eight, Milsom Street. Anyone will give you my direction. You will be there I hope, your grace?" Without waiting for a reply she stalked off.

"Caroline Besborough was always the rudest woman I ever met," commented Lady Hyde.

"Will you be going to her musical evening?" asked Mr. Fortmain.

"Oh, of course. She may be rude but she gives lovely parties. Besides, we were bosom bows when we were girls."

"Good heavens," Mary said with a small shudder. "Must we stay here, Aunt? It really is so dull."

They left at once and Mary didn't so much as notice Mr. Frobisher-Coke and Mr. Cooms just coming in the door. They turned to stare after her in dismay. Both had received strict orders to attend the Pump Room in good time this morning in order to meet the duchess again, but had sat up over their wine until a late hour the previous evening.

"Do you think you will like Bath, your grace?" asked Mr. Fortmain.

"Oh, I am determined to do so. But I shall miss my exercise."

"Why should you do so? There are lovely rides in every direction, as well as good walks."

"Well, I did not bring my mare—"

"Nonsense, Mary," interrupted her aunt. "If you want your mare it shall be brought here at once. I will speak to Shrubsole about it when we reach home."

"Perhaps in the meantime you would like to take a turn in the Crescent?" suggested Mr. Fortmain.

For the first three days after Mary's mare had arrived in Bath she had wonderful rides with Adrian Fortmain, accompanied by a groom, of course. He had found rides outside Bath where she could gallop full-tilt to her heart's content. Then the other young men, most of whom had been ordered to Bath to try their luck for her fortune, learned of this activity and began to request the pleasure of joining her on her rides. Soon there were seven young gallants trotting in her train, and the lovely gallops became less easy of achievement. Apart from this, she felt

she had become something of a spectacle trotting along
the streets of Bath with such an entourage.

To counteract this she invited several young ladies she
met on her round of parties to join her, and at last it
became a party of young people who joined together for
a morning ride each day.

Adrian Fortmain seemed to take it all in good part,
whether the earlier "spectacle" or the later riding party.
He always held to his place at Mary's side regardless of
the jostling among the other young men for her attention,
and though always perfectly courteous, he never left Mary
for the charms of the other young ladies when they joined
the party. He was the clear favorite and this caused some
grumbling among the other disgruntled swains.

Adrian was very happy to see that her spirits seemed
to have improved since he had first seen her when he
came to Bath. He thought then her quiet, abstracted air
the result of some bout of ill health for which she had
been brought here to recover from, never dreaming of
the real reason. After all, how should he? He had never
heard any name mentioned in connection with hers, nor
seen any sign of preference on her part stronger than
that she had shown to him at Mallows and here. He
began to feel extremely hopeful about his chances.

He was too wise, however, to begin making love to
her while she was in low health or until he had been
given a clear sign from her that she would accept it. She
certainly could not doubt his own feelings, and in the
meantime it was best to allow her to get to know him
well and feel safe in his company.

His antecedents made him acceptable to the hostesses
of Bath, and his intimacy with the family at Laura Place
made him sought after, so that he was sure to be found
at any entertainment attended by the duchess and Lady
Hyde. Before many weeks had passed it became a fore-
gone conclusion among the matrons who arbitrated such
matters that the duchess meant to have Mr. Fortmain,
and several young men left Bath in a dudgeon.

Mary kept her resolve not to mope and entered as

lightheartedly as she could into the entertainments offered. There were dinner parties and parties to Sydney
Gardens to see the fireworks and listen to the band,
dancing at the Lower and Upper Rooms, concerts and
carriage parties to Wells, as well as morning attendance
at the Pump Room, visits to Duffields or Meyler and
Sons to look over the new books or read the newspa-
pers. Every day seemed packed to its fullest with activity, and she had, in fact, very little time to mope. She
was aware that her acceptance of Adrian Fortmain's
continual company was by way of being a passive acceptance of his suit. She did not encourage him in any
other way, though she did allow a light flirtation on his
part. She dreaded the moment she knew very well must
surely come, but stood by her resolve to be open to
Adrian Fortmain, and if he would have her when he
knew the true state of her heart, she would marry him
and try to be a good wife to him.

Adrian had begun to feel that the time had come for
more positive action and contrived one day to lure her
into a race to detach her from their party. In a few moments they had left them all far behind. He allowed her
to get ahead at the beginning, but then took the lead and
pointed out a tree standing apart in the distance as the
end of the race. She nodded and urged her mare on, but
she could not catch him up, though he beat her only by
inches. They sat laughing and gasping for breath for a
moment before he dismounted and held up his arms to
assist her down. She hesitated a moment, but then put
her hands on his shoulders. He held her by the waist and
lifted her down, then continued to hold her, looking into
her eyes. She flushed under the intensity of his look and
lowered her eyes.

"My dear," he murmured.

"No! No, do not—" she began wildly.

"Yes. I must. I will. You must surely be aware of my
feelings. I have loved you for so long without speaking.
I hardly dared to hope. I know it will be thought pre-

sumptuous by most people to hope to make you my wife, but I do so hope. Will you marry me, my darling love?''

''Oh, Mr. Fortmain, I—I wish—''

''Yes, dearest, what do you wish?'' he asked eagerly, his arms going about her to pull her closer.

She pulled away, but gently. ''I wish that I did love you, Mr. Fortmain, for I like you so very well.''

''Ah, I will teach you to love me, my angel. I know you will love me. I know it,'' he cried exultantly. He pulled her into his arms again. She allowed him to embrace her, but turned her head aside when he attempted to kiss her so that his lips only brushed her cheek. ''Say yes, Mary dear, say you will marry me,'' he urged softly.

''I cannot say yes. I do not know. I—''

''Then say you will think about it. Will you, my love? Will you think of it and give me an answer as soon as you can? I do not know how I will manage to exist until then, but I will wait any time you say if you will only give me hope. May I ask you again in a week? Two weeks? Oh, beautiful one, do not make me wait any longer than that!''

She smiled a little at the plaintive note in this last plea. ''Very well, Mr. Fortmain. In two weeks I will answer you.''

By the time she had returned to Laura Place she regretted her answer. How could she decide in two weeks? Even in two months? But this was the wrong attitude, and she was well aware of it. She must be open to his love and believe seriously that she would learn to love him. With this thought she threw herself across her bed and cried until she could cry no more. After a time she sat up, dried her eyes, and sat down at the dainty escritoire with which her room was furnished. It was the hour before dinner, sacred to her for writing her daily letter to Robin.

Not entirely unaware of a deep but not consciously acknowledged motive, she wrote to Robin of the day's event, adding rather ingenuously, ''. . . my aunt is very anxious for me to marry, and since Mr. Fortmain has offered for me and I do not dislike him, I have told him I will give him my answer in two weeks."

That evening she told her aunt of the proposal. "Oh! Oh, my dear child, I am so very glad!"

"I have not said yes, Aunt," said Mary with a sad little laugh. "I have only said that I would think of it and give him my answer in two weeks."

"Well, I am sure that is very wise, but I could have wished for a more romantic answer from you. But still . . ."

"Oh, romance," Mary said, brushing away the notion, "you know very well this is not a romance, Aunt. My heart can never be given before my hand now."

Lady Hyde sighed. "Well, my dear, and what will your answer be?"

"I have not decided, Aunt. I have two weeks to think about it."

It was long before she slept that night. They had gone out after dinner to a musical evening at Mrs. Frobisher-Coke's and there had met Adrian Fortmain. His face had lit up when they entered and he had hurried to her side. He took Mary's hand and pressed it, giving her such a look of ardor that she blushed, knowing every eye in the room was upon them. He stayed by her side all the evening and escorted the ladies home, walking beside Mary's sedan chair.

She retired to bed to stare sleeplessly at the ceiling for hours. She could not help being touched by the love that shone out of his eyes, but her conscience smote her. Was it fair to encourage such a fine, true gentleman to hope when she had not yet told him the whole truth? Would such a man want her still under such conditions? Nevertheless, she decided at last, she had no choice in fairness. She must tell him immediately, not keep him dangling for two weeks then saying yes if he were willing to take someone who loved another man. When that decision was made, she turned over and fell asleep at once.

The next morning, when he came to take her riding, she asked him to step into the library for a moment first.

He followed her apprehensively, afraid she had already decided against him.

"Mr. Fortmain," she began resolutely, "yesterday you honored me by asking me to be your wife. I told you I would give you an answer in two weeks, but now I realize I was guilty of—of a lack of openness with you. I have a confession I must make before this goes any further." She turned away from his unhappy look. What could it be? he wondered. Madness in the family? A fatal illness only now discovered in herself?

"Please do not turn away from me, my darling. Whatever it is we will face it together. You know you may tell me anything. It will make no difference in my love for you," he said fervently.

"I am very much afraid that it may do so. I . . . The fact is my heart has already been given to another," she said bluntly at last.

He stared in stunned surprise. At last he faltered, "But—but then, why . . . I do not understand."

"There can never be any happiness in it for me. I am trying to forget it and go on with my life. I thought it necessary to tell you this at once when I realized how unfair I was being. Of course, I will forget your—your offer to me yesterday and hope that we may go ahead as good friends as before."

"This is my answer, then? You cannot marry me?"

"I have not given an answer to that, sir. I think it is now more a matter of whether, under the circumstances, you still wish to—to—"

"Of course I do! Oh, Mary, my love, do not take all this so seriously. It is not unusual for very young ladies like yourself to develop a *tendre* for some unsuitable man and believe their hearts to be broken forever. Then, when someone comes along who truly loves you, you realize that what went before was merely an infatuation. Why, my cousin used regularly to fall in love every two weeks. She still does so, I believe," he added wryly. Mary could not help laughing. "Believe me, my dearest love, you will love me, I promise. Now, will you marry me?"

"I will answer that in two weeks, sir."

They went off for their ride. He was convinced she had fallen in love with a married man, though who it could be he could not imagine, unless it was someone she had met in London. Certainly it could not be anyone at Mallows. In any case, she would get over it once she made up her mind to marry him, and she would marry him at last, he was sure of it.

Despite himself, however, as the days passed, her confession bothered him. He tried to brush it aside when he thought of it, impatient with himself for foolishness, but found it coloring his thoughts and laying a fine mist of depression over his previous happiness and dimming his optimistic belief that she would learn to love him, once she had decided to marry him. He would so much have preferred his love returned heart-whole, with rosy blushes and confusion and finally a shy, maidenly acceptance, followed by an eager offer of lips for kisses to confirm it.

He tried to tell himself it didn't matter, but somehow, insidiously, it did. He saw her everyday and knew he loved her, and told her in every look and word, but even she felt some subtle change in him. She thought it was only worry about her decision and felt more for him than she had so far.

In the meantime her letter to Robin went on its way to Hatchett's End and was read to him by Mrs. Heaven. She then had to explain to him what "married" signified.

"But why should her aunt want her to marry? She would not let her stay here with me because she wanted her at home. Will she not have to leave her aunt to marry?" demanded Robin.

"Not necessarily," said Mrs. Heaven warily. One had to be so careful what one said to him, he was that clever he could catch you out in no time.

"Why not?"

"Sometimes married people live with their relatives or have them to live with them."

"Oh," was his enigmatic response to this. He

climbed down from her lap and went away to think of it all in the open air.

That afternoon his Uncle Charles took him up before him on his horse for a ride into the village, where he had some business to attend to. As they rode along, Robin chattered away about all they saw, asking endless questions. Suddenly he remembered what had been bothering him earlier in the day.

"Uncle Charles, why must people marry?"

"Good heavens!" Charles laughed. "That is a very weighty matter to be bothering your head about at so early an age."

"Yes, but why?" persisted Robin.

"Well, of course, it is not a matter of must. It is usually by choice. Two people, a man and a woman, like each other and decide they want to be together for the rest of their lives. They probably want to have children and—and all that."

"Are you married to Mrs. Heaven?"

"Good Lord! What an idea! Where do you come up with such things? No, I am not married to Mrs. Heaven. She is my housekeeper. She works for me, just as Scroggs and Betsy do, and I pay them wages. Is all that clear to you?"

"Yes. But why are you not married? Do you not want children?"

"I have you."

"I suppose that is why Mary's aunt wants her to marry."

A short silence followed this statement. Then Charles said gruffly, "What are you talking about?"

"In her letter today Mary said that her aunt was anxious for her to marry, and this gentleman had offered for her and she did not dislike him so she was going to think about it."

"I suppose it must come sometime," said Charles hollowly.

"And I was thinking, if her aunt is so anxious for Mary to be married, and since you are not married, why do you not marry her and then she can come here and take care of me again? She can bring her aunt if she likes,'' he added magnanimously. There was so long a silence after this proposal that at last Robin tugged his uncle's sleeve impatiently. ''Why do you not, Uncle Charles?''

''I—I cannot. It is impossible,'' said Charles in a strangled voice.

''Why?''

''Well, it is just not possible. She is—she is a duchess!''

Robin thought this over for a moment. He didn't know what a duchess was, but it was clear from the way his uncle pronounced the word that it was something quiet, quite dreadful, like a liar, or something even worse! At last he said judiciously, ''Well, I would never hold it against her if it isn't really her fault. I would forgive her if she would only come back. Mrs. Heaven says we must always forgive people when they say they are sorry and I'm sure Mary would say she was sorry and would try never to be a duchess again if we asked her to.''

It took some time before the import of this speech penetrated Charles' misery. When it did at last, he looked quite stunned for a moment and then suddenly gave a great whoop that caused his horse to start violently. Charles leapt to the ground and lifted Robin down into his arms and hugged him so hard the boy cried out in protest. Then he threw the child up into the air and caught him, causing Robin to shriek in delight.

''What a monstrously clever boy you are! And what a fool am I! A great dunderheaded fool! You would not hold it against her for being a duchess. Out of the mouths of babes, indeed.''

''Then you—'' Robin began as he soared once more into the air. When he was safely caught, he said breathlessly, ''Then you will forgive her, Uncle Charles?''

''Forgive her? Yes! Yes, I will forgive her. What is more, I will marry her!''

19

It took Charles the rest of the week to put all in train for his trip to Bath. He had to set out all the work to be done while he was away, and assign the various tasks. His London clothes, so long in disuse, had to be aired and pressed and his shirts and neck clothes to be laundered and freshly starched. He decided to ride his own horse rather than take the stage, as being cheaper and also providing him with a mount while in Bath. He had asked to read all of Robin's letters from Mary and had seen that morning rides figured large in them, and he didn't want the extra expense of having to hire a hack while there.

The visit, he knew, would be an expensive one and he could ill afford it, but he was determined not to count the cost. He had given some little time to thinking of what manner of approach would serve him best, and knew that he could not simply knock at her door and propose marriage, but must spend some time winning her confidence and showing her he was not the ogre she must undoubtedly think him.

She might very well loathe him now, though he knew very well he had not mistaken her response to his love-making. He had too much experience himself to doubt that she had never been kissed before. He knew also that she was not an experienced flirt as he had accused her of being in his anger. Never in all the weeks she had stayed at Hatchett's End had she flirted with him.

He had resolved that though she might detest him now for the advantage he had taken of her at their last meeting and for his cowardice in not facing her again before she left, he would still go to her, court her in the most rigidly correct way, and take his chances that he might have roused some feelings for himself in her heart that could be revived if he went about it in the proper way. He would attend the Pump Room and the assemblies, and he knew enough people to get himself invited to dinners and parties she would be attending. He would be excessively courteous while allowing her to see his intentions, and he would make the agreeable to her aunt, no matter how starchy she might be. Most of all, he would make it clear that his blood was every bit as good as the Marshall blood and that the Leighs had been titled gentlemen some hundred years or so before the Marshalls had risen to prominence, though they had at last attained a duchy.

As for the young pup who had been dancing attendance upon her, he would soon send him to the right-about or know the reason why. Some jumped-up young fashionable from the *ton*, no doubt, who made her pretty speeches and buttered up her aunt and was only out for her fortune.

The thought of her fortune bothered him, though he refused to allow him to stop his plans. Damn it all, he had forgiven her for being a duchess and all that that implied, had he not? He had fallen in love with her when he thought her but a poor governess, and he had been willing to marry her and make her his countess and share his fortune with her, poor though that was. He was not interested in her money. She could give it all away or put it in trust for her children as far as he was concerned. He was not always going to be a poor man. This year's crop was most promising and his sheep and cattle were doing very well. He could now see his way clear to begin repairs on the house in another year, and the year after that, if all continued well as he meant it to do, he could set her up with her own carriage and take time for a Season in London is she desired it. Oh, yes, he was well able to take care of his own wife, be she duchess or governess.

Robin was beside himself with excitement and followed his uncle about all day with hundreds of unanswerable questions, mostly to do with how soon Mary would return. He entertained no doubts at all that she would return as soon as his Uncle Charles asked her to do so. After all, did she not tell him in every letter how much she missed her darling Robin and how much she had enjoyed her days with him at Hatchett's End? It was only natural that when Uncle Charles told her he forgave her for being a duchess, she would joyfully agree to return at once.

Mrs. Heaven, of course, had heard the news, despite Charles' strict injunction that Robin should tell no one, and had thrown her apron over her face and cried, then laughed, then cried again, all the while calling Robin her blessed, clever little boy. He had questioned her carefully about what a duchess might be, without in any way mentioning Mary's name, for he felt the fewer people who knew of her aberration the better. He was much relieved to learn that it was only her title, nothing like a liar at all, but found it difficult to believe that anyone could have a title greater than his uncle—except for the king, of course.

He dictated a letter to Mary telling her the good news of his uncle's forgiveness and his approaching visit to Bath to bring her back to Hatchett's End, but Mrs. Heaven did not write this letter. She felt quite certain that Lord Leigh would prefer not to have his plans announced and that, if he did, he would prefer to do it himself. Instead, she wrote the sort of letter she always wrote for Robin, telling of the pond and Old Meg and of going to the fields with his uncle, and had Robin sign it in his shaky capital letters and sent it off.

So Mary was completely unprepared for the appearance of Charles Leigh in Bath. It had been a day of intermittent showers, unpromising for riding, so that when a watery and uncertain-looking sun finally appeared, Mary and Lady Hyde had put on their bonnets and walked to the Pump Room. Lady Hyde never missed drinking a glass of the waters every day, and had convinced herself it had benefited her health enormously, though it is probable that the daily walk to and from the Pump Room was equally responsible for her sense of well-being. She was very much in charity with Bath and everyone in it for having, to her mind, turned Mary away from moping and smoothed the way to what looked like being a most felicitous match with Mr. Fortmain.

Adrian Fortmain had arrived only moments after their own arrival this morning and obligingly fetched Lady Hyde's glass of water and then walked with them about the room for a while before finding a bench for them to sit.

It was then that Charles came in. He saw Mary the moment he entered the room, and his heart thumped painfully as he looked at her. She was half turned away, talking to a gentleman who stood beside her bending over her in a most possessive way. Charles' dark, heavy brows came together in a frown and he marched across the room to stand directly before her. She turned with a pleasant smile.

For a moment she continued to smile and then it faded and her mouth fell open and her eyes widened, then all the blood drained from her face and she swayed. Then, in a rush, the color came flooding up her neck and over her face up to her hairline.

"Good morning, your grace. I hope I find you in good health?" said Charles with a bow.

Lady Hyde, who had watched in amazement Mary's strange reaction to this stranger, bristled at his words, while Mr. Fortmain drew himself up and stepped protectively closer to Mary's side. Mary only continued to stare speechlessly.

Charles turned to Lady Hyde with his most charming smile and bowed. "Allow me to introduce myself to you, Lady Hyde. My name is Charles Leigh."

Now it was Lady Hyde's turn to stare and for a long moment she made no acknowledgment. Then she nodded. She could not have spoken had she tried. Indeed, her head was spinning with this unexpected apparition here before them. In Bath! Just when all was going so well and Mary in a fair way to forgetting him . . . and such a good-looking creature! The very sort of man to capture a young, inexperienced girl's heart without even trying . . . the way he carried himself, centuries of breeding there . . . there was the wastrel father and brother, but still, all families had those, look at her own uncle . . . Oh, Lord, what was she thinking of? What was she to do? She glanced at Mary, still pink and gaping, and then turned to Mr. Fortmain.

He sensed an appeal for help in her look and felt called upon to take some action. It was clear both ladies were at a complete nonplus. That they knew the man was evident, but it seemed also evident to Adrian Fortmain that they were displeased, even appalled, to be accosted by him. "See here, sir," he began forcefully, "may I ask—"

Charles swung around to face him and slowly inspected him from head to foot. "I beg your pardon?" he drawled.

This insulting treatment so confused Mr. Fortmain that he became flustered. "I—I said—well, I mean, you seem to have disconcerted the ladies and I—"

"Your name, sir?"

At last Lady Hyde found her tongue. "This is our friend, Mr. Adrian Fortmain," she said hastily. "Mr. Fortmain, this is the Earl of Leighford."

Both men bowed briefly and stiffly and Charles turned back to Mary. "Have you found the waters beneficial, your grace?"

Mary was still in the grip of shock and could not speak. Lady Hyde became aware that their little party had attracted the attention of nearly everyone in the room and felt it was time to remove Mary from their interested speculation. "Come, my dear. I think we have had enough of the Pump Room for today." She had to put her hand under Mary's arm to rouse her to move.

Before anyone quite realized how it happened Charles

inserted himself between the two women and held out an arm to each. Taken unaware, they both took the arm offered to them and he led them away, leaving Mr. Fortmain to trail along behind. Lady Hyde recovered herself almost at once and would have liked to withdraw her hand before they had taken five steps, but that would leave him with Mary, who seemed to be in a trance, and might also give rise to more conjecture among the assembly than simply going on as they were until well away from prying eyes.

Once out on the street, Lady Hyde removed her hand and faced him. "Thank you, Lord Leigh, but we need not trouble you further."

"No trouble at all, I do assure you, Lady Hyde. You will allow me to see you home, I hope?"

"No," she said emphatically, but then softened her words by saying, "it will not be necessary as we have Mr. Fortmain to escort us," at the same time glancing at Mary with a troubled frown.

Charles also looked at Mary and saw that she had still not recovered from the shock of his unexpected appearance. Perhaps it would be as well not to press himself upon them in the circumstances and give her time to grow accustomed to the idea of his presence. Besides, it would be rude to insist when the old lady was so very determined against it. There was no point in antagonizing her at the very outset. Therefore, he murmured his good days, raising his hat and bowing, before turning and marching briskly away. He had a number of calls to make upon old London friends, as well as old friends of his mother's, from whom, no doubt, he would learn all he needed to know of Mary's social engagements for the next week, as well as obtaining cards to those parties for himself.

Mr. Fortmain, meanwhile, escorted Mary and her aunt to their door and bade them good-bye until the evening, when he was to dine with them before escorting them to the Upper Rooms for an assembly. He was aware that Lady Hyde's effusive leave-taking to him was a cover for

Mary's total silence. She seemed unaware of his being there or of his going away. He was much puzzled. Who on earth was this Lord Leigh whose appearance had had such an effect on Mary and, to a lesser degree, on Lady Hyde? He had never even heard the man's name mentioned. He could only be some London beau, though the names Bath gossips had connected with Mary's as being possible suitors from her London Season had not included that of Lord Leigh. Where, then, had she met him? His aunt Fortmain had assured him that she had never been in society before London, and he himself had been the occasion for the first entertaining she had done upon her return—and he knew there was no Lord Leigh in the neighborhood of Mallows.

Of course, there was that malicious rumor promulgated by his cousin Emma about Mary having worked as a governess, but that had been for a farmer, if he remembered the story correctly. No, the man simply could not be fitted into Mary's history, yet there could be no doubt she knew him.

Mary made her way slowly upstairs to her bedroom, where she sat down on the side of her bed without even removing her bonnet and stared intently into space. Lady Hyde watched her progress and heard her door close and felt a spasm of irritation with her niece. Really, the girl had displayed a shocking want of conduct this morning in behaving in such a shatterbrained way before everyone. And now just to wander upstairs as though there was nothing to be said on the matter . . . Well, she would have to speak to the child. She marched purposefully upstairs and entered Mary's room after the most perfunctory of knocks. Mary still sat on the side of her bed and seemed unaware of her aunt's presence.

"Mary!"

Mary started and turned to her aunt. "Yes, Aunt?"

"Whatever is the matter with you, Mary?"

"What do you mean, Aunt?"

"What do I mean? Are you so far gone in your wits

that you do not realize what a spectacle you made of yourself at the Pump Room? No doubt all the gossips are busy with the story already.''

''What did I do?''

''You sat with your mouth open, staring, turning first white then red as a beet, and never said a word from the moment he entered until this moment.''

''Well, that does not sound so very bad. I did not go into strong hysterics,'' said Mary with a smile.

''Mary, for heaven's sake! This is no time for jokes. You must pull yourself together and think what you are to do.''

''Do? What would you have me do, Aunt?''

''Well, I . . . In the first place, what is he doing here?''

''I cannot imagine. I have been trying to think. I do not see how he managed to leave Hatchett's End. He always hated anything that called him away from the work, even if it was only into the village for an hour.''

''Oh, what does all that matter? The point is, he cannot have any business in Bath, and you must make that very clear to him.''

''I? How can I do so? I am sure that, whatever his reason, it has nothing to do with me. He quite despises me. I am surprised he even brought himself to speak to me. I doubt we will see him again, for he will make quite sure to avoid me.''

''Nonsense. The man came in search of you and marched right up to you when he found you. It did not seem to me that he despised you at all. Now, my dear, you must decide how you are going to behave and be firm about it.''

''I do not entirely understand what you—''

''Oh, give me patience! Must you be so want-witted? You had decided to put all that business out of your mind. You have done so very successfully so far, it seems to me. You have encouraged Mr. Fortmain and he has proposed. You are to give him your answer in a week. Is all this to be forgotten because that man appears?''

"N-o-o," said Mary, but hesitatingly, "but I am convinced his visit has nothing to do with me. Oh, Aunt, do you really feel that he does not despise me?"

"Oh, dear heaven!" cried Lady Hyde, throwing up her hands in despair. "What can I do? You will go your own way, I suppose, no matter what I say."

"But of course I will do just as you want, Aunt. You will see, though, that you have nothing to agitate yourself about. We shall see no more of him, I'll wager."

She lost her wager the moment she entered the door of the Upper Rooms that evening. He appeared before her like magic, plucked up her hand, bowed over it, pressed a kiss upon it, and turned to bow to Lady Hyde before Mary quite realized what was happening. She stared at him in a dazed sort of way for a moment, then pulled herself up sharply. Her aunt was right. She must not make a spectacle of herself again. If only he would not keep popping up before her like a jack-in-the-box and taking her by surprise . . .

"Good evening, Lord Leigh," she managed to say, quite creditably, she thought.

"Your grace. I hope you will honor me by allowing me to lead you out for the first set?"

She sensed, rather than saw, Mr. Fortmain stirring in protest at her side and spoke before he could say anything. "I have already promised the first to Mr. Fortmain, my lord."

"Then the second, your grace?"

She nodded in acquiescence, wondering how she would be able to stand up at all when the time came. Just the sight of him brought all the forbidden memories flooding back into her mind. How, then, would it be possible to dance with him? She felt her knees quivering at the very thought.

The music began and Adrian Fortmain led her out onto the floor. He did not speak at once and she could tell by the slight contraction of his brows that he was not pleased. Perhaps Lord Leigh's perfunctory nod of recognition had affronted him. At last he spoke.

"I do not believe I have ever heard you mention Lord Leigh. An acquaintance from London, I take it?"

"No. He is . . . I met him when I went to visit my cousin Maud Bryce after I returned from London," she improvised, congratulating herself that it was not quite a lie.

Adrian wanted very much to ask a great many more questions, but felt it would be rude. If she wanted him to know more—for instance, why his appearance this morning had affected her so profoundly—she would tell him. Once they were betrothed, he would have the right to question her, and he would certainly do so.

When the set was over, he led her back to her aunt, who was seated by now with Lord Leigh attending her politely. Several other young men were hovering around waiting for Mary's return to engage her for dances, and she was happily too busy for some time to have to confront him. But then the music struck up for the second set and he was beside her, holding out his arm. Unable to look at him, she placed her hand upon it and was led onto the floor. She knew he must feel her hand trembling and was humiliated to exhibit her nervousness to him but could not prevent it.

"How—how is Robin?" she asked to divert his attention.

"He is very well. He sends you his love."

Her eyes flashed up, startled, then dropped. She could think of no reply. What did he mean? He was so—so different, and yet there was a warmth in his voice that she remembered from those tea times together before he learned the truth about her. What did it all mean? Why was he here?

"Do you make a long stay in Bath?"

"Only until I finish my business here."

"Ah, business. I see. I wondered what could have dragged you away from Hatchett's End. I know you never like to go away from your work and it must be busy there at this time of the year, though, of course, I know very little about crops and things of that sort."

She was chattering like a fool and could not stop herself, she was so nervous. She glanced up again and he was smiling down at her. That smile of his that was so devastating, changing his stern face, causing one to realize how very blue were his eyes as they glinted with humor. She felt her pulses pounding and became more flustered than ever.

"I do not like being away, but there are sometimes things more important than Hatchett's End," he said at last in a low voice, gazing down at her so intently she could feel it and could not resist looking up. Their eyes met and locked together—for what seemed forever. Then the set ended and reality intruded. She turned away dazedly, her knees trembling so that she faltered. He took up her hand and placed it firmly on his arm and led her back to her aunt. He does not despise me, she thought. He does not despise me!

Charles bowed to her, bowed to Lady Hyde, nodded carelessly to Mr. Fortmain, and took his leave. He had accomplished his purpose for tonight and did not feel inclined to be part of a jostling crowd of young men awaiting her favors. The evening ended there for Mary also, though she carried out her obligatory dances. She remembered nothing of it, however. Lady Hyde bit her lip to keep from speaking sharply to her, and Adrian's brow contracted into a permanent frown.

Confound the fellow, he fumed silently. Coming here out of the blue and interfering in my courtship. Everything looked to be going so well, too, and now . . . well, something had definitely happened today and it was disturbing, though even now he could not quite put his finger on it. He had never seen Mary as she was at this moment. Abstracted, yes, but he had seen her that way before. Never, however, with those glowing eyes, that sort of exalted look. She turned that look upon him as they danced again later and he was convinced she didn't even see him. He didn't like it, by heaven, he didn't like it one bit.

20

They had arranged to ride the next morning if the weather was fine and Adrian Fortmain was at Laura Place as early as permissible. He was relieved to see no signs of other visitors as he was shown in. He lingered in conversation with Lady Hyde for only a few moments before Mary came down dressed in her habit and they went out at once. As they started out, several young men joined them and then two young ladies—but no Lord Leigh, thank the Lord.

However, as they cantered along out of town, he was suddenly among them, blandly bidding them good morning and commenting upon their good fortune in so lovely a day. Mary turned pink and began chattering away to the young ladies over her shoulder.

From that moment there was no peace for Mr. Fortmain, for Lord Leigh seemed to be everywhere, every dinner party, every entertainment of any kind to which the duchess and her aunt—and of course, Mr. Fortmain— had been invited. Lord Leigh spent some time being gracious to his hostess, was the soul of courtesy to everyone, but he spent most of his time with Mary, or if she were engaged, with Lady Hyde, whose initial frostiness, Adrian noticed with chagrin, had thawed considerably as he bent his charm upon her. But it was Mary Adrian watched closely, and he saw the change that came over her when Lord Leigh appeared and slowly he began to form the suspicion that this must be the man to whom Mary had confessed to have given her heart. Adrian had been convinced that it was a married man, but Lord

Leigh was unmarried. What, then, if she loved him, had been the obstacle to her happiness? Adrian turned the matter over and over in his mind, now telling himself it was impossible this could be the man, since clearly Lord Leigh was pursuing her, then telling himself that despite all this he must be the one, otherwise she would not be behaving so. Surely if her heart was given to someone else, she would not be flirting with Lord Leigh after half-promising to marry himself. Mary was a well-brought-up girl and would not behave so indecorously—Lady Hyde would not allow her to do so.

At first Mr. Fortmain was bitterly angry with her. She had never blushed and flirted with him! Oh, yes, he knew the look. His thoughts came to dwell more and more upon the young lady he had previously thought he would marry. She had looked at him in that way. It comforted him to remember that.

Lady Hyde had, indeed, come to like Lord Leigh very much, and found herself becoming almost fatalistic about what she was sure would happen. After all, if he was attempting to attach Mary, he would have so little difficulty there was no point in fighting it herself. He might be penniless, but he was certainly personable and clearly acceptable to society, and he was the object of many flirtatious looks from other young women wherever he went. The town was in a delightful ferment of gossip, arguing first for Mr. Fortmain's chances and then for Lord Leigh's. Nothing so exciting had happened in Bath for years.

Then, two days before the end of the week and the time when Mary was to give Adrian his answer, Lord Leigh did not join the morning riding party. He came instead to pay a formal call upon Lady Hyde.

She started violently when he was announced and dropped the novel she had been reading. He entered and bowed. She managed to greet him and motion him to be seated. Before he sat down, he bent to retrieve her book and hand it to her gravely.

"You do not, ah, ride today, Lord Leigh?"

"No. I wanted to speak to you, Lady Hyde."

"Oh," she said.

"Yes. I have come to ask your permission to pay my addresses to your niece."

Her hands fluttered up nervously and then fell back into her lap. "Have you—have you spoken to her?"

"No. I thought it correct to have your permission before I did so."

She was tremendously flattered by this. It was, of course, correct, but the old courtesies were dying out and these days such formality was rarely practiced. Mr. Fortmain had not seen fit to ask her permission before speaking to Mary, nor had he done so yet. Perhaps he thought that after he had Mary's consent was time enough.

"Well, my lord, I think you must be aware of the difficulties. Mary's situation is, ah, an unusual one, and there is a very great deal to take into consideration."

"Lady Hyde, my case is very simple. I fell in love with Mary when she worked in my house as governess to my nephew. I was not then aware of what you term 'Mary's situation.' I did not then hesitate to consider marrying her and making her a countess. My fortune was small but I was happy to think I might share it with her, penniless though I thought her to be. I am not boasting of this, only stating the facts as they were."

"And what were Mary's feelings, my lord?"

"I believe Miss Marshall would have had me. I am not sure if she was aware of her feelings then, but I think she would have come to love me if I had spoken. Unfortunately I learned of her true identity and lost my temper and my wits at what I considered her deceit. I felt I had been made a fool of. I have learned since that I had not needed her to make me a fool." He smiled ruefully as he said this, and she nearly fell in love with him on the spot. Here was romance at last.

"And now, sir? What of now? Do you know her feelings? Has she given you any reason to hope she cares for you?"

"Yes," he said simply.

She was so taken aback by the bareness, but conviction, of this reply that she didn't speak for a moment. She could not deny his statement, for she knew the answer herself only too well. "Well, of course, I cannot answer for my niece, but if it is so, you must know there are many weighty matters to be considered. Her fortune—"

"Can go hang," he interrupted rudely. "She can do what she likes with it, for all of me. Burn it, give it away, put it in trust for her children. I want none of it."

"I was going to say," she said chidingly, "her fortune does not come into her own hands for another seven years, when she is five-and-twenty. Naturally I have wanted her married to someone trustworthy before that moment comes. It is very large, you see, and she knows nothing of money matters. However, her dowry is apart from that. I hope you are not so altruistic as to refuse to be concerned with that?"

He changed his position uneasily, his heavy brows meeting in a frown. "Well, I suppose it can be tied up in some way for her own use."

"I believe you are struggling now to restore your estates. Any husband may be forgiven for using the money his wife brings into her marriage to help him in such a project. If Mary is to spend part of the year in your home, I am sure you will want it to be an establishment suitable to her position."

His frown did not abate, but he made no reply to this.

Lady Hyde went on blithely. "I was sure you would see the force of that. I do not doubt that were Mary penniless, you would not allow that to deter you, nor should it deter you that she is not. I do not for a moment look upon you as a fortune-hunter and I have no fears about entrusting you to do all that is necessary for her comfort and happiness. You have my consent to speak to my niece."

He rose at once. "Thank you, Lady Hyde, for listen-

ing to me and not rejecting me out of hand. I will bid
you good day.''

"Lord Leigh, there is one other thing: the title, you
know. Her son will be the next duke, if God wills that
she has one.''

"He will also be the Earl of Leighford, madam. I
have always found that title an honorable one,'' he said
proudly. "I will call tomorrow morning, if I may. Perhaps you will ask your niece to receive me?''

"Certainly, my lord.'' He bowed and left and for
some reason Lady Hyde found herself inclined to tears.
"Old fool,'' she sniffed, groping for her reticule and
then for her handkerchief, "but still . . .''

Mary returned from her ride distinctly out of sorts.
Not exactly cross, for she had never been the sort of
girl to behave crossly, but she was definitely not her
usual self. She hurried past her aunt, who met her in
the hall, without a smile or a greeting, saying only that
she must hurry to change her dress for she was late for
Lady Graves' "breakfast.''

Lady Hyde, bursting with her budget of news, had no
chance to speak at all. What on earth could have happened to the girl to make her behave in so rude a way?
Lady Hyde went back to the drawing room and sat down
to compose herself. There was no point in pursuing her
and insisting upon an interview when she was in such
a mood, and besides, Watts would be with her now.

Mary bit her lip to keep back the tears as she was
helped out of her habit and into a gown by Watts. Her
morning ride had been miserable from the beginning and
had ended worse. First of all, Charles Leigh had failed
to appear. She was so sure he would join them she had
persisted in believing it all the way out of town, which
made the disappointment all the greater. This past week,
though he had never said a word to her that could not
have been overheard by anyone, she had felt—and knew
he had meant her to feel—that he was making love to her
with every syllable. It was the tone he had used to her

when they had taken tea together at Hatchett's End, and behind every word they exchanged had been the memory of his arms holding her closer and closer and his lips upon hers. Had it been so for him? She had thought it must be, from the way he looked at her, a look that made her heart pound and her knees weaken. In just these few days she had become as addicted to these passive but explicit exchanges as the worst victim of a drug. Had she only imagined all of it?

His nonappearance this morning had created such a feeling of deprivation in her that she could hardly speak or attend to those around her. She had become more and more nervous and distracted until at last, when Adrian had asked her if she was feeling unwell, she had almost snapped at him.

"Certainly not. Why do you ask?"

"Why, my dear, no need to bite my head off. Surely I have the right to inquire?"

"Right?" she queried sharply.

"Does not my love for you give me some rights?" he said in a low, almost angry voice.

"This is hardly the time for such remarks, Mr. Fortmain," she said loftily, looking about to make sure no one was near enough to overhear.

"You seem to be continually looking for someone. Perhaps you are piqued that your latest conquest has deserted your train today," he said pettishly, snappish now himself.

"How dare you say such a thing to me, sir?" she said, pulling up her horse with a jerk.

"Well, it does seem to me that you are not content unless all of your admirers—" he began, most unwisely.

"Mr. Fortmain, I assure you I am quite content to ride alone!"

"Perhaps you would prefer it if I did not accompany you?"

"I certainly would prefer not to have anyone accompany me who persists in making himself disagreeable," she said coldly.

On the point of a tart reply, he caught it back. Taking a deep breath he said, "Mary, why are we quarreling? I beg your pardon if I have offended you. Come, let us be friends again. Have you forgotten that tomorrow you are to give me my answer?"

She rode on at that without replying. She was on the verge of telling him at once that she could never marry him—not now, when she had fallen in love even more resoundingly than before with Charles Leigh. For she knew now that even if Lord Leigh did not return her feelings, she could never marry another man while she felt so. But with the whole party strung out behind them and someone likely to ride up alongside at any moment, she knew it would be cruel to go into the matter now.

Adrian Fortmain rode silently at her side. Despite his conciliating words, he still smarted from her cutting remarks to him. Surely this was not the way a girl spoke to the man she was about to bestow her hand upon? He could almost wish she would throw him over. He, of course, could not as a gentleman back out now, but he was becoming more and more unhappy with the situation. He wanted very much for his beloved to be in love with him—now. Despite his confident words to her that she would learn to love him, he felt deprived at not having her first love, and the thought of having to teach someone to love him depressed him immeasurably.

Suddenly Mary said, "Come, ride ahead with me, Mr. Fortmain. I must speak to you," and she galloped away. He followed, and presently, when the others were left far behind, she pulled up and turned to him. "I must give you my answer now, sir. It is pointless to leave the matter hanging in this way for even one more day. I cannot marry you, Mr. Fortmain. I am very sorry for any unhappiness I may have caused you. I thought it might work out for both of us, but I know now that it cannot. I wish I could make amends, but I do not know how I may do so. I hope that you will forgive me and always remain my friend."

"It is that Leigh fellow, I suppose," he said, not very graciously.

She drew herself up. "I beg your pardon, Mr. Fortmain?"

"Oh, very well, I'll ask no questions. Perhaps it is for the best, after all. I have begun to feel I would not care for a wife whose heart is not given to me wholly from the start," he said gruffly, aware he was behaving badly, but his *amour propre* was too badly dented at the moment to control his tongue.

"I am sure you are right, Mr. Fortmain. Shall we rejoin the others now?"

The ride home had been uncomfortable. Adrian had remained broodingly silent and she had been forced to pretend nothing had happened and to present a tranquil face to the rest. He had escorted her to her door and bowed, still silent, in farewell and gone away. She was left feeling bruised and uncomfortably in the wrong, though she knew she had been honest with him from the beginning to the end. Perhaps it had been wrong of her to ever have given him reason to hope, but it was too late to mend that now. At least she had always been truthful.

When she came downstairs she found her aunt entertaining visitors and unable to go with her to Lady Graves. By this time Mary had recovered a bit of her composure and was beginning to look forward to the party in the hope that she would see Charles Leigh there. Surely she would, for had he not been in attendance at every party since he had arrived in Bath? Perhaps his business had detained him this morning. After all, he had said he had come to Bath on business. She wondered what business he could have in Bath? But perhaps he had concluded his business and returned to Hatchett's End! No, no, surely he would not just leave without so much as a word. Unless—unless she had only imagined everything she had thought she was seeing in his eyes because she had wanted so much for it to be there. Or unless it was some game he was playing to pay her out for deceiving him. Could he be capable of such treachery?

No, she could never bring herself to believe that. That he had a temper and could be violently angry she knew, but he was too much a gentleman to play such tricks as that. Besides, he could not afford to leave his work and take an expensive trip just to pay off old scores.

It was still possible, however, that she had only imagined everything. After all, he had said not a word of love. He was just always there, wherever she was; he always danced only with her and rarely even spoke to anyone else when she was in the room. Surely that must be some indication of something? On the other hand, farmer though he might be now, he had been well-known in London society before he had inherited his title and debts. Every hostess in Bath was acquainted with him and had invited him to their parties. So it was perfectly possible he had meant nothing particular in being always where she was, but had only known the same people. Her head was beginning to ache from all this speculation.

Her arrival at Lady Graves' was greeted by a press of people, all eager to claim her attention, but he was not among them. She did her best to be gay and lighthearted and to ignore all the buzz of comment she could not help overhearing about the unusual circumstance of both Mr. Fortmain and Lord Leigh being absent. She could not prevent her eyes repeatedly seeking the door, sure that he must come. But he did not.

She escaped at last, her head throbbing with pain by now, and went back to Laura Place. She asked Salcombe at once if any messages had been left for her, but there was nothing. She went to her room, where Watts waited to help her change for dinner.

"No. I will not go down to dinner tonight. I will have something light on a tray up here later perhaps. I have the headache. Please tell my aunt that I cannot go out this evening. She will have to send my excuses to—to . . . Oh, I have forgotten where we are promised for tonight," she said wearily, tears of self-pity starting into her eyes.

Watts was alarmed. She had never known Mary to

behave so. She helped her into bed and bathed her temples with eau de cologne, but Mary finally pushed her away irritably, saying she only wanted to be left alone.

Watts hurried along to Lady Hyde's room and urged that a doctor be sent for at once to attend her grace.

"Why? What is wrong?" cried Lady Hyde, starting up from her dressing table. Watts explained all she had observed and Lady Hyde drew on a dressing gown and hurried across the hall.

"Mary, my love! What is this? Watts tells me you are ill."

"No, no. I have the headache only," said Mary, but she sounded so dispirited Lady Hyde became alarmed.

"I think I had better send for the doctor," she said worriedly.

"Oh, please! I do not want a doctor. I only need to be alone." And with this Mary burst into tears.

"My dear—" began Lady Hyde tenderly.

"Please, please, just leave me alone for a little," sobbed Mary.

Lady Hyde reluctantly withdrew. She did so long to tell her about Lord Leigh's request, but certainly this was not the moment to go into all that. The child had overdone her engagements and tired herself out. Let her have a good night's rest and she would hear it all very early in the morning in plenty of time to prepare her mind for his visit. He would not come before ten.

Mary woke feeling better. After all, there was nothing physically wrong with her and she was young and healthy. When Lady Hyde tapped and peeked around the door, she found Mary sitting up, drinking her chocolate, her eyes clear and her color good.

"There, child, a good night's rest was all you needed. You look much more the thing this morning. I think we should cancel all our engagements and stay at home for the day. You have been doing too much. Why, it is as bad as a London Season!"

"Oh, no, Aunt, there is no reason for that. I feel perfectly well now."

"We shall see. For the morning at least you shall stay at home. I have accepted an engagement for you here this morning."

"What is it, Aunt?"

"Well, you see, Lord Leigh called upon me yesterday while you were out riding and—"

"What?" Mary dropped her cup and chocolate splashed all over the coverlet. She didn't even notice it. "Here? He was here? Why did you not tell me before?"

"But I had no chance, my dear. When you came in you rushed up to change, and when you came down I had callers, and when you returned you were ill and wanted to be left alone," Lady Hyde replied in aggrieved tones.

"Forgive me—forgive me, dearest Aunt, but I beg you to tell me now," Mary cried, leaping out of bed and throwing her arms about her aunt's neck.

Mollified, Lady Hyde said, "Well, as I said, he came to call on me to ask my permission to pay his addresses to you. So *comme-il-faut*. Such a gratifying attention that I—"

"He . . . to pay . . ." Mary said faintly.

"Yes, my dear, and I gave him my permission. Of course I told him that I could not speak for you and that he must make his proposal in form to you for his answer, but I find I like him very well and I think he will suit you even better than Mr. Fortmain. Such an old family, you know. The Leighs have been earls since Edward the First or someone like that. Penniless now, of course, but that need not be a drawback to my mind when all else is well. Anyway, he is coming this morning to see you."

Mary stood still, staring wide-eyed and unseeing at her aunt. Suddenly she spun around and ran to the door, calling, "Watts, Watts!" She then opened the cupboard doors and began to throw out her gowns onto the bed.

"Mary—Mary, for heaven's sake," protested Lady

Hyde. "You must come down and have some breakfast and calm yourself. This is most unseemly. He will not be here before ten or half-past and it is only eight."

Mary paid no attention at all and at last Lady Hyde went away to have her own breakfast. Really, she didn't like seeing girls behaving in this eager, thrusting way, preparing to throw themselves at a man. In Lady Hyde's day girls did not behave so. Of course, she was madly in love with him and had suffered all these weeks, and it was only too clear he loved her and had done so all the time, but had been too proud to admit it once he discovered who she was. So romantic, really, but still . . .

Mary ordered a bath and then had her hair brushed until it shone before Watts arranged it for her. At ten, when the footman tapped to whisper to Watts that Lord Leigh had called and Lady Hyde requested that her grace come down to the drawing room, Mary had still not decided upon a gown. She darted about the room picking up one gown and then discarding it in such a distracted way that at last Watts picked up a sea-foam-green muslin and held it out in a decisive way and Mary stepped into it and allowed it to be fastened up.

Dressed at last, she hurried out, but at the top of the staircase she was brought to a dead stop by a horrible thought. Suppose he was only offering for her because he felt honor-bound to do so after kissing her and really didn't love her at all? After all, he had never said one word of love to her. Her chin came up proudly. She would certainly never want him under such circumstances! Her nerves stopped fluttering and she trod regally down the stairs. When she entered the room, Lady Hyde was happy to see her niece looking so calm and collected. I should have known a Marshall would be too proud to throw herself at him, she thought approvingly.

"Your grace," said Charles, rising and bowing.

"Lord Leigh," she said stiffly.

"I was sorry not to see you at the Huntley's dinner party last night," he said.

"I felt like a quiet evening for a change."

A silence ensued. Lady Hyde rose abruptly. "Will you excuse me, Lord Leigh? I have some matters to attend to."

"Certainly, Lady Hyde. My purpose this morning was to have a private interview with her grace, as you know," he said politely, but without beating about the bush.

"Oh—oh, yes, of course," said Lady Hyde, much flustered. "Well, I will just . . ." She hurried out of the room, closing the door firmly behind her.

Mary stood looking stonily before her while Charles eyed her quizzically. At last he said, "May we not sit down, Mary?"

"Certainly, Lord Leigh, please have a chair." She crossed to a straight chair and sat down. He seated himself on the sofa facing her. "You wanted to speak to me?"

"Did not your aunt tell you?"

"She told me you wanted to speak to me," she said ungivingly.

"Now, what is all this? Are you playing some game with me? She must have told you that I want to marry you."

"Why should you want to do so?" She faced him now squarely, challengingly.

"Well, surely after what happened the last time at Hatchett's End you must have realized—"

She gave an artificial little laugh. She knew it all now. It was just as she had suspected. "Oh, dear, Lord Leigh, you must not be so old-fashioned. A kiss! Good heavens, people do not feel obligated to marry for that in this day and age. Why it is nothing—"

Suddenly he had leapt up and snatched her out of the chair to face him, her wrist in a grip of iron.

"Nothing, is it? We'll see that!" Then she was in his arms, his mouth demandingly upon her own. Her pride fought only a moment before her senses took over and she was swept up on a tide of passion fully as great as his own. When at last he drew back, he grinned and said, "Nothing, eh?"

"Oh, Charles," she said breathlessly, "you do not despise me?"

"Despise you? For what?" he said between little soft kisses all over her face.

"For being so—so forward that first time you kissed me?"

"Little idiot," he said, kissing her again to prove how stupid she was.

When at last she was able, she said, "But you rushed away so . . . Oh, I was sure you despised me for behaving that way."

"If I had not rushed away, I might have been unable to stop myself from—"

"From what?"

"Never mind. I will tell you what after we are married. You will marry me." It was more of a statement of fact than a question, but she answered just the same.

"Yes. Of course I will. You know I will. But you have not said that you love me—not even once," she complained.

He proceeded to tell her how much he loved her between demonstrations that left her weak, with trembling knees.

Lady Hyde, hovering outside, felt at last that her duty to her niece demanded that she return to the room, and she opened the door with a loud clearing of her throat and a rattle of the handle. They did not hear her. She stood staring for a moment, aghast, and then backed away and closed the door softly. Really it was . . . Well, it was indecorous, hardly within the bounds of what was permissible to display such feelings when they were barely betrothed. When she was a girl, such embraces were never allowed before marriage. Of course, there was the time Hyde caught her in the shrubbery when her mother had stopped to speak to the gardener, but still . . .

SIGNET REGENCY ROMANCE
COMING IN SEPTEMBER 1988

Sandra Heath
An Impossible Confession

Laura Matthews
Miss Ryder's Memoirs

Caroline Brooks
Regency Rose

The New Super Regency
Mary Jo Putney
Lady of Fortune